# GLASS PRISON

## PRISONER SERIES: BOOK ONE

# M.J. THOMPSON

Crystal Eye®
Absolutely Unprofessional®

Print and distribution through IngramSpark at ingramspark.com.

Paperback Printing: 2023 **(Format & Date)**
ISBN 979-8-9879-116-0-0
Crystal Eye®
crystaleyepub2022@gmail.com
Absolutely Unprofessional®
absolutelyunprofessional.com

This book is dedicated to
my husband, Justin,
and my four incredible children,
Gabe, Aidan, Maddy, and Aidan (yep... there are two),
who always encouraged and supported me to get this done.

And to my parents, sisters, brothers, and multiple friends
who offered invaluable feedback and encouragement
as I muddled my way through.

A special shout-out goes to my brother, Richard,
who believed in me enough to become my
partner in publishing this first of
hopefully many more books to come.

# Chapter 1
## Zoey

*Dying in the dirt. No. Not after the glass prison. Body frozen. Mind awake and screaming for help. This is not how it ends.*

"No!" Zoey gasped, sitting up in a bed of tangled sheets. Her night terrors tended to lack people. When they started it was nothing but darkness and silence, but lately, she'd wake up screaming, blinded by all-consuming white lights. To add to it, there was a pain so fierce it would leave her bruised for days. It felt like being in someone else's skin. She had heard some dreams have meaning, but the significance of these escaped her.

Last night was filled with that agony, and her legs were still sluggish as she swung them off the bed. The cracked linoleum felt cool on her feet as she made her way into the living room.

Aidan noticed her hair was more wild than usual, which meant her nightmares were in full swing. He decided to start the day off with sarcasm. "Looks like you spent the night flying on your broomstick," he badgered in a low voice muffled by the couch upholstery. His appearance mirrored the sound of his voice with his red hair matted on the left side of his head and the cushion pattern imprinted on his cheek. It added character to his freckles. The twelve-foot walk to his bed would've taken too much energy.

"Uh-huh," said Zoey, channeling Stevie Nicks after her long night. Aidan and Joe were the only ones around to hear her middle-of-the-night screams. They'd been friends since the world went dark only five *excruciatingly* long years ago and were her brothers of choice, even if not blood. They were getting used to the solitude, or so they pretended.

Her nightmares began the same night the explosions had taken out the power. Since then, her dreams had blossomed into full-on nocturnal battles. Zoey could still hear snoring from the back bedroom; that meant her screaming must have been short-lived. It clearly hadn't broken Joe's sleep.

"You're just jealous of my swoopy red locks and keen fashion sense." Aidan raised his right eyebrow a few times to ease the tension, but today was a chuckle-under-her-breath kind of day.

It was all she had in her.

"Your knee-high yellow Minion socks beg to differ," she said with all the sarcasm she could deliver.

His jokes gave way to concern, and he cracked an eye open to look at her. "You must've had a pretty rough one last night." The lightness in his voice didn't hide the underlying sympathy, and it was killing her.

"I like you more when you *don't* coddle." She cut her gaze to him. After a full ten seconds battling it out in a staring contest, he let his eyes roll to the sky in mock misery.

His fingertips grazed the ceiling as he stretched his six-foot one frame. "Why me, God! Why am I trapped with the Wicked Witch of the West!" He feigned heart failure and landed hard on the wooden chair by the kitchen table. The palm-tree-print cushion ripped open further, allowing more stuffing to puff out at the side.

"Drama queen," she mumbled, walking to the open floor space in their tight living room.

"Hey!" Aidan's expression showed him fighting his natural urge for a dramatic response. "I think I'm more like a beefy Prince Harry circa 2013." Holding an invisible M-16, he flashed a killer half-grin.

"Or Vision in Avengers—"

"What? Paul Bettany didn't even have eyebrows in that movie."

"Oh, you have eyebrows?" Zoey could feel his grunt brewing before he made a sound. A smile crept across her face. His biggest pet peeve was his blond-white eyebrows being mistaken for *no* eyebrows.

When they first met, life was all about survival. As time passed, he'd become more like an annoying brother. The kind you wanted to throat punch.

Zoey arched deep into a yoga pyramid, causing several vertebrae to pop. She'd never taken yoga, but several months back, she found an old Rodney Yee's Power Yoga DVD and pretended to follow… mostly improvising. A sigh of relief left her lips as some of the aching demons escaped her body. Slowly she leaned down to the ground to stretch out her back. She pulled herself into upward then downward dog poses before returning to her feet in mountain position. She was pretty sure it was called that. If Mr. Yee saw her interpretation of morning yoga, she'd likely be banned from the craft for life.

Exhaustion cut her usual morning routine short. Even her bones were tired. Her dreams were physically as well as mentally taxing.

Feeling slightly less stiff, she shuffled her way to the bathroom and stumbled over the one-inch-raised threshold stubbing her baby toe. "Dang. Every time."

Just as she thought, 1980s hair. Her mirrored reflection was not on her side today. Zoey's natural jet-black, pin-straight hair always curled into ringlets on mornings like this. Aidan was right. Much kinkier than her typical morning wake-up look.

After washing her face and attempting to tame the madness on her head, she pulled off her shirt and exchanged it for a clean one—a clean-*ish* one.

She jumped away from her reflection in the mirror as her abdomen came into view. "What?" Her fingers trembled as she touched her stomach lightly. The pain seared like a burn. A small spider web of angry, bright purple lines interlocked under her skin to the right of her belly button.

Grabbing a washcloth, she tried rubbing at them, but nothing changed other than them just getting angrier. She turned and looked at the bathroom door as if she could see the boys on the other side. Anxiety skyrocketing, her breath came in shallow bursts.

Joe and Aidan were already on high alert with her these days since her nightmares had become more fierce.

"Crap." Zoey managed to calm down enough to think a little more clearly—until a knock on the door scared her back toward the sink, where she slammed her hip into the porcelain. "Hey, Zoe? You almost done in there? My bladder's at the breaking point."

Grabbing her soon-to-be-bruised hip and clearing the fear from her throat, she said, "Yep. Yeah! One sec."

Her options were limited: tell them and have them freak out, or not tell them and see if it would go away on its own.

She opted for number two. There was no reason to get them all riled up. If the purple lines didn't spread—or kill her today—then maybe she'd fill them in.

She glanced back down at her belly, "Like I need another problem."

Zoey decided to do what she always does. Ignore it.

Putting her hands on the cold, hard sink edges, she lowered her head to steady her thoughts. Stilling the air in her lungs, she glanced back into the mirror connecting with her own eyes. Meeting their reflection, the moment of calm dissipated.

Zoey's pupils dilated. She felt her body being compressed. A bright light blinded her. The faint sounds of screaming paralyzed her.

Was the screaming her own?

Without warning, it was gone. The silence seemed somehow louder.

She blinked.

Zoey gasped as if no air had entered her lungs for the past few minutes. The porcelain sink held her upright as tunnel vision closed off everything around her. Whatever had just happened nearly knocked her out.

Grabbing at the faucet, she splashed water on her sweating skin for a second time. She avoided eye contact in the mirror again and quickly opened the door for Aidan.

*That was new.*

"Playtime's over, kids," Joe yelled as he pounded on the bathroom door.

Aidan flung it open before the final knock and almost got a fist to the face. "I heard you!"

Joe was out of bed and on a mission. "Our generator is on the fritz again. We need to go do some test maintenance."

He was 200 pounds of muscle and HoHos. Mostly HoHos. He filled the room like a giant but was truly the geek of the group. He held the essential role of handyman and fixer of all things tech.

He could also out-beard anyone she'd ever met. If any man could pull off a rusted red beard with a silver stripe down the side, it was him. Zoey had heard that on occasion when a person experienced a significantly traumatic event, a patch of their hair would turn white or silver. She didn't really know if that held true for beards, and he had never come out and fully explained the circumstance that had left him with that stripe. If he wanted to share, he would.

The rusty beard gave him a 'soft' Viking-like quality. He had a stocky build with a face that should have smiled with laughter. Yet, for as long as Zoey could remember, his eyes had never truly danced with life.

"Is it malfunctioning? I thought it was holding out longer than usual?" Aidan asked around a mouth full of stale Fruit Loops.

Not fully awake and without her morning sugar-laced coffee, she stared at Joe blankly. He was about to answer when she held up her hand to stop him. Pointing to her mug on the counter, Zoey said, "Coffee first. Generator pause."

He turned and grabbed her mug, filling it with a murky, water-like substance, and took a deep breath as he handed it to her and said, "Okay. Pause over. Yes. It's still working. The alarm should've gone off about 23:45 last night to be re-gassed. It didn't."

"Normal human-speak," Zoey said with her eyes closed, breathing in the bitter fumes.

"Eleven forty-five p.m. no alarm. I woke up around three, thinking I forgot to fill it up. When I came out to the kitchen, all the lights were still on." Eyes like daggers at Aidan, he said, "*Someone* forgot to switch them off again last night."

Aidan threw his hands in the air. "*What*? I fell asleep on the couch!"

Barely missing a beat, Joe came back to the point. "And not just on... but brightly lit." He stood by the wall and flipped the switch.

"Holy—turn it off!" The light was so bright Zoey worried the bulb may burst. Her hands crossed over her face trying to block the shock of light, and almost spilled her coffee. The glare burned her stubbornly tired eyes. Stumbling to the switch, she swatted Joe's hand away and smacked at it.

Aidan said nothing at first, then nodded his head toward the door. "Maybe we should go down and have a look-see at the equipment. See if some 'good Samaritan' is filling the generator with the high-octane stuff."

Joe grunted. "Right, and I'm going to open the fridge to an entire stock of porterhouses and A-1." He grabbed his headlamp and jammed it on his head.

"Never know." Aidan took a moment to process the thought of those steaks.

They walked down the six flights of stairs to the basement of their apartment building. The basement was the width of the building but with multiple rooms branching off. The DuroMax generator, affectionately called 'Gennie,' was located in the main entrance room you walk into from the stairwell. There's a small ventilation system built for the generator's fumes to release, but it was otherwise a dark cemented-in area, with only one access point at the stairs. The ventilation system was big enough for a person to shimmy through. Zoey knew that all too well, as she was often the person of choice to snake inside it when it got clogged.

Joe's vocal confusion mirrored their facial expressions. "I just don't understand. It's not as if the power grid has come on lately to avoid using the generator, but the gas level has only moved two centimeters below the last time I came down here." He spun in a slow circle as if looking for clues. "Makes no sense. Not that I'm complaining, but this isn't rocket science. No one should be able to get in here, so how is Gennie still running?"

Joe's grease-stained fingers lifted some of the tubing on the side of the generator while pointing his penlight at the target. He leaned down to inspect it closely. "Check this out. The gauges are cleaned out, and it's, uh, almost like the tubes were replaced."

"Joe, you're in charge of security. There's no way anyone could've gotten in here with all the tech you have rigged for monitoring." Aidan tried to sound nonchalant, but his darting eyes gave away his nerves. "Maybe it *is* a good Samaritan?"

Ignoring Aidan, Zoey answered Joe's question. "Yeah. I see what you're talking about, and there are no *good* Samaritans out there willing to give up gas." She could feel something was coming. "Nothing around here comes free. Somebody wants something."

"You're right. I do." A voice rang out from the dark.

# Chapter 2
## Purgatory

April 9, 2028  |  6:50 a.m.

*I awoke to darkness. I've been waiting for the lights to come on—knowing they won't but allowing myself to hope for it anyway. I strain my ears to hear something. Anything.*

*On a clear, windless day, the sound of a hummingbird's wings can be heard. At least, it's the closest image I can visualize trying to make sense of the hum. My body feels uncomfortable, crushed, but by what? I'm not sure. I don't struggle against it. That struggle ended a long time ago.*

*This isn't the first day I've tried to determine if I'm alive, dead, blind, drugged, or just placed in purgatory with no defining life, death, heaven, or hell. Closer to hell than any of the former. I couldn't say how many days it's been. Or how many times I've tried to feel even one small part of myself physically or mentally. I also doubt this is the last moment of questioning I'll go through. My mental state of calm-to-crazy comes in and out like the slow, quiet waves of an ocean on a moonless night. I have trouble recognizing when one turns into the other.*

*I can't quite feel my fingers, but somehow, I know they're there. Nothing seems to want to move. I can't tell if I can't feel what's around me or if I just can't feel me.*

*The thought's disturbing but not distressing.*

*I attribute it to the reality that this has been my 'life' for some time. I just wish I knew how much time.*

*I spend a great deal of energy trying to focus on any change around or against my body. The pressure in my ears makes it difficult. My ears seem blocked, like after swimming in a pool for hours and needing to tilt my head until the water runs free. I can almost remember swimming in a pool—the cool water as I sink into it with goosebumps on my arms. The image is grainy, like an old picture, but I'm almost certain it's a memory.*

*Maybe I* am *drugged. That would explain the lack of feeling in my body, the pressure in my head, and the humming in my ears.*

*But if I'm drugged, how am I able to hold an entire conversation with myself like this? I can't possibly be dead. Energy never disappears or stays in one place. It has to go somewhere. If I'd died, would it be possible for me to be mentally trapped like this? Mentally intact? Or so I feel. Yet, non-existent?*

# Chapter 3
## The Compound

Fed. Building, PA | April 9, 2028 | 6:50 a.m.

"**B**lepharospasm."

"Bless you?"

Gavin's evergreen eyes cut to Justin in annoyance. "Her eyelids are twitching. She almost appears to be dreaming. Justin, are you seeing this?" Gavin said as he slid his glasses up his long, arched nose. It was a clear sign it had been broken many years ago. He immediately followed the action with a hand through his black hair, which made it stand on end. After putting his Galaxy tablet for medical monitoring on the kiosk, he pulled down the hand-held imagery monitor for the magnification video camera. Disbelief was etched on his face. He watched the screen intently as her eyelids spasmed. At that exact moment, the blue-alert light in the corner of the room flashed once, then stopped. The shock of the dusty light flashing created a sense of urgency Justin wasn't wholly recognizing.

"Wait, what?" Justin's attention immediately swiveled in disbelief to Gavin. In his mind, the words kept repeating, *she's moving... she's moving.* His brain kicked into gear as he searched monitors for activity. "I don't see anything," he said before practically jumping over the counter from a seated position, nearly knocking over the useless equipment showing their unwavering graphs. Justin's face was pressed against the glass before he could see her eyes shift. His mind raced back to the few times he'd thought he had seen minor eye movements in the last few months.

Flickering.

After all this time, he thought it might be his *own* eyes playing tricks, but now… it was real. Justin sucked in a breath. "When did it start?" he asked, trying to sound like his insides weren't twisting.

Gavin's eyes flashed toward him, "The same millisecond I said her eyes were moving." Vocal angst didn't detract from the hard lines of scientific study in action on his face. Without diverting his gaze from his patient, Gavin typed in all the possibilities this change could mean on his tablet.

Justin couldn't believe her eyes were still moving, and it had been more than thirty seconds. "Each time she looks up…" he said on the release of a breath taken eons ago. Too late, he realized what he'd said wrong.

Gavin's eyes opened wide, and his glasses slid further down his nose. "What do you mean 'each time,' Justin? Have you seen this before?" They stared at each other for two seconds too long. "How long—"

"No,"—he cleared his throat— "I haven't seen her *move*. It's just something about the direction of, of... of the flickering." He wanted to break the glass and shake her awake, but instead, he turned away to avoid Gavin seeing him directly. "I just meant, the fact that her eyes are moving under her lids is already improbable enough. It could just be random misfirings in her brain. It could be her body preparing to shut down after being in a vegetative state for so long." He picked up his own pad to take note of the data from the last several minutes, ignoring Gavin's intense glare.

Gavin blinked. "We haven't seen a blip of movement in two years. Now all of a sudden, she's having... what? Electrical impulse movements or involuntary muscle contractions because her body is dying?" He peered through the glass at Justin on the other side. "Or it could be that she's trying to wake up."

Those were the words Justin had been waiting years to hear but knew the consequences if she was. Instead, he deflected the comment. "I wouldn't call what she did two years ago 'moving.' Her eyelids barely flickered, and there was hardly a breath of movement in our data."

Everyone else wanted her to remain comatose to be studied. The regulation was that if she showed signs of waking, they would have to ensure she ceased to exist.

*He…* would have to kill her.

The measures they were required to train for in case she ever woke up were absurd. The story behind what she 'might' be capable of was even more so.

Gavin grabbed his Galaxy again and started editing information as his five-foot ten frame narrowly missed walking into objects in his way. Justin knew Gavin was inputting his statement of their patient potentially 'looking up.' Notes Justin had not taken down himself previously. At least not anywhere Gavin would see them. He had been patiently waiting for his co-worker and only friend to witness it for himself. Or worse, that blue light to go off. The risks of her moving were too high despite his great need to see her open those eyes again.

*Damn.*

"It's over," Gavin stated matter-of-factly. Justin's frustrated brain didn't comprehend. His mind skirted toward the worst.

"What do you mean *it's over?*" His defensive reaction caught Gavin's attention.

"The spasms stopped." Gavin's statement took a moment to register in Justin's brain. After all this time, finally seeing a change of any kind had nearly pushed him over the edge. He needed to get a grip.

Three long strides took Gavin to his computer. He began searching for any anomaly in her neurological graphing. Justin shook off the last bits of anxiety and followed his lead. "I think this is it. This slight rise in the Raw EEG data, but… barely."

Gavin squinted. Shoving the pencil between his teeth, he typed a quick note on the graph line to annotate the change difference.

Justin verified all the leads that fed from their equipment into the glorified incubator were secured. Then he further checked that the lines leading inside the glass encasement to their patient were attached. "All's good here." He stopped and glanced over at Gavin. They both took a deep breath, not knowing what to make of the situation. Had anything even happened at all?

"What about changes in electricity levels in the building? Did the grid come on and boost the output?" said Justin, throwing out options.

"Even if it did increase it, this change was to her physically, not just to the readouts." Gavin put the perfectly sharpened, barely used pencil behind his ear, then leaned down to inspect the monitor that spits out brainwave activity. "The small spike of activity occurred at 6:49 p.m. for 47 seconds." They simultaneously glanced at the non-flashing light in the corner. It had only blinked once. They wondered if that would be enough to bring down the twelfth floor.

Without another word, they both began scouring the readouts for the hour before the spasms. Justin refused to lift his head as he asked the question they were both thinking, "Do you think it will happen again?" He masked his heart beating out of his chest by reviewing activity logs for changes in air density or temperature variations. He was afraid Gavin might actually see the thudding behind his t-shirt. Gavin always wore his white lab coat, but Justin had given up the pretense of stereotypical doctor's attire for the more comfortable T-shirt and jeans long ago.

Gavin gauged his response for a silent moment before saying. "I don't think it's an unreasonable assumption."

They began saving data to different file locations and even printed off a hard copy to archive. To the untrained eye, the blips of activity would not be evident or seemingly important. However, to those above their pay grade, changes by any degree were considered critical pieces of information.

The high tension in the room wasn't just because of the recent anomaly. Justin's out-of-character defensiveness had not gone unnoticed.

After three hours of analysis, Justin couldn't take it anymore. Leadership didn't show, so they knew they were safe for now. Frustration and hunger were two things that did not go well together, and he was more than happy to use them as an excuse to get out of the room. "I need food," *and a drink,* he thought. "Let's get chow." He watched his friend push his glasses once more over the bridge of his nose, only to see them slide back down. His remaining bits of frustration came out. "Why don't you just get Lasik? You can go right up the hallway. They'll do it for you in thirteen seconds, and you can come right back to work. Those glasses fall off every time you bend over, and you end up stepping on them." He knew it was a ridiculous argument to stir up.

Gavin pushed through the door, effectively positioning Justin's face just millimeters from being schwacked by it. "My eyes are my biggest asset. Not risking the loss, tool."

He deserved that.

Despite the widespread electrical black-out most of the world experienced daily, their little compound was light years ahead. They had the elite of the elite in doctors, physicists, engineers, all the way down to the janitors. All personnel had their area of expertise, but Justin and Gavin had only one focus: the girl in the glass box.

"So tell me about this upward eye movement you think you've seen," Gavin said in a low voice as they waited for the elevator. He was by far one of the greatest young neurologists on the planet, which is what landed him in this glorified prison. They needed doctors like him: young, intelligent, and able to think outside the box, especially when it was *this* particular box.

"Justin?" Gavin held the elevator door open as Justin stood planted to the floor. He hadn't realized the doors had opened. Memories came flooding back—memories of a lifetime before this.

"Sorry, no, I'm listening. I'm going." Justin's skinny legs moved forward onto the elevator just before the doors closed. He didn't say another word until they exited the elevator. Ears were always listening.

He breathed in slowly. "It's not just that her eyes were flickering," he said, deciding to take a chance. "Did it look to you like she was casting them up in just one direction toward the top of her head?" He left the question hanging while Gavin gave it some thought.

He felt Gavin had something to say but was holding his tongue until they made their way across the sterile hallway and into the dining hall. Justin was crawling out of his skin, anticipating the upcoming discussion. Still, he kept his patience in check, if only by a thread. He could tell Gavin wasn't comfortable saying anything further just yet.

After each grabbed a sub that would've put Jimmy John's to shame, they took a table in the middle of the room with the greatest ambient noise. At this point, Justin's glare could've fried an egg in the center of Gavin's forehead.

"Over the past few months, I've noticed it only a few times. I've played back the recordings during those moments, yet you can't see anything significant. Each lasted less than a second. The last thing I was going to do was alert anyone to a millisecond of movement that likely didn't happen."

Justin ground his teeth, and his lips barely moved. "So you never thought to ask if *I'd* seen this flickering before?"

"Have you?"

Both men seethed, but Justin said nothing.

Gavin had never shown a temper. His incredulity took Justin's anger down a few notches when he realized Justin had been keeping similar information from him.

Knowing he was just as much to blame, he whispered, "It was such a minute change that the few times I *thought* I saw her eyes twitch there was no proof I could have even provided you. The datasheets for those instances showed only anomalies on a very almost *non-existent* scale. A literal breath of a wave on the monitor. Muscle-wise, there's no definitive increase or decrease."

Gavin's voice didn't change in volume but definitely increased in intensity. "I kept a personal log on my computer with dates and times only."

Justin nodded, indicating he had done the same.

Both men got up from the table and dumped their uneaten food in the trash chute. Not wanting anyone to acknowledge their irritation, they calmly made their way back to the elevator and down to their lab. Once inside, each spent the next six hours pulling up all assessments from the dates and times they'd individually witnessed possible changes in readings. There had to be some correlation based on time, changes in electrical outputs—hell, even inclement weather. Finding it was going to be the hard part.

She couldn't be just a shell. Calla Lily had to be in there.

# Chapter 4
## The Stranger

Zoey, Aidan, and Joe jumped back from the stranger's voice, hidden in the darkness of the generator room.

Although a hood partially covered his face, his scarred fingers were touched by the excess of Joe's penlight. Zoey's nine-millimeter was pointed at his head with her finger on the trigger.

He didn't make a move toward them, but he didn't back down from their weapons either. Aidan's military-grade rifle, adorned with a laser sight tweaked to target perfection, was surveying the surrounding areas for anyone else hiding deep in the shadows.

"I'm alone."

"Then you're stupid—" Aidan snorted.

"What are you doing here? What are you doing with *our* generator?" Zoey spoke out over Aidan's words.

He stood quietly, patiently. The anxiety increased with each second. "Yes, maybe that's a stupid move. To be here alone. I'm not here to hurt anyone, and your generator will now last more than three times as long as it used to. You're welcome."

"I'll take a pass on the *thank-you* for now." Aidan showed no inclination of standing down. "How about you remove your hood so we can see your face?"

After a beat with no movement on the stranger's end, Joe said, "If you come into our home providing such a great gift, you're going to have to show your face. We'd like to know who we're 'thanking.'"

Ignoring Joe's comment, he said, "I came here to see you for myself. I have a proposal for you." He was focusing solely on Zoey. All three of them noticed it. As if he knew she was the unspoken leader of their unusual pack. He lifted his hands to his hood, pulled it away from his face, and let it fall onto his back. There was odd anticipation as if they were waiting for disaster to strike, but nothing strange happened. He was plain. No significant features to even recognize him on the street if they were to pass in broad daylight.

Sarcasm-laced, Aidan replied, "We have nothin' to give. Three people living on the edge of the city spending our days just tryin' to keep both our generator and stomachs filled." These days, generosity was only a mask. Zoey's crew had nothing to offer outside of quick wits and pessimistic attitudes.

Not to mention they kept their building heavily secured, and this stranger appeared to have just opened the front door and walked right in.

"I know what you are capable of. I've been tracking you for several years, and all of you have specific skill sets my team and I need. We are willing to provide you with whatever *you* need in exchange for your assistance."

"Our *assistance*? We have nothing. Our skills are based on survival." Zoey had always been the most straightforward of the three of them, and she got frustrated when people talked around a subject. "I'm putting my gun back in my pocket. My damn arms are tired. Spit it out."

He didn't move. For ten seconds, no one did.

"Zoey, your ability to quickly assess and judge a situation is one of the things that makes you unique. In fewer than fifteen seconds, you determined I wasn't a physical threat and holstered your weapon. Despite any visual verification from me to make certain."

Both men contemplated his words, then flicked their eyes at their weapons. Aidan slowly lowered his gun to his side but didn't release his hold on it. Joe's short-barreled sidearm was less pronounced. He preferred subtlety, but his sure-shot capability to put a bullet on a target from almost any angle was an exceptionally handy skill to have around. He also didn't have nearly as much faith in people as Zoey did, so his bullet launcher remained at the ready.

"That's not exactly an uncommon ability for these times, stranger. Years of practice in the city will give you that." Zoey was in conversation mode now. Ever since she could remember, she'd had this innate ability to gauge when someone was lying to her or not. He was not here to harm them, but she was also not giving him the satisfaction of knowing how right he was. "However, you showing up in our home uninvited, bearing gifts, and asking for help before giving us your name seems a little sketchy."

"True. Very true." He turned to Aidan, then cast a glance at Joe. "Nonetheless, the three of you have an appreciation for the truth, a respectability for human life, and, as I said before, skills we are searching for." Aidan began to speak, but the stranger cut him off. "I will explain in more depth in your apartment if you'll allow me that much courtesy?"

Joe squinted at Zoey. "You're the truth-teller. We good?"

Zoey gave him a lone stare back. "Yes. We're good."

With only a brief hesitation, Zoey cocked her head toward the stairs and led the way. The other two pulled up the rear behind him as a fail-safe. It was a practiced move they'd used many times when vagrants and thieves had broken in to steal food, clothes, and other comforts. That was primarily before they installed their security features. Those learning curves were the catalyst for all the safety upgrades.

Clearly, they would need to find another one.

Most people did not live as the three of them did. Life was more of a struggle outside of their small apartment building. They'd reinforced it over the years with Joe's engineering talents, and it had been a while since someone had made their way in. Joe was like a human Swiss Army knife. Every time you thought you'd pulled out all his neat little tricks and talents, another one popped out of a crevice to surprise you.

The three of them and a few selected others were the only people living inside the walls of the eighteen unit apartment building. They lived from the third all the way to the top floor, where their favorite tenant, Dr. Sheila, and her medicinal garden reside. Their 'tenants' forced them to become the maintenance crew, caretakers, and protectors of every life in the building.

They led him upstairs into one of the sparsely furnished apartments. They'd designed it for a visitor's semi-comfort, equipped with concealed cameras and sound equipment to record and playback conversations with shady individuals. Though more so for Joe's entertainment value. All too often, there were delinquents, called *jackers*, who attempted to break in. Joe would throw them into the room and proceed to scare them out of a life of crime with noises from hidden speakers. Entertainment was hard to come by.

"Comfy," he said, observing the room.

Aidan, bouncing with impatience, said, "Alright, man, what's your name? Why are you here? Why are you keeping track of us, and what are these skill sets you talk about needing? Need for what?" Although Aidan wanted answers, he was always a sucker for attention. Zoey knew he wanted to hear someone highlight the skills he so obviously possessed. She snickered at the thought. Joe caught her almost silent laugh, and the corner of his mouth also kicked up a notch.

This unknown man peered around the room as if taking

mental notes of all the hidden devices. They hadn't told him they were recording his every move and word, but Zoey could tell by the way his head cocked slightly that he had a sense of their existence. Most people have no clue, but there were a few folks out there who were either more in tune with their surroundings or just intelligent enough to know when they were not entirely alone.

"My name is Rice Jahnsen. I work with a team of individuals that want to bring the world back to before the fall of the grid. Before the death and hunger we've witnessed firsthand ever since. All we want is for life to go back to normal. No—" He paused. His left hand trembled slightly. "Not normal. Better than before the grid failed."

"'All we want,' he says." Aidan scoffed loudly.

Jahnsen held Aidan's gaze. "I do want more. More freedom. More of life. However, I want *less* of a lot of things too. Less disease, less starvation, less chaos, and I think you do too. I also think you three may be our key to the 'less' factor. I don't expect any of this to make sense at the moment, but it will. If you are willing to help us, we will take care of your needs and security."

"We don't need anything from you. We don't know anything about you. You've told us nothing of consequence." Zoey started to feel the pin-prick tingles on the back of her neck just before he spoke again. Those needles had guided her reactions over her entire life and had been more sensitive the last few years. She knew they weren't failing her now. He wasn't necessarily a threat, but there *was* something off about him. "Are you a Breaker? Or just a wannabe? We have no desire to jump on that train." Her eyes didn't falter from his.

Rice stood up and slowly walked toward the door. "No. We are not part of the lunatics taking down the grids. We do not have anything to do with them. They are fighting against everything we want." He took another step. "The Breakers have never shown any interest in putting society back together. They believed the world was so overpopulated with ignorant breeders, and people had grown so incapable of taking care of themselves, that taking away technology would collapse humanity.

"You're right. I haven't said much about why I'm here, but I had to make sure with my own eyes that you three were, without a doubt, who we thought you were. I've seen that you are. I will provide you with all the information you need over the next several months. Hopefully, you will believe as we do that we can work together to get that life back. With any luck, it will be even better than before."

Joe spoke out, "We haven't made any sort of decision to help you."

The corner of Rice's mouth lifted. He gave them a little nod and turned to walk out the door.

Aidan stood up to follow, but Zoey raised a stopping hand. He'd gotten into their building just fine, so ensuring that he was actually leaving seemed moot. They heard the front door of the building open and close.

She stared at the empty apartment doorway and whispered, "I don't think he was giving us a choice."

# Chapter 5
## Purgatory

October 11, 2028 | 5:17 p.m.

*What is that light? I can almost see it just over my head. I just need to see where it's coming from. Come on!*

*I now know I'm seeing this light. I honestly thought I was losing all semblance of control, but this is real. And it's getting louder in here—the humming. Like a running printer or refrigerator slowly being moved closer to my head. But the light. The light! I just want to see it. Where's it coming from?*

*I've been in the dark for so many days. Months maybe?*

*My thoughts or memories, whatever they are, are clearer all the time. I'm not as dazed as before, yet I'm more confused than ever. Now this light! I just want, I just... where is...*

*Why is there no one else here with me?*

*There's the hum again. It's stronger now. Before, it was like an ocean wave coming in and out, louder and softer. But it's different now. More poignant. Sharper edges to the tones.*

*A fierce pressure on my ribs both reminds me of what pain feels like and traps me in a horror I can't escape. The fear intensifies, which somehow causes the vise-grip on my body to increase pressure. The pain would rip a scream from my lips if I could manage to make a sound.*

*After what seems an eternity, I feel the iron hold releasing. The fear subsides. The pain begins to dissolve. I know with more certainty now that I am somewhere. This can't be purgatory. If only I could remember something.*

*I desperately try to think back to my last living memory… all I see are two little girls. Playing in the dirt. Climbing trees. Someone, somewhere, is yelling, but we just keep playing.*

# Chapter 6
## Inside the Gate

Justin set the pressure distribution test to Begin 30-Minute Full Body mode, then sat back to review his notes. He was comparing them to Gavin's from the last six months of potential activity after witnessing that first eye flicker. A rapid beeping sound he'd never heard before came from the stimulus monitors. "Gavin? Gavin, *where are you?*" Papers flew from the clipboard in his lap as he launched to his feet.

The blue strobe light in the corner began to blink, only this time it didn't turn off. That meant the clock was ticking on the arrival of their twelfth floor leaders and lackeys.

Justin ran to where Calla Lily lays prone inside her glass prison and saw Gavin standing nose to glass on the opposite side. His eyes wide, mouth open. It was as if the wind had been knocked out of him. Gavin put his hands on the window, "Oh my God. But how? Justin, this isn't possible." A brief moment of terror—or joy?—crossed Gavin's face before he could mask it. The ever-professional scientist was missing. Justin was momentarily stunned by Gavin's facial expression.

Justin had to yell over the sound of the monitors for Gavin to hear him. "What were you doing just now? Right now. Before it started, what were you testing?"

"Nothing. *Nothing!* I just flipped the light on at the head of her tank and almost instantly—" Gavin's words faltered.

"Her eyes. It's like she's moving them toward the light behind her head." Although her eyelids were sealed shut from the pressure of the stabilizer unit she was in, her eyes beneath would not stay still.

The few times they'd noted movement, it was minimal spasm activity. *This* could be described as having a significant purpose.

"Her eyes are forced upwards, and her body is almost imperceptibly shifting with the strain of it." Gavin could barely force the words out.

It had been months since her eyes had begun flickering for only seconds at a time. Still, no other signs of increased functioning had occurred with or without the pressure distribution running. Justin's heart was beating so quickly that he was in danger of passing out. In the back of his mind, he thought it would be incredibly un-manly of him to faint in front of his younger counterpart.

"The subject shouldn't be moving. There's been no discernible movement of her body, or even so much as a spark in brain activity for years." Now all the needles and numbers around them were moving rapidly, despite her almost complete physical stillness. Almost. Gavin grabbed his tablet off the kiosk and began pulling up the analysis feeds. He was comparing her visual movements to what the graphs were depicting. "What were you testing when the monitors went off?"

Justin eyed the documents strewn across the floor. "I had just finished Calla Lily's daily Glasgow testing for motor response and began the full-body distribution pressure tests." As he said the words, he realized they were still in progress and ran back to his computer to see what the pressure was currently at across her body. She was suspended in a glass box that allowed for pressure changes on each part of her body, either singularly or all at once. The pressure was set to cause a pain response but not enough to cause injury. The test began by sealing her eyelids before applying pressure to the left, right, top, and bottom portions of the eye. It exerted enough force to help them determine if she could feel it, causing her to move her eye away from discomfort. From there, the computer compressed her sternum down through her exterior limbs, palms, fingers, and toes.

Until that moment, she had never once attempted to recoil, withdraw, or escape from the pressure. They'd begun to believe the spasms of her eyes were an anomaly. But now…

Impossible.

"We need to prepare for Jones. He's going to want answers. He's going to be ticked."

"We don't have time. He'll be here any minute. The blue light has been going off for the past—" Justin's words failed him as everything went still.

Silence. They looked around at the once spasming machines disconcertingly going off mere seconds ago. All of it was silent. "What happened? Where'd she go?"

Gavin began moving in circles, racing from screen to machine and back to the glass, but nothing. No movements. No eyes straining. Just nothing.

"Do you think this was a one-time deal?" asked Justin.

After a few moments of speculation, Gavin shook his head. "No. I think this is just the beginning." His eyes flashed over to their silent, immovable patient. Both men were astonished with slightly terrified expressions. They had been at this for quite a long time together—four years, in fact. Gavin was hired to work alongside Justin about a year after he arrived. He had been watching, testing, and—for Justin, at least—waiting for any sign of life since.

Their positions were not simple. They were instructed to keep her alive, test the chemical compounds in her blood, and note any triggers that may cause movement or signs of mental and physical functioning. Blood, hair, and other samples were drawn weekly and sent to different sectors within the building for testing. The two of them were the only ones privy to all the data. Every other lab performed analyses without knowing why or how it all fits together.

Ultimately, though, Justin and Gavin were required not to let her regain consciousness. They had to keep her alive but comatose, and if she did somehow wake up despite their capabilities to keep her under, they were ordered to *pull the cord*.

The dichotomy of the regulations they were required to follow was unrealistic, to say the least. She had been comatose since the day the grid failed and kept alive every day within a glass coffin with no defining conscious functions.

According to those they worked for, as long as she stayed non-functioning, they all lived. If she began to function, they died. However, if they were to "pull the cord" as leadership dictates, they live, but they lose the opportunity to learn from her supposedly higher-level capabilities. Granted, in all these years, they hadn't learned much. Without any physical or mental activity, only her biology could be studied. As far as anyone could tell, she was no different than any other little girl.

Outside of their compound, this girl was a myth. She was supposed to have capabilities beyond the norm. Everyday folks used her story as a theory as to why the grids failed, and power plants exploded. No one truly believed it.

Inside the compound, personnel had several working theories about the power failure, and she was theory one.

To them, she wasn't a human being—she was a research subject. Even Justin had grown so accustomed to the objectivity of his day-to-day life, the complete lack of human compassion for her, and the callousness with which she was discussed that he often succumbed to their belief that the world was safer with her asleep. The compartmentalization of his wish for her to awaken was tucked tightly in a box in his mind.

There was some truth to the generally accepted theory, but there were many, many lies as well. Justin had become her protector and guardian before the end of normal civilization. Another lifetime ago. Sometimes he believed it was a dream, but he knew deep in his soul that it wasn't. She lay still in front of him, each day unconsciously pleading with him. Gavin sat ten feet across from him, peering through the same glass with the same expression of longing, obsession, and fear. His fear was he would have to kill her. Justin's was that he would have to save her.

"What's happening down here?" Director Jones' words rang loudly through the silence.

# Chapter 7
## Ice Cream

"**L**et me just try to understand you for a minute here, Aidan. Your infinite wisdom and life experience led you to believe that scientific enhancement could *not* have played even a small role in the development of this magnificent entity?" Joe's eyebrows lifted in skepticism.

"Correct." There was no mistaking Aidan's dogged belief on this issue.

"Humans have spent centuries trying to enhance medicine, uh, technology, the—" Joe spluttered as he tried to reason with Aidan. "*Life,* for crying out loud! Technology is or was involved in basically every part of life as we know it. How can you sit there with a relentless belief that, in this particular case, it's *au naturel*?" Joe gripped his knees to keep from strangling

Aidan. He was a man of few words, but certain topics he would not shy away from.

That red hair and those pretending-to-be-lazy eyes didn't hide Aidan's internal joy for riling Joe up at every opportunity. "Yup." He gazed at Joe with all the innocence his devil's soul could muster. "It's ice cream, man. Ice cream is the most amazing gift God has blessed us with, and *He* wouldn't taint it with unnecessary chemicals and scientific garbage." He leaned back in his chair, causing the front two legs to lift off the ground. After taking an absurdly large bite of delicious homemade ice cream, he followed it with a spoon salute.

"There are so many flavors! How do you think they even— how do you explain the colors and the— the— You are the most idiotic s—"

"—Stupid, pain-in-my-arse human on the planet," Zoey finished off his statement for him. This wasn't the first pointless argument they'd had, and it always ended with the same ridicule by Joe. "Joe, technology did play a small role in the design and augmentation of flavored ice cream. Aidan knows it, but you let him get to you. Aidan one, Joey zero." She cut her eyes to Aidan. "And you're an idiot." She kicked her foot under the front part of his chair.

He careened backward. His arms shot out to grab the table and side of the fridge, trying to stop his momentum. And he was almost saved.

Almost.

His ice cream bowl began tipping off his right leg, and he made a judgment call. Would it be his body or his ice cream hitting the floor? The answer was easy.

The groan of pain as his back hit the peeling linoleum gave her the little smile she needed. "You need better arguments. Lame." Her attention moved to Joe. "Any news?"

Aidan held his bowl of ice cream up to the ceiling as he dropped his head to the floor. "SAFE!"

"You're a junkie," Zoey said.

"Nada," Joe said around a mouthful of organically delectable ice cream, ignoring the scene that had just played out. On every other issue, Joe was fairly devoid of emotion regardless of if he was for or against something. But when it came to science and technology, he could get a little feistier. And when it came to ice cream, both men's love for it was held most high, so the verbal carnage between them significantly enhanced.

Their fight over it never made any sense, really, but it gave them a reason to argue when trying to avoid things like a world in chaos. It'd been quite a few years, and the pain had faded. The reality of it all, however, was present in every moment of their lives. Right now, their most forefront discussions had been on the stranger's visit, Mr. Rice Jahnsen, and why they hadn't heard a word from him in six months.

Zoey walked around Aidan, trying to get up from his tangle with the chair on the floor. She felt the rush of cold air graze her skin as she opened the fridge. It was glorious having food that was always cold. They'd done a lot of extra security work around the Sanford, NC, area. In return, they'd scored bananas, honey, and cocoa in order to make ice cream, only made possible with their more stable electricity. Sanford was about thirty-five minutes from their apartment building. It was a small town, but not a lot of crime unless you count the significant drug trade that kept the townspeople a little better off than most.

They had long spring and fall seasons, hot summers, and short winters. There were plenty of other places where they could live decently enough. However, with unreliable electricity, meaning a lack of a consistent heat source, they found that being in a place where winters were measured primarily in days was helpful. Further south, they'd be hit with hurricanes. West, they'd have tornadoes, severe weather, and earthquakes. And up north, it's cold. Plus, they were right off Highway 95's main artery for moving produce and supplies of all kinds. That, of course, included narcotics, but that particular trade brought up bananas too, so who were they to complain? Most would think the drug trade would crumble after a technological apocalypse. Considering it was there before tech, it stood to reason it would be around after. In fact, it seemed to have flourished and cast a wider net. They didn't do drugs, so they didn't much care... and frozen bananas made ice cream.

Zoey thought the ice cream tasted almost like the old Wendy's Frosties. So delicious.

She pulled the entire Rubbermaid from the freezer and relished every frozen spoonful.

"How come you get the whole bowl? You only let us take a small scoop!" Aidan's whining made her want to eat all of it just to spite him.

"Maybe that's because I'm the one that makes it." She didn't even crack an eye open as she savored the flavor.

"What if I—"

"Nope."

"What do you mean n—"

"Nope."

"You suck."

She smiled around the spoon in her mouth.

They let the silence sit for a few minutes before Aidan brought up the topic on all of their minds.

"So our theory is that this Jahnsen guy isn't one of the Breakers."

"Right. Sounds like he wants electricity back, too," Zoey said, shoving in another heaping ice cream scoop.

Putting her bowl down, she held her hand out to help Aidan up. His voice strained as he pulled his chair, along with himself, back upright. "Sucks without electricity."

Joe arched his eyebrows in agreement without taking his eyes off his bowl. "It would take decades to undo the global damage. We've been out of continuous power for, what... five, six years almost? There are almost no children for the next generation to take over for ours. Nearly all of the old and wise are dead and gone." Joe said aloud, though it seemed like he was talking more to himself.

Zoey felt her heart clutch a little as she remembered watching her Grandma Cecile pass away through the square window of the door to her hospital room.

That first year after the power loss, a sickness spread the

globe. Even without the violence and chaos caused by the outage, the illness took those whose health was already in decline since medication was limited.

Joe's eyes seemed far away, momentarily reliving his own pain during those terrible few years. None of which he'd ever spoken to them about.

He glanced back up at her, the sadness replaced by determination. "So if not Breakers, then who? Do we have any faith whatsoever that *Rice Jahnsen* is on the right side of this? Could he, or anyone for that matter, bring back a stable environment? A world with electricity, restaurants, and schools? He said he wants it to be better than before. So what, no crime? No hate?" He let out a wistful sigh.

"You mean a world where love and patience rule instead of defensive driving and movie-theater shoot-outs?" Zoey was in it to win it today. She laughed under her breath, fully knowing the ridiculousness of a future where love could reign. "Wonder what faction we'd be."

Aidan blurted out, "Dauntless, duh."

*Divergent* was still one of her favorite movies.

Was it even possible to have faith in others? Even the ones you believed you truly knew? She was the one that had a knack for spotting liars, but genuine trust was a whole different ball game. "Yeah, well, I don't know. We need more information. Joe, anything back from your cyber buddies?"

"Nothing yet. I've got a signal out, but it depends on if they can receive it. It's always intermittent at best." Using his finger, he swiped out the last bit of ice cream on the sides of his mug.

"You think this has anything to do with that girl? The one they say supposedly brought down the grids?" Aidan was now sitting back in his chair with the front two legs off the floor again. Zoey was itching to tip him over but decided not to give in to temptation. He made it too easy.

"Not sure. Seems like a myth. One person taking down the world? One small girl, to be exact. Seems ludicrous. Do you remember when that Lizard Group—"

"Squad," Aidan cut her off.

She rolled her eyes, "Or whatever they were called took down that gaming system, Xbox, years ago?" One thing Zoey did *not* have was a knack for remembering things like bands, actors, or anything gaming related.

"Ohhh, Xbox," Aidan groaned. "Oh, how I miss you." He slammed his chair back down and put his head in his hands.

Joe stopped just shy of licking the remnants of sticky ice cream from his finger. "And you thought I was bad." He gave Aidan the once over. "Lame."

He put his hand out to collect Zoey's bowl. She could see his mind spinning. "What are you thinking?"

Joe didn't turn around but said, "Everyone thought for years it would be a war that would take us down. Then it was nuclear war, just waiting for some ignorant, greedy SOB in North Korea or Iran that would push the proverbial red button. Not just killing their enemy but also themselves in the fall-out. After hundreds of years of face-to-face war and peace talks, we then go from tech-less to tech-savvy in a matter of decades."

Joe dried off the bowls and then continued:

"We saw it coming. At least those of us in the nerd world. We had every spectrum of good, bad, indifferent, and ignorant in our community. Some folks wanted to make the world better, easier. Others wanted to take it over through technology. And *then* you had the young and stupid that spent their time trying to break things just for the hell of breaking it.

"They were the scariest because they had no sense of mortality, no purpose, and no life experience to recognize there was so much more waiting for them outside their mommy's basement. A world full of families, kids, and friends. Instead, these kids were staying up all night wearing headsets, talking to strangers in a *Total Recall* world. Their ignorance of social reality lent to having no concept of how the pizza and soda they were sucking down even came to be through hard-working men and women. They were stupid geniuses."

He turned around to face them and perched his hands behind him on the counter. "It was never going to be a battle fought by tanks or airplanes in the sky. It was always those kids. Kids with the means and opportunity to do something outrageous. They were governed by one group, smart enough to lead them by giving them what they needed. Their next fix and ultimate challenge. Prove they could take down the world. I'm pretty sure they aren't laughing now after their final triumph of controlling and taking down the power grids. Hard to stay up all night binge-eating pizza and playing *World of Warcraft* without electricity."

Aidan and Zoey looked at him with mouths open, shocked

he had so much to say.

Joe took no notice of their reaction and sat back down in his chair across from them. He sipped his tea, which had no doubt, by this time, turned cold.

Zoey found her voice and said, "So you think it was those tech kids that took down the grids somehow?" She could see his point but was unconvinced.

"Eh, I don't know. Just a theory I've been toying with. There have been rumors, but nothing concrete from anyone."

Aidan couldn't resist. "That's dumb."

Joe cocked an eye at him.

"Well, it is. They might've been idiot kids thinking they could take down the world, but wouldn't at least *one* of them have been smart enough to realize that taking the power out meant no more games? I mean, you are kinda smart and all, Joe, but, on this, you're dumb." Aidan should've stopped while he was ahead.

Joe glared at him long enough for Aidan to contemplate if he should be worried.

"Yes, Aidan. Someone, I'm sure, thought of that. However, some kids are too stupid for their own good and can't see beyond the tip of their nose." He pointedly looked Aidan in the eye.

"True. True," Aidan said.

Joe released a deep breath. "Alright, so we'll label that option as possible, but less likely. Either way, there's no good answer." He gave up, recognizing that as much as he'd like to have an easy answer for laying blame, there would never be one.

"How did we, or the electric companies, not have fail-safes?" Zoey knew they did, but it all seemed so mind-boggling to think everyone, everywhere, could be affected all at once.

"They did. Every country had its own. But every country also has people who, for some reason, hate their own country. They weren't exactly hard to find. Half of them posted their anti-whatever country on their Instagrams, intermixed with pictures of their dogs walking around in socks."

Aidan nodded in agreement with Joe. "True. Man, those were some funny videos, though."

Zoey took a moment before coming back to the question at hand. "So the verdict is we don't get involved? Is that our answer?"

Both men nodded slightly, but a small amount of uncertainty still flitted around the room.

"Do you think that girl truly exists? The one they flashed across news stations as everything began failing?" Zoey felt somewhat naïve for asking, but something about the little redhead in her memory from that day felt off. She absentmindedly rubbed the now-less-painful purple webbing on her belly. The lines had spread, but only to the right side of her body. It was worse after her more fierce night terrors. She still hadn't said anything to the boys. As the days passed, it didn't seem to be killing her. At least not that she could tell anyway. Showing them would come with more questions she couldn't answer.

She just didn't want to deal with that.

Neither man said a word, so she kept talking.

"You know, I can still remember that day," she said quietly. "The TV was on in my living room. I finished making some toast and jelly before running to class, packing my books in my bag as I went, and wondering why I wasn't just taking online classes like all my friends.

"I was reaching for the front door when the sound of the news anchor's voice shut off mid-sentence. I turned back to look at the TV as the screen came back with frenzied commentary—anchors talking over each other about power fluctuations around the country and internationally.

"The last image I remember seeing was a crystal-clear picture of a young girl—or young adult maybe, but she seemed tiny. The girl was standing in front of that power plant down off Highway 1, the old Harris plant. She was standing completely still. The image had a fake quality to it, maybe because it was so clear. Like they were using it as a background image until the television stations could get back on the air."

Joe and Aidan looked at one another in confusion as she spoke about the image of the girl.

"That's when the blast happened. Even though I was watching through a TV screen, the explosion was such a shock it made me fall backward. When I got up from the floor, the image on the screen flashed a few more times. The girl was on the ground, motionless. Then everything went dark. Power grids everywhere failed."

"Zoe, you saw a girl? On your TV?" Aidan's body moved

slightly forward.

"Yeah." She looked at him, unsure what he was asking, and then continued, "At first, no one did anything. They just waited, assuming the power would come back on. After a few days, people started talking. Irritation turned to anger, and anger turned to action. There was just nothingness. No messages from the president saying everything would be fine. No, 'This is a test of the Alert Broadcast System.' Within a week, looting and killing began."

All Zoey could see in her mind as she spoke was the chaos.

Several minutes ticked by, and the silence got to Aidan. "Alright!" He didn't have to hear the words running through their heads to know what they were thinking. "Let's blow this popsicle stand. I need some fresh air. Let's irritate some neighbors, shall we?" He grabbed his M4 and slung it over his back.

Zoey smacked her hands on her thighs and pushed herself up. "I'm in. Maybe we need to start considering our options. A nice beachfront property would be a good change for us."

Aidan always had a way of re-focusing their attention. Maybe that was his addition to their skill sets?

"Yeah, we could make spears and hunt sharks!" Aidan sounded pumped. Joe's expression of horror at the idea gave Zoey the laugh she needed.

"For now, let's settle on finding the meat-man and pray he found a lost cow." Her voice showed ease though her mind still raced. Even now, she could see the girl's silhouette on the TV screen in her memory. They weren't going to get out of whatever it was the stranger wanted from them that easily. She just hoped they could ignore the hunger they all felt to find change in their lives. Something about this potential adventure seemed like it may be difficult to walk away from.

49

# Chapter 8
## Inside the Gate

**"S**ix months of this, and you're just now telling me? Have the two of you lost your damn *minds*!"

Justin had known this was going to happen. He and Gavin had placated Jones when Calla initially began the eye twitching. They'd provided him with just enough information to give him hope that she would fade back to her normal, motionless, non-functioning existence.

But she didn't.

Gerard Jones, the Director of Valuable Interests of Special Persons—otherwise known as VISP—was not a prominent man. He was the kind of man you may not notice walking down the street. Yet here he was, in charge of likely the most classified organization left on earth.

VISP was one of the multiple windowless buildings on their compound housing scientists like them. They should have at least made it a three-letter organization like the CIA or FBI. An attempt at looking like they belonged with the cool kids. But no, the powers that be went with VISP.

Jones was raving mad. They had sent up their weekly and monthly situational reports—SITREPS—on Calla Lily but hadn't exactly gone out of their way to make her changed condition known. After six years of nothingness, any sort of something was a big deal.

"Jones, she never woke up. She isn't moving," *much*, "and we never thought there was any reason to contact you for some minor eye movements."

"Minor? I'm not an idiot, Justin. I can read the charts. Some days the brainwaves are high enough for her to be yelling through that glass!" His face was red, his anger palpable, and the buttons on his shirt strained against the overlapping belly. That had always been a mystery considering the only food provided on site was organic, nutritional sustenance. It was surprisingly excellent food. No one could complain, yet his stomach *screamed* Twinkies.

Justin and Gavin had come up with elaborate stories that Jones was the leader of an underground railroad for preservative-laced foods. Obesity was negligible anymore. Except for Jones, of course. They *would*, however, prefer to be part of the underground railroad peddling their old friends Belvedere and Hennessy.

"JUSTIN!"

*Huh?* "Huh? Yes, sir?"

"If I'm going to come all the way down here to yell at you, at least have the courtesy to stay in the moment and listen," Jones said calmly, but his glare was lasing through Justin's corneas.

"Right. Absolutely." So lost. "Yes, as far as the brainwaves, that is what finally brought us to call you. We didn't previously because we wanted to make sure it wasn't just a one-or two-time event. We were gauging if her physical movements would increase before bringing it to you. Basically, we wanted answers to the questions we thought you'd ask before you asked them." He took a breath, "Such as:

"Has this happened more than once? *Yes.*

"Where exactly are the movements occurring? *Started with eye movements beneath the lids, primarily rotating toward the top of her head. She has begun to show signs of upper spinal motion, yet no significant bodily movements are occurring at this time. Still too early to tell if electrical impulses in her brain are the cause or if she is consciously causing the movements.*

"Has her brain shown signs of increased activity with or without eye movements? *Definitely with the eye movements, but now the activity increases about an hour before and an hour just after the eye movements thents. According to the monitors, the activity within her brain is not otherwise consistent with the physical activity, or lack thereof, that we can see. Separately though, her brain activity is equivalent to a grown adult male maxed-out in a fight or flight response. Which... is high. Yet she shows no real physical sign of that energy.*"

"Get to the point, Justin. What does that *mean*?" Jones was standing stock still, but the redness rising from his neck seemed to intensify.

"This could mean the function of her body is essentially broken just as a quadriplegic might be, though with considerably more energy coursing through her brain. Or, it could be the beginning sequence of her body reviving. The increase in brainwave activity is growing in intensity during the periods of eye movement." Justin walked away from Jones and toward the glass encasement, subconsciously putting himself in a defensive position in front of Calla Lily.

Taking a deep breath, he said, "As far as her potential to wake up? Right now, we do believe physical functioning could increase, but the pace so far suggests a very long process—as in years. Based on all of this evidence, our primary concern or suggestion, sir, is to plan for the most likely scenario and begin preparations for her" —he didn't want to say it but knew there was little choice—"awakening." He quickly continued, "We believe we have several years to plan, but the discussions should begin now." Justin could sense the fuse being lit, but someone had to entertain the reality that killing a young woman on the off chance she had the capacity to murder everyone else was asinine. They had plenty of time to make a forward-thinking plan. While it was true that that was all he'd been doing for years, the acknowledgment of it had to come from someone with a higher pay grade.

Jones took a moment to walk over to the glass case

encompassing the primary topic of conversation. His breath hitched as the corners of his mouth turned down. A sadness was evident in the expression.

Jones's chest puffed up as if giving himself strength, then turned around. "She doesn't wake up. We don't plan for her *awakening,* we plan for the end game. It's your job to keep her silent and still and asleep." Despite his quiet words, the heat rising on his neckline showed he was nearing the verge of a heart attack.

"The end game? That's a little extreme, don't you think?" Justin steps closer to the glass case.

"Sir," Gavin deflected focus, "I realize that's been a possible plan since the beginning, but no one knows what the fall-out would be if she were to all of a sudden *not* be here. That's one of the main reasons we were pulled in on this: to sustain life. *All* life. There was only so much testing we could do without any physical functioning of Calla over the past several years. Things have changed. We need to continue our work and see where it leads us. Assuming the human race would be lost if she wakes up seems illogical." Saying those words out loud created an almost volatile silence. Justin decided to pull the attention back on himself, seeing his partner's attempt had fallen short.

The hum in the room was the only sound cutting through the silence when Justin's voice rang out. "On that note, we would like to set up a meeting with you, sir, to go over the contingency plans. Based on what we *do* know about Calla Lily, we don't feel there is a significant threat. Allowing us the opportunity to discuss those plans and possibly adjust—"

Gavin cut in on his thought, "Wouldn't it make sense to fill us in on our part of the coordinated contingency plan, at the very least? Other than… the plug part?"

Jones glowered from one man to the other. "Yes, there is a plan, and you already know why you aren't involved. We can't risk a third party somehow finding out. Your job is to leave the planning to us. If it ever has to come into action, you'll be informed of exactly what you need to do and where to go based on the circumstances. For now, you know what your job is should she wake up."

"When you say 'third party' finding out,'"—Gavin skeptically assessed the catatonic young woman prone in the nearby enclosure—"you mean Calla—" He didn't finish his thought due to the sparks flying from Jones' eyes.

He just stood there. His eyes seared into them.

As they waited for Jones to explode or start firing them en masse, Justin started to get very nervous. Jones wasn't yelling yet.

Jones inhaled slowly, and on his exhale, he sat down in the nearest chair. He was known for being somewhat bipolar, but thankfully their anticipation of him yelling and walking out the door, even possibly firing them on the spot, did not come to fruition.

"Gents, we've been at this a really long time, and you've done an amazing job. Truly. I can't begin to know how tedious your work can be, and if we could easily bring more people in here to assist you in some way, we would. But as it stands, you're it. The two of you know more about the fate of this world than God himself. If there is a collective triad of God out there," his gaze met Justin's... "I'm looking at the Father," then Gavin, "the Son," and turned toward the glass holding a beautiful, small young lady, "and the Holy Spirit."

Deep.

"First time compared to God, Gavin?" Justin whispered, *not quite* under his breath.

Gavin's mouth opened, but Jones cut in, "Just find a way to make her stop moving!" He stood, turned, and exited, mumbling, "I thought I'd be long gone before having to deal with this. Damnit…" That was the last bit they heard as the pressurized door closed behind him.

"Well?" Gavin's eyebrows rose in the universal, what-do-we-do-now? gesture.

"Not a clue, brother." They walked up to the glass prison. Her tiny frame was about five feet tall, maybe eighty-five pounds. Her light-red hair had grown long over the years and was wavy, as opposed to the curls they once held. The luster was somewhat gone from it, but it still shimmered like sunlight. At twenty-one she wasn't much bigger than when she'd been placed in their care. The stabilizing unit had somewhat suppressed her growth into the woman she should be now. For so long, Justin had watched her from outside the glass, blocking out the ache of being unable to free her by stuffing it deep into a box within his soul. She was safe. He would keep her that way.

Even now, they could see her eyes cast up to the light

slightly behind her head. Lids closed. Like she was praying to the heavens. Jones christened them as gods, yet they weren't answering Calla's prayer.

Justin paced his small living room, half-filled with furniture he'd never have picked out for himself. Furnished living quarters were a *perk* of choosing this life of solitude. Beige. Why was *beige* the universal color? Beige sucked.

It was one in the morning and sleep was taking a backseat to Justin's endless internal conversations. Pacing around the beige couch in his cramped living space had yet to offer a spark of insight into what was taking place twenty floors below him. What changed? Was there anything they'd done differently within the last year that might have been the catalyst causing Calla to start moving again? Was she actually waking up, or was this a precursor to her death?

It seemed it was a precursor to death either way at this point.

That thought drained the energy from his limbs. Sinking into the couch, he drug his hands down his face in frustration. He clicked on the barely used 60" TV to erase the reflection staring back at him. A shell of his former self. There were only two channels. The VISP news of government activities on one, such as updates of what was happening here on their compound: technology conferences, new equipment testing so 'prepare for the occasional explosive,' and, of course, mandatory fun events. For morale. Sometimes he would even catch the weather lady, MJ Thompson. She came on every day at nine a.m. to tell them it was sunny and seventy-two or that a storm was brewing. She'd stay on to give them the 'up-to-the-minute' updates, which were much more entertaining during hurricane season. Weather lady. What an easy job. He'd be overly blessed to have her job. You could be wrong all day yet still get paid.

The other channel was on-and-off news updates on the outside world. On occasion, someone outside the walls would find a way to break through the communication barriers and broadcast reports from around the globe. Generally, those broadcasts didn't reach very far, but a few organizations out there still had the know-how and equipment to pop in once in a while.

The techies on the compound could pick up frequencies from just about anywhere because they had sole access to the satellites. The communications division could monitor anyone with the right equipment to broadcast. They were also able to retrieve satellite imagery worldwide, but only when the satellite's trajectory placed it overhead of the location they wanted to see.

Justin felt smothered glancing around his one-window apartment. Slamming his hands on the glass coffee table, he pushed himself to his feet, grabbed his jacket, and reached for the door. His reflection in the mirror beside the coat hanger stopped his forward progression.

It was a pale face with a stranger's eyes. He used to live in the sunlight each day, as the sweat from mowing lawns cooled his skin. Earning cash on the weekends put him through college. Skinny, yes, but strong. Now he was just skinny, as well as pale and lifeless.

There was no recognition of that former man in the mirror.

He threw his jacket onto the couch, changed direction, and put workout clothes on. He took a deep breath and told himself, "This guy is about to get back to basics." How could he possibly protect Calla if the most energy he expended in a day was to walk to the elevator and back again?

Justin's workout clothes hadn't gotten much action lately, now draping over him where muscles used to be. His sister told him once upon a lifetime ago that muscle shirts were for men with muscles.

Time to make good on her sarcasm.

# Chapter 9
## Purgatory

*T*ime's standing still.

Agh, why can't you hear me?

I'm not alone. I know I'm not alone. I can hear you talking right now. Why can't you hear me?

Ahh! I'm breathing. I know I'm breathing. I can feel my lungs expanding against the pressure in my chest. I can hear the whir of the air holding my body in place. I know my eyes are being held shut, but my eyelids can't stop the light from penetrating.

And neither the dark nor the pressure keeping my body still can stop the voices around me. Most of the time they are muffled, but occasionally they are close enough that I can grasp a few words.

"... she would be... movement is suppressed... breathing on her own... no stopping progression..."

*They are talking about me. I can hear their words. It feels like ants are crawling all over my body. There's a screaming in my head raging against the inability to move an inch. I'm vibrating with the will to move, but I just can't get my muscles to cooperate with my mind.*

*Wait... what... someone is listening, Hello? Hello! Please hear me! Please hear me....*

*I know you can hear me.*

*My eyelids. I can feel them begin to spasm. I can almost....*

# Chapter 10
## The Newcomer

VISP | March 9, 2029 | 7:17 a.m.

"How's our girl today? She's been kind of fidgety lately." Maria was the newest addition to their lab team. She was quite possibly more intelligent than Gavin, which left Justin as the rock of the group. She was also very amusing in a semi-man-bashing sort of way. Justin was grateful for the new levity. Gavin was less appreciative. The two men had been working together for so long humor was hard to come by.

It had been close to a year since Calla had started moving her eyes beneath her lids. Despite Jones' disparaging words about being the lonely God-like duo protecting the planet, twelfth floor management had finally listened to requests for more brainpower in the lab. Since they showed that they were able to keep her comatose for all intents and purposes, Jones finally agreed.

Gavin and Justin were able to vet Maria's capabilities and agreed she could bring a great deal of expertise to the table.

Plus, she was a woman....

Which didn't hurt.

They weren't privy to exactly *where* Maria had been found. They knew there were limited options considering the condition of the outside world. There were still hospitals, but only the bigger ones were able to continue functioning on generators as long as they could secure the fuel.

Hospitals located near solar panel fields were able to survive once generators were no longer an option. People came from all over to assist in security for hospitals, granted it was not out of the kindness of their hearts. Instead, it was a service they could provide in exchange for food and shelter. Over the years, small compounds were built around hospitals to protect the medical providers. Naturally, communities developed surrounding those compounds.

Without power, worldwide communication dropped to a standstill. That first week or so, everyone waited with growing impatience for repair technicians to fix the problem. By word of mouth, rumors began to spread. The primary and most prevalent story was that a terrorist group had something to do with it. There was so much chaos already that terrorists seized these opportunities to wreak havoc across western civilization.

Initially, the elderly and immunocompromised became gravely ill with an untreatable pneumonia-like sickness. There were no good answers. As the months went by that first year, many folks passed, whether by illness, violence, or heartbreak. With the world having turned on its end, finding someone with the medical expertise to work alongside them would've been daunting at best.

Justin looked for a very specific trait in a newcomer that neither leadership nor Gavin needed to know about. And here she was.

He hoped and prayed that her maternal instincts would provide a buffer for not killing Calla if it came down to it. A man in this scientific role would be more likely to compartmentalize and follow protocol.

Sexist? Sure, but Justin had a mother. She would righteously tell him compassion wasn't a man's strong suit in a crisis. She wasn't wrong.

Also, Maria *was* the best candidate by far.

She had specialized in working with both comatose and traumatic brain injury patients. She had worked with patients inflicted by trauma, tumors, and unexplained phenomena. She had continued her research even after the power plants failed because there were still people who needed medical care despite the devastation. As medications quickly dwindled, her biggest asset became deceased patients. Having electricity meant she could still accomplish brain scans through MRIs and CT scans. She may not have been able to enhance livelihoods through medications, but she managed to learn a great deal from her patients—both alive *and* dead. Autopsies reveal a great deal about a damaged brain.

Plus, there was no shortage of marijuana, so... she wasn't *totally* out of medicinal options.

The United States had just started legalizing it the year prior, but it turned out they didn't need to. With the world torn down, the most accessible medication became marijuana. Easy to grow. Easy to get. Most diseases and injuries were now treated with it.

Maria's personal history was unknown, but showing up here typically meant you were family-less. Orphaned in some way. An orphaned genius in Gavin's case. Justin barely hit the genius mark... truth be told, he was probably the least likely person to be found at VISP. That's not to say he wasn't worthy. He had a connection. A connection that no one there could claim to have despite all of their education and training. Granted, no one other than Jones knew about his past with Calla. Some of his paperwork may have been altered, if not entirely manufactured, to gain him access.

For Maria to be brought in on this meant she'd have also undergone a rigorous investigation. VISP had to be sure she was not a rogue saboteur. Also known as a Breaker. Simple enough term. To some, it meant terrorist. To others, sympathizer. Breakers had different factions too. Some wanted peace, some anarchy, and others power. Regardless of their goal, they all felt that breaking in here and killing or kidnapping the alleged Calla Lily would prove an end to their means. The closest a Breaker had ever come to Calla was working in one of the above-ground offices. Standard paper-pusher. It was difficult to find an overly intelligent person willing to be a pawn—specifically in a game where even half-truths about what went on were nearly impossible to come by. Most intellectuals had a little more pride than that.

Maria, however, was a lay-it-all-out-there-from-the-get-go kind of woman. Her spiced-up attitude brought some much-needed color to the mix. She quickly became part of the fabric of their team. Then again, some Russian spies were known to meld into society pretty well too.

They were keeping an eye on *Mata Hari.*

"Did you just ask if our girl was fidgety?" Gavin said around the pencil clenched between his teeth. "You've likened the life-sustaining power of our world to a kindergartner that has to pee," he muttered.

Maria and Justin peered over at him. Her eyes rolled so far back in annoyance it was a wonder she didn't fall. Justin chuckled.

She turned her sights on Gavin. "So?"

Justin opened his mouth to cover for him, but Gavin took the bait. "She's doing better or worse. Still *fidgety,*" he said, lacing that last word with sarcasm. "Her arms and legs aren't yet twitching, and her spinal movements from yesterday have calmed down. It feels like she's becoming more aware of us. Despite the air pressure and acoustics within the unit depressing our voices, it's as if her vitals change in tune with our activity out here."

Maria, unlike her male counterparts, held little back. "Well, *my* thoughts are that we don't have as much time as everyone around here thinks. They keep talking as if there are years or even decades left before this little girl makes her entrance to the world known. I'm not sure we have the capabilities in here to stop her if she decides she's ready to let loose."

"If there's even a need to stop her," Justin said nonchalantly. Maria's openness gave him more courage to speak his mind. Even if it was simply to defuse her thoughts. He wasn't quite ready to deal with the fallout of an awakening and what that could mean.

She acknowledged his response with an eyebrow lift. "The air depression in the tank keeping her from moving makes me think she's much further along in the revival process."

Maria had just vocalized what the two of them had been thinking for the last year. Leadership believed Calla waking up was a possibility so far down the line that significant preparation wasn't yet needed. "Anyone care to chime in on this? I know I'm the fledgling here, but I'm also a set of fresh eyes."

"I think that's a plausible reality. The fact that she is moving at all puts serious holes in the theory of permanent catatonicism," Justin never truly believed in it being permanent to begin with. Calla's coma had ceased in his eyes, but he held his tongue on that point. The permanence of her staying asleep was pure fiction. The explosion that occurred over seven years ago caused many casualties. There was one crucial casualty that was likely the reason she ever went into this deep sleep state.

Those that know of Calla's existence believed she would

never recover. For Justin, this belief was a good thing. As long as he was in the lab with her, the research would continue, her life was safe, and leadership had every intention of keeping her protected. The importance of Justin being with her was critical. VISP leadership was clear that their concern was for the safety of humanity. Justin worked toward that also, but it fell second place to Calla's safety.

Despite the last year of activity, no one outside the three of them, and a *very* small circle of people, even knew of her true existence, let alone the conceivable implications of her waking up. The researchers on the four sub-ground levels all worked in specific areas related to Calla. Many weren't specifically aware of *her*, just that they were continuously testing and analyzing data from Justin's lab. The rest of the folks on the protected compound had no idea what went on in this building. The world, as a whole, only considered rumors of her to be just that: rumors.

The devastating crumble of the power grid and her proximity to the initial blast seemed to be the only catalyst for her presence at VISP. At least in Justin's mind. There was still information being held back even after all these years about what truly put her in this position. That was one topic Jones made sure to keep close to his chest.

People tended to believe the worst of others far quicker than they considered the good or probable. An individual could be bright, but a group of people could be led by emotion with little effort. Anger being the quickest.

"Maria?" Gavin said, not taking his eyes off his computer.

"Yes?"

He paused for a moment, causing Justin to glance his way. Gavin was generally very poignant, so his hesitation was out of place.

"What is it like now?" He asked without slowing his typing.

"What's what like?"

"Civilian life? Being outside of this cement prison we spend every day in?" His sarcasm barely masked the embarrassment of asking.

She leaned back away from her desk. "You know, not much different. Kids mouthing off, thieves stealing from the rich, murders in the alleys." Her saucy comments brought a disappointing look to Gavin's face. It was rare for him to ask questions like that. He had been more introspective the past few months, especially after Maria had come into the picture. It made Justin wonder if he had ever been on a date. Ever been in love. Ever been laid.

Sadness flickered across her features as she noticed his now withdrawn manner. Letting out a breath, Maria knew he probably hadn't had any sort of real life in quite a while. He deserved at least a partial answer. "No. It's not really like that. Some areas are better than others. Some worse. Individuals who are lucky enough live well out into the country. People trade and barter with each other. Live off the land. Other fortunate ones are smart enough to work in a place like this—the complete opposite of those in the country. Kind of like where I was before I came here.

"I worked in a large hospital in New York. Even with the power loss, the hospital was able to keep going for a while on generators. As time grew short on the generators, the hospital was able to tap into a solar panel field.

"We had our share of attacks, but many people stepped up to play security for us. Thankfully, we were able to be self-sufficient. Compared to ninety percent of the world, it was like living in the lap of luxury. And it was life with a sense of purpose." She moved over and sat down next to him. "Most people primarily live in cities near rivers. Power would come on, sometimes weeks at a time. Then it's gone again for months. The Breakers control the power grids. We were able to circumvent them with our solar fields. The worst of the killing, gangs, and death waned back in '25. In my opinion, it was because the only people left were those that had a purpose. Something specific they brought to survival.

"The last of the non-perishable foods were used up by '26. Everyone remaining realized it was easier to join with other skilled groups to support each other instead of killing for territory."

Gavin was openly curious, although he remained silent, taking it all in.

"Granted, there are still some bad ones out there, but humans are humans. Most people have found their niche. There are still techies smart enough to hack the hackers and get the power back for a while." She sighed. "But, the Breakers always regain control.

"For a long time, it was like Zombieland, or what was that

show? Dead Walk… Walker… Walking Dead! That's it. Without the zombies, of course. Well, shoot, most people acted like zombies."

"You're rambling—" Justin said. She ignored him.

"—walking around dazed, hungry. Shut it, Justin," she said with a smirk.

Gavin looked wistfully away from Maria for a second and mumbled, "I always loved that show."

Maria's eyebrows lifted. "Somehow, I'm not surprised." She abruptly stood up, attempting to kill the conversation, but Gavin clearly missed the memo.

"So what happened to your…" He left it hanging a moment too long, but Maria knew where he was going.

"Family? They're gone." This time her tone got his attention. She lifted her empty water bottle and pointed it toward the hallway, effectively cutting off any further questions.

Justin could feel Gavin's disappointment. He had a little of his own, but there was not much he could say. He'd been in this box almost from the beginning. Outside of the rare news stories on TV that he even more rarely watched, he had no idea what was going on out there any more than Gavin did. He picked up his digital notepad and walked over to see what Calla was up to. As he peered through the glass at her steady breathing, it dawned on him that her body was still. Not still like in sleep, but more the frozenness of a cat waiting in the shadows.

She was alert.

He sucked in air so quickly that his heart stopped beating. Her eyes weren't flickering at all. They were completely motionless.

Gavin heard Justin's deep breath and jolted to his side.

No one moved. No one breathed.

Gavin slowly expelled the air in his lungs. "She's looking right at you."

# Chapter 11
## Connected

"**Z**oey?" Joe awoke to Zoey's labored breathing. Her eyes were pinched shut. Moving quickly to her side from his recliner he touched her shoulder. Her body curled into a tight ball.

*So dark in here. Feels so thick. The air, the sounds, and my breath are all suffocating. Oh God, oh please. So much pain. I can feel her anguish! All I can do is cry and plead for it to stop. I push my hands out to block the onslaught of crushing agony, but I realize my arms aren't physically moving. They're trapped, crushed. I can feel my bones grinding together, splintering as the blackness presses them.*

*Without warning, a voice whispers in my head, "Hello? Hello? Please hear me! Please. I know you can hear me."*

*Her intensity in knowing I'm with her breaks my heart to a million pieces.*

*She knows I'm here.*

*Blindingly bright. The darkness disappears. It's so piercing, my eyes burn.*

*There are people. Maybe three or four. Some staring, some yelling. But she's different. Just out of reach, gazing directly into my eyes. Everything's foggy, but her eyes are clear. Bright. Crystal blue. She's trying to tell me something. Her lips are moving, but it just doesn't make sense. I can't hear her beyond the roaring in my ears and the splintering of bones reverberating up my body.*

*Again, she repeats herself. She's telling me to wake up? I am awake. I want to scream it at her! Yell at her to help me, save me, stop the crushing, but all her lips tell me is to wake up. I AM awake, for God's sake! Aren't I?*

*Her body's getting closer, but yet she's perfectly still. She's so close now it's as if I can feel her breath on me, but her face no longer looks menacing, just pleading. Pleading to me? I'm the one trapped, unable to breathe.*

*Then she screams at me, "Wake me up!"*

"It's not me!" Zoey screamed into the dark. Her arms and legs thrashed, trying to break free from the agonizing pressure.

"What's not you? What's not you, Zoey? Zoey calm d—"

"IT'S NOT ME! OH MY GOD, IT'S NOT ME! Let me up, dammit!"

She grappled with the covers wrapped around her legs. Flailing about, she was trapped. Joe tried to grab her before she hit the ground with no success. She careened off the side of the bed.

"Jesus, Zoey! Stop! I've got you!" He climbed off the bed and grabbed Zoey's face between his hands. "You're okay. You're alright. We're in our apartment. You're not trapped. You're breathing." They'd been through this before. He knew when Zoey woke up from one of these episodes she needed someone to remind her of who she was. Where she was. And that she was alive.

Sucking thick, hot air into her lungs from the gratuitous heat in the bedroom, her rigid body began to relax. With every worsening night terror, it seemed to take Zoey longer to come out of it fully. Joe had started to sleep in her room so that if—when she had these dreams, they wouldn't find her hours later huddled in a ball in the corner of the room. She would spend half the night rocking herself, not knowing what was happening but feeling the residual pain deep within her bones. Not to mention the nosebleeds. Sometimes even bleeding from her eyes and ears. She would end up with bruised and cut limbs from thrashing through those dreams.

They'd found her one too many times in that state, and the fear it brought to both men had them taking turns at night to keep watch. Trying to wake her from one was even more terrifying, so instead, they just tried to keep her safe from herself during the outlash she caused.

Zoey clutched his arms as his hands held her head more

gently. "I get it now." Her eyes locked onto his, a crystalline clarity shining through a hazel tint. He had never seen anything like it. "It's not me, Joey. It's not me. It's her."

Aidan burst through the door, minutes late as usual. "Everyone good here? I heard a ruckus and considered briefly that the S-E-X was happening in here—oomph!" A pillow struck him straight in the face. "But—" He recovered quickly. "—obviously, that's not the case, Grizzly-Adams." Aidan tossed the pillow to the bed and put his hand out to help Zoey.

Joe tried to stand up while untangling himself from the covers. Stretching his limbs in the process, he said, "Zoey's alright, in case you were wondering. But that was the worst I've ever seen." He paused. "Your eyes were open, Z, and yet you weren't in there." Joe's eyes locked onto hers. "You were… lost." He wiped some of the blood off her cheek with his thumb. He was afraid to lose her attention, for fear she'd disappear.

Tears forming, she walked into his big bear of a frame and was encompassed by his genuine worry. None of them were openly affectionate—specifically Joe. So for him to show this level of concern was a significant awakening for all of them.

"What? I don't get no love?" Aidan quipped. He walked forward and pulled the two of them into a true embrace before breaking the moment. "So none of the sex?"

Two pillows slammed into both sides of his head.

"Such a jerk," Zoey muttered as she walked into the

bathroom to do her customary *after-nightmare* de-sweat routine.

As she turned to close the door, Joe said, "Zoey, what did you mean? 'It's not me, it's her.'"

Her breath felt shallow, but she didn't answer his question, "I need a minute." She finished closing the door. Her reflection was haggard and dazed.

After the door closed, Aidan asked, "does she know yet?"

"Know what?"

"Brother, you need to tell her."

Zoey reached blindly for the sink and the water streaming from the faucet. Cool water drenched her face, leaving trails down her arms and dripping puddles onto the floor. This one was bad. Very bad. This dream felt so real she could still feel the pain in her body from the sense of bone-crushing pressure. The lights in the bathroom were so intense her eyes could barely open. The blue irises of the woman that had stared her down, begging, pleading for Zoey to wake *her* up were still so vivid in her mind.

While she assessed herself in the mirror, it all came back with such realism that the oxygen felt stripped from the room. Soon, the floor rose to meet her hands, then her face. That's when she heard it. The voice from her dream, *"I know you can hear me,"* said in the softest whisper, *"I can feel you. I can hear you. Please, say that you hear me."* Her quiet voice tore Zoey to pieces.

No, this isn't right. It was just a nightmare. I'm awake right n—

*"Please… just hear me…."* The pain in the voice was so tangible that it wracked Zoey's body with a wave of agony.

"But I—"

*"I need you. I need you to wake me up. Don't leave me here."*

"I hear you." Zoey's voice sounded strangled. This is not a nightmare. "I hear you."

"She's getting worse." Aidan stood in his power pose. Feet spread out, arms crossed in front of his chest. He wore the face of a man trying to look like a stern parent but not quite pulling it off.

Instead of finding humor in that thought, Joe's concern for Zoey was a weight holding down any levity.

"I know she's getting worse."

"We need to do something!"

"What do you propose? A mental facility? Know any good ones still open!" They were rage whispering now, knowing the water in the bathroom would turn off any moment, and the conversation would be cut off.

Aidan took a long breath. "She loves you, man. Love worked for Sleeping Beauty."

"Not like that, she doesn't. She loves me like a brother. So a brother is what I'll be. Drop it, Aidan."

"How many years have we been doing this? Take a damn

chance, man—"

Joe cut him off with a wave of his hand and cocked his head. "Why's the water still running?"

They walked to the bathroom door. Joe turned the knob, but the door wouldn't open. "Zoey, you alright?" No answer. "Zoey? Open the door." Both of them felt the same panic.

"Move out of the way, Aidan!" Joe took a few steps back, ready to throw himself at the door when Aidan's body appeared on his periphery and smashed into it. Aidan held onto the handle to keep it from fully swinging in.

The men pushed carefully into the bathroom, where Zoey's body was blocking the door in a heap. Joe grabbed her arms and head while Aidan helped lift her off the ground, pulling her back into the bedroom.

Joe was the first to see the side of her jawline. "Grab ice, Aidan. She must've hit her face." Aidan gently finished laying her on the ground and ran into the kitchen to grab a frozen water bottle from the freezer. Running back, he caught sight of a strange shape next to the front door and hesitated for just a second before Joe called out to him.

"We need to see if Doc is nearby. I think she's broken her jaw. Maybe she hit her face on the sink." With careful movements, he began to turn her chin into the light. He saw the dark lines trailing down her neck at the same time Aidan walked in to see Zoey's shirt hitched up, showing her abdomen.

He stopped short. "Joe… look at her stomach." Aidan traced his sight up to the neckline of her shirt, where the dark, purple spider-web lines navigated up along the side of her face and jaw. "I don't think it's anything caused by broken bones."

Stopping mid-motion while he tried to determine what may be wrong with Zoey's face, Joe let his gaze also follow the pathway of crisscrossing lines. He tracked it down her neck to where her ribcage and belly showed above the edge of her cargo pants. He reached down and slowly peeled off the sweat-soaked shirt Zoey was wearing, careful not to hurt her in her unconscious state. They could see the continuous web design of deep purple and red lines reaching from below her pants and up the right side of her navel, with the brightest red lines reaching her face.

"What is this? Have you seen this before?" Aidan's voice trembled for just a moment, then he checked himself. "What is it?"

"I have no idea. I've never seen anything like this."

"Any chance I can have my shirt back?" Zoey's voice startled them from their shock.

Her eyes were mostly shut, but at least she was coherent.

"Zoey! Zoey, don't move. Hold on, Aidan's getting you some water."

A moment later, Aidan realized Joe was talking about him. "Yes! I'm getting it. Water." He took off out of the room again.

"What's going on, Zoey? What happened?" Joe helped her sit up but kept his hands around her shoulders.

Their gaze locked, and he couldn't hide his awe. Her eyes had always been a type of hazel color—sometimes almost green when she was happy and darker brown when she was mad. Now they were luminous like hazel crystals with flecks of both green and now blue.

"Your eyes." He said in a whisper.

His startled look caused her confusion to wane and refocus her thoughts. "My what?" She pulled herself up off the floor with his help. Zoey saw herself in the broken mirror on the old German dresser as if for the first time. She wasn't sure if she was still dreaming. At first, she saw the web of lines up the side of her face and was taken aback by her reflection.

She saw a stranger's eyes looking into her own from the mirror.

Her breath caught in her throat as she realized the similarity of the crystal colors in her own eyes with the woman pleading to her moments ago as she lay on the bathroom floor.

Aidan came back in and froze.

"Zoey." He could barely breathe out her name.

Her body gave way, and her knees fell out from under her. Reaching for her simultaneously, the men softened her descent and carried her to bed.

Zoey whispered, "We need to find the woman with the crystal blue eyes. It's her. Something terrible is happening to her, and whatever is happening to her… is happening to me." Her voice was a strange mix of pain, exhaustion, and fear.

"Then we'll find her," Joe stated, sounding matter-of-fact. "Zoe, what do you see? Is anything different when you look around? Do you feel different? Are you in pain?"

She lay there momentarily with her lids closed, taking a few deep breaths. When she finally opened them, they watched her take in every detail.

Everything seemed hazy at first, but then she focused out the window. At the sky. The clouds. The haze started to ebb away, and everything became much clearer. Very clear. Her pain was temporarily forgotten despite the evidence her face and body projected.

"Everything is just… open. Bright. I don't know." She shook her head as if to remove the cobwebs from her mind.

Aidan lowered his head for a second, then got up and walked out of the bedroom. Within a minute, he walked back holding a package.

"This was sitting inside our front door. I didn't notice it until I ran in here with the ice. It might have nothing to do with what is going on with you, but coincidences of this magnitude don't really jive as unrelated in my book." He sat down on the bed next to Zoey with Joe looking on from the opposite side.

Joe gave him the go-ahead nod. After turning it around a few times to ensure no odd wires or oil stains were on the box, he ripped open the seam. A letter sat on top of the filler inside, and Aidan read it out loud:

Zoey, Joseph, Aidan:

I realize I've given you very little information, but the details will come with the journey. The contents of this package will provide enough information to get started. Even before the grid failed, our world was crumbling, and we believe we've found the key to making a change for the better.

As I stated in person, all three of you are gifted in a way our organization significantly needs right now to get through the first and most important mission. We can't do it without you. I know I can't ask you to believe in us or to have faith that our agenda will lead to a better future. For now, the only thing I can ask you for is your help, and I believe that what you are looking for aligns with our agenda.

I realize you are waiting for a further explanation, and the only thing I can offer is that we need you to rescue someone. Any details beyond that, I cannot provide, as the level of importance of this person's safety is too high to risk anyone else intercepting these details. If you're willing to take on this challenge, I trust you'll be able to determine the best course forward based on the data within.

With that, I ask you to please burn this message once you've finished reading it.

What you'll need to find the location of this person is in this box along with a cell phone. When you've rescued the individual, your phone will be active. We'll have eyes on you to pick you up and transport you to our location for safety.

R.J.

"Little information? Try no information," Joe said under his breath. Then with greater conviction—and irritation—"Target date? What's the target? What are we special forces?"

Aidan, who would typically be ready to jump into any new adventure, stilled his hands on the sides of the package. "We don't have to do this. We could just stay here. Or walk away from all of this. Go find a beach somewhere and live our lives away from whatever all of this is." His hands rested on either side of the box, hoping Zoey or Joe would say *anything* that might change what he knew they would do all along.

"You're right," Zoey said. "We could. Everyone has a choice, and this is ours." No one said anything else, as they could tell Zoey was trying to process. "You know, I have spent too many nights without sleep, sitting in this apartment wondering only one thing: what's the purpose? What is *my* purpose? Before all of this happened—before the fall of the entire economic world order, I had a plan. Grow up, go to college, and start a career in criminal justice, even though I had no idea what that really meant. I wanted to help people. Keep folks safe. Make life better somehow. At the time, I thought it meant I would be stopping bad guys and bringing justice to all. Ridiculous. Even as vague as it was, I felt I had a purpose.

"Now? We sit here day after day just surviving. No other reason for living this life other than just to breathe air and become worm food when we die. All people die. At least that's the rumor I'm going with until I see Lincoln and Elvis sitting at our table drinking coffee together.

"How does our life or death even matter? Would it make or break how the world functions if the three of us died right now? There's got to be a reason we exist. Right?" She stared out the dusty window. There was not even a slight breeze to make the old curtains ruffle on either side of the window. After a few breaths, she found a little more strength for her next words.

"All I know is, right now, I am being crushed by a force I can't see or touch, yet it's killing me just the same, which seems ludicrous. Am I possessed? Is it aliens? Is there something deeply wrong with me, causing me to manifest physical signs of bodily harm because my brain is broken? None of this even seems possible, but it's happening. Despite the fact that it thoroughly sucks, it has opened my eyes somewhat to my sense of purpose.

"I *know* that I have to help this person that cries out to me—not just for her sake, but for my own. If doing that somehow invokes a change for the better in this world in some small way, then that tells me I'm doing the right thing."

Zoey looked slowly from one man to the other before saying, "I have a sense of peace about it. Doesn't mean it'll be easy, but at least I know something about this is right. I can't live as a zombie day in and day out anymore. If I can believe that finding her and helping this woman is the right thing even though I can't physically understand it, then I can believe there's an even greater purpose for our humanity and existence outside the cycle of eating, sleeping, procreating, and dying." Her desperation bore into each of them.

"So, no. No, we can't, Aidan. I can't even begin to comprehend what is going on, but whatever is happening to me"—she gestured to the violet web interweaving up along her rib cage—"it won't stop if we walk away from this. This—this is happening because of her." Her arms dropped to her sides, and she stood there, spent.

"How do you know that following this insane path, guided by a person we know nothing about, will *actually* bring us to her?" Aidan asked the question even though he knew it really didn't matter.

"I don't. But like you said… this many coincidences don't jive in my book either."

"Open it up, Aidan," Joe said quietly. "If they wanted us dead, that box would've blown the place up well before we woke up to find it inside our door."

With a nod from Zoey, Aidan pulled the top stuffing out of the box. Inside were three different types of keys, a cell phone, a set of blueprints, and a map. He handed the phone to Joe, "I suppose this will be easier than a message in a bottle."

"Do cell phones still work?" Zoey followed the phone transfer from Aidan to Joe.

"Yup, in the right places." Joe was nodding while he opened it and turned it on.

He handed the keys to Zoey, then pulled out a set of maps and opened them.

"It almost looks like a forest, maybe? Or a farm? The map doesn't show much other than roads around this circled area here." He pointed to a hand-drawn circle on the map over what might be an empty property. "Hold on, lemme see… yeah, this second map is of whatever that blank area is on that one. These numbers correspond to something. Are there supposed to be buildings here? There's no name for this area anywhere from what I can see. Here, you take a gander," he said, handing the first map to Zoey.

Instead, she pointed to the third document. "Are those blueprints? Here, move that second map out of the way… yeah, there, hand me that, Aidan." Zoey slid from the bed to the floor and unfolded the third document into a two-foot-by-four-foot blueprint. "Again, no name, but it could be a large building. Here, on the bottom, it says it's 700,000 square feet. Dang. That's a lot of space." Taking a moment to scan the blueprint, he finally shared his thoughts. "Each cordoned-off area on here has an identifying character set of a letter and number. Granted, there's nothing explaining what the heck it means. See how this one is circled? LR17 is written on the side. Maybe a floor number?" She wasn't asking anyone in particular.

Aidan pointed to the bottom-right corner next to the map legend. He gestured toward a handwritten date. "Look, it says eight, ten, twenty-nine," he snorted before saying, "So apparently, we do this thing in August? That's such a random date." Shaking his head, he looked around for confirmation. "Right? That's random, isn't it?"

"Uh-huh," Zoey said without really paying attention. She was lost in the maps and prints in front of her. Joe stood up and stretched his legs before bending over to pick the keys up off Zoey's lap, and then he walked out of the room. He headed for the fire escape window and stuck his head outside to survey the alley. A large four-wheel-drive gunmetal gray Mercedes Benz G550 sat there clean as a whistle and not so incognito.

"I figured out what at least one of the keys is for," he called back through the window.

Aidan popped his head outside and followed Joe's gaze.

"Damn. Dibs!" They hadn't had much need for a car in a while, and the one they did use from time to time sat sadly a few feet away from the flashy Benz behind it.

Snatching the keys from Joe's hand, Aidan tried to jerk backward through the window but only managed to whack the back of his head on the frame. A long howl of pain erupted, followed by a few foot stomps.

Joe said, "Y' okay, Aidan?" Not even trying to hide his laugh.

Aidan punched him in the arm before turning on his heel to head outside. Zoey's voice echoed from the hallway as he grabbed the knob on the front door. "Hey, guys?" She walked slowly out from the back with her face buried in a map. "This map is of someplace in Pennsylvania."

Aidan tipped his head up and said, "Is that the place everyone talks about, you know, where super-secret squirrel testing is going on?" He turned back around with excitement in his eyes. "Wait. Is that where that girl is? The one people say will 'doom us all and kill the world'?"

"Oh, right! That almost makes sense." There was hardly a trace of sarcasm in her tone as her new crystalline eyes were filled with interest. Aidan and Joe momentarily froze when her eyes peeked over the map in her hands. It was an unbelievable sight.

Aidan filled the short silence with, "We're going to have to get her some sunglasses." Both men nodded their heads in unison.

Joe blinked at her to clear his thoughts, then chimed in,

"You mean the girl named after that plant? Rose? Or wait—Calla Lily? If it happened at the Harris Plant, wouldn't she be somewhere here in NC?" He walked over to his computer to see what his contacts could tell him.

"Maybe, but Pennsylvania was where the electric company blew up. The first one before all the others around the globe started detonating. The Blue Ridge Summit or Raven Rock Complex is out there. It's where they had those old WWII Nuclear fallout bunkers. They could've transported her up there." Aidan paused for some introspection. "Come to think of it, I bet that's where the president is hanging out right now. I bet they equipped it with sweet underground waterfall showers, spas—oh, and freezers full of thick juicy steaks. If that's where we're going, I call dibs on the executive suite! Gonna have a beer with the VP. Think he'd let me date his daughter? Imagine, I could be the *Son-in-VP!*"

Zoey and Joe rolled their eyes as he continued his monologue. "Would make sense they'd have her there. I bet they're training her to be a secret weapon."

"Who? The Veep's daughter?" Joe snickered.

"*Calla Lily.* You know, the girl we're all talking about? And actually, Joey, Rose is correct too. Depends on the circle you're in. Some call her Rose. Some call her Calla Lily. Both are beautiful with hidden dangers. Whatever. It's a freakin' flower." His frustration told them that they should be following his train of thought. Sometimes it was surprising to hear Aidan speak intellectually. It was rare that he paid attention long enough to catch details. "What? Don't look at me like that. I know things."

Zoey blinked once, then stared silently for so long that both men took notice.

"Zoe?" Joe's voice came only as a whisper, barely revealing his concern.

"I think... I think that's it."

"What's it?" said Aidan, quiet as Joe.

"The girl. They are looking for her." Her gaze traveled between them. Surer of her thoughts, she blurted out, "They really are looking for her. I think they believe they've found her."

She took in a deep breath, then released. "And they think we can save her."

# Chapter 12
## Inside the Gate

"Her eyes are open," Maria said in awe. "They are… her eyes…." She couldn't put into words what she was witnessing.

She lay there still in all ways, except for her eyes. Initially looking straight ahead, they drifted left, settling on Justin's. Immediately he knew. She was seeing him.

The three of them just stared as her eyes began to close again.

"She's fading. Her eyes are closing. How was she able to even open them? Print out all the stats for the past twenty-four hours. We need to see the overall change pattern in the neurological processes leading up to her eyes opening." Gavin was going back and forth between talking to himself and spouting out orders as he raced around the room, tapping keyboards, swiping at digital files, opening data sheets, and swearing as the printers moved too slow for his warp-speed movements.

Maria finally pulled her eyes away from Calla's closed lids. She realized the full, topless water bottle she had forgotten to screw the lid onto now dripped down the front of her dress into a puddle on the floor.

"God Bless America." She chucked the empty water bottle to the side of the room while moving toward Gavin to assist in saving and printing. "Did you see her eyes? The color? Were they glowing?" She was now talking a mile a minute.

Justin couldn't believe it. He had known in his heart it was only a matter of time once she started showing neurological movements that she would eventually wake up. Now that it's happened, it felt surreal, and... they didn't kill her. It dawned on him as he watched Gavin bark commands (even though Justin was the senior tech) that no one made the call. No one turned off the oxygen or flipped the switch on the lethal dose that would've killed Calla within moments. All he could do was stare at them.

Gavin finally noticed. "What are you doing? We are going to have a lot of explaining to do in no more than ten minutes! Start saving before they come down here and take all our data away to burn!"

"Burn? What?" Maria watched the exchange between them but never stopped what she was doing.

"I don't understand. Why didn't either of you flip the

switch?" Justin wasn't sure whether to prepare to fight them or hug them.

Gavin stopped what he was doing and stood up defensively. "Why didn't *you*?"

Staring each other down, neither knew the others' motives for letting her live. Any minute, Director Jones and who knows who else would be bearing down on them. After all of these years of wondering what Gavin would do in this situation, Justin realized that despite having spent almost every day together for six years, he honestly did not know what this man was really here for. Now was not the time to try to figure it out.

Justin opted for the easiest and least informative answer. "She's my life."

"Mine too."

After a few seconds more, Maria broke the strain. "Now that you've cleared that up, could the two of you help me out here!"

Both nodded, unconvinced but with an unspoken agreement to deal with it later. They then paused to discern Maria's reasoning. "And you?"

She put her hand on her hip and said, "I have never in my life killed another human being despite how long I was on the outside before coming here. I don't plan to be the one that potentially kills off the planet by killing that little girl. Can we get back to business?"

Solid answer.

"So, what's our story?" Gavin said as he finished putting the rest of the printed files into a nondescript folder. Racing around, he shoved it between the archived folders in the dusty cabinet at the back of the storage room. As soon as he reappeared, so did Jones. Followed by five other headquarter twelfth floor suits.

Gavin's questioning look immediately turned to a calm, almost nonchalant demeanor that he had no ability to pull off. "Geez Jones, you got down here pretty quick from when that buzzer went off. We were just about to head up—"

"Upstairs? To let me know that our girl is running *sprints* in her cage?" Palpable anger.

Maria froze at the word 'cage.' "Cage?"

Justin cut her off before her reaction could turn feral. "Everything's fine. She's not awake. It was our fault."

"What do you mean it was 'your fault'? That buzzer only goes off when the sensors are peaked for movement!" After the last visit from Jones, in which he was informed of Calla's increased neurological functioning, they re-calculated all of the sensors only to read higher-than-normal movements. Hers had become significantly higher, and that was in a state of complete paralysis.

Gavin jumped in and put his hands up in surrender. "We know. With the eye movements we've seen and the increased brain function over the past year, we've adjusted and created new testing procedures. In the past two months alone, we've seen significant rises. We wanted to try and test her ability to physically move other parts of her body even if she's not consciously aware she's doing it. Today as the sensors started peaking and brainwave activities reached levels for a potential physical movement, we were able to conduct these new tests." He glanced at Justin to take over.

"Yes, uh, we upped the return flow of electromagnetic energy from the sensors placed on her temples. This increased stimulation to her brain and specifically to her eyes. Although we couldn't determine if she was physically 'aware' of her eyes being open or if she could even see, the capability still exists within her brain to *make* her eyelids move. That is, if she *were* mentally capable of doing it herself."

Jones and his five lackeys all blinked in unison.

"I don't recall signing off on new tests. Why did you not warn us then that you were conducting them?" Jones was slightly calmer after the explanation. However, he was not a doctor or scientist, so it was really a wag if he even knew what they said.

Maria could no longer hold her tongue and stepped in using her haughtily superior voice. "I wouldn't think your team of elite scientific specialists with the ultimate responsibility in Research and Development as well as survival and care of our infamous and potentially cataclysmic 'Being' needed to ask for permission to do what we're being paid for." Hand on hip. She fearlessly stared him down.

He had the careful eye of someone who could see through flawless vocal garbage a mile wide. However, he said nothing. Walked up to Calla's unmoving form. Observed her from head to toe. Then he turned and said, "You only get one. This was it." He walked past them and through the doors with a train of confused men following in his wake.

They waited until the sound of the door's pressurized seal completed its hissing sound to expel the air in their lungs. "*What*... did we just tell him? And what is '*you only get one*'? Holy crap, I thought they would be dragging us out of here in body bags." Maria sat down in the seat behind her and leaned her head back.

"That was the only lie he'd let us fully get away with. He knows she's waking up. We know she's waking up. At the end of the day, no one really knows what to do about that. Or what the consequences of that mean for all of us." Gavin sat down in the closest seat and dropped his head into his hands.

Justin's breath poured out with the words, "I don't think he wants to have to kill her, just as much as we don't want to."

Gavin paced Justin's apartment further wearing down the carpet in the same manner Justin usually did; counterclockwise, round and round the cramped furniture. Maria just sat on the couch, legs tucked under her, deep in thought over the day's events. She hadn't been here nearly as long as the men, but the impact of what transpired was deeply impactful, nonetheless.

"It's incredible. Her eyes were open. *She* opened them. She was staring right at us as if she wanted to say something. Then she just fell back to sleep? I've been over every second of what happened, and I can't find any triggers to give us a clue as to why she would've opened her eyes like that." She took the bottle of water Justin held out for her, opened it, but just held it in the air as she said, "Why then? Why that moment? What's the activator?"

Gavin walked over to the miniature screen overlaying the news on the TV. They could see Calla at any given time on their personal monitors in their room. It's a screen only they could log into using secure codes—that way, no one could find their way into their apartments and gain visual access.

Maria was staring into space when she said, "How is it that you ended up with all those kitchen appliances, and yet, based on the layers of dust, there's no evidence you cook." Both men looked around, surprised by her random declaration.

"Uh." Justin looked from her face to his kitchen and then back again. "What? There's food in the cafeteria." His mind couldn't change directions that quickly.

"I'm sorry, but I love to cook. Especially when I'm stressed, and I don't even have half of what you have in your kitchen. So unfair," she muttered. Unfurling from the couch, she walked into his rarely used kitchen to grab three glasses. Then reached into her so-called purse, which any *man* would call a gym bag, and pulled out three small bottles with a clear liquid in them.

"Wait. Please tell me that's what I think it is?" Justin grabbed the armrests on either side of him in a death grip. *Please, please, please, please…*

With a twinkle in her eye, she winked. Putting her attention back on the bottles, she dumped each into a glass with a few ice cubes from the fridge. Gavin was in his own world when Maria reached out and put the glass into his hand. "What?" His startle caused a small spill.

She puckered her face. "Well, now that's just wasteful."

Maria was a hero.

"Bottom's up, boys." Maria raised her glass, then tapped it on the counter in front of her. Finally, Gavin realized what was happening, smiled, then followed quickly with eyes that said, 'Hell yeah!' They all took a sip, planning to savor the liquor burn that had been missing for what felt like eons.

Unfortunately, tolerance wanes over time, and both men were found wanting by Maria. Choking, they tried not to spill any of what remained in their glasses. That would be alcohol abuse. Unacceptable.

Maria couldn't hold back. "That's just ridiculous. Possibly the two sorriest men I've ever met." With that, she turned, walked back to the kitchen, and pulled out several dusty appliances into a pile on the counter. "These," she gestured to her mountain, eyebrows lifted and daring anyone to object, "are now mine."

As the last of their coughing fits faded, Gavin said, "So now I get it." Their eyes locked.

"This is 100% why you got hired."

From the kitchen came a distinct *humph*.

"Maria? Where have you been all my life?" Gavin said as he stared at his now half-full glass.

"Underground. Making this," she said, pulling out another three bottles. Gavin felt the weight of the day subside.

An hour later, the three of them had fully crossed the line of sobriety, yet only on their second glass of Class M liquor.

M for Maria since she wouldn't tell them what it was exactly. While it did get their curiosity juices flowing, they were coming up with more questions than answers.

Gavin was standing by Calla's vital readouts on the screen. They could even print them out in raw data form within their apartments using personal codes. He watched as the monitor lines peaked and bottomed out. "So strange. Two years ago, this line never even moved a hairsbreadth. As if she wasn't alive at all. Just another inanimate object in the room." He paused, taking in all of the potential outcomes this little graph could mean. "Now she's human. Alive. And one day, she'll be truly awake. It seems surreal."

Maria was in Justin's kitchen making a panini. Justin watched in awe, recalling how he'd wondered what that contraption was for when he first moved in. Her masterpiece looked delicious and was light-years beyond the sandwiches in the chow hall. She placed a plate in front of him and one on the table for when Gavin decided to stop pacing.

Though she looked relaxed, Maria was burning with questions about the events in the lab ever since they walked into Justin's room.

Standing at the kitchen counter about to take a bite, she lobbed the first question at them. "So why is it that we quickly saved and 'stored' the data before the Director and his Sandlot crew came into our lab? You said they would burn it if they had it?" She bit into her sandwich. So blasé.

Neither man immediately chimed in, unsure of how to explain.

Gavin cleared his first bite and wiped his hands on his khakis as he leaned back in his chair. "Several years ago, we had a significant spike on the digital readout specific to her mental functioning. None of the other monitors showed any changes, but that one had four distinct spikes. Troubleshooting the equipment, we verified with every diagnostic that nothing had changed. Still, we couldn't explain the four spikes in mental activity. About fifteen minutes later, as we were printing and scrutinizing every detail, in walked Jones and a similar group of individuals to the ones you saw today. He walked directly up to us, asking what had happened. If it was a problem with our systems or some other error.

"Honestly, we weren't one-hundred percent sure, but initially, we believed the equipment linked with her brain had malfunctioned. We never had the chance to investigate more thoroughly because Jones took all the read-outs we'd printed. Then one of his lackeys went into our computer systems to delete that last hours' worth of data." He shook his head incredulously.

"That doesn't make sense. Why would they do that?" The mouthful of panini didn't stop her from asking the question.

Justin chimed in, "We don't know. As two of them collected the printed data, and another deleted the files, Gavin and I asked those same questions... loudly. But the only explanation we got from Jones was that if it was an error, then we didn't need the data anyway. It would stir up trouble if the information got beyond his office."

"But—"

Her 'but' was completed by Gavin. "—but yes, that data may *not* have been an error. Maybe it was a clue. Maybe it was a lead into something coming. Maybe it was the start of a pattern showing us she was coming out of her coma. We never had the chance to figure it out."

"And you didn't raise hell about them interfering with your data and how you do your job?" Putting her sandwich down, she was furious at the thought.

Gavin kept his eyes on the floor, not wanting her to see the anger in his own eyes. "Oh, we did, and they made our options quite clear at that point."

Justin filled in the blank. "We could continue to be well-paid security guards impersonating scientists willingly or by force."

"But we wouldn't be relieved of our duties." Gavin shook his head. "We know too much, and honestly, I wasn't going to leave regardless." Justin nodded his head in agreement. "I guess we both willingly decided to change things as we went along to keep those above from realizing how far she had come. Until today anyway."

Maria was confused. "If that's the case, why didn't they come in and erase the data when she started moving her eyes?"

Justin leaned forward with his chin on his fists. "I think they learned from their initial mistake. That coming in and deleting data could make us turn on them, and they need us as much as they need her. Too hard to find people with our qualifications to replace us. I also don't think Jones is as stupid as he looks." Gavin grunted at that comment. "I know, G, but

I have a feeling he's very good at split-second decision-making. He grilled us for less than two minutes when we had that first spike in brain activity. We told him the *only* data affected was that one particular lead. I mean… we gave him that information as soon as he walked in the door, which made it easy for him to determine he could erase its existence."

"So what you're saying is, he made the decision then and there to destroy it since it was the only piece of evidence we had. But when her eyes started moving, *all* of our equipment was linked to that small show of life, which would've been more difficult to ensure it was erased." Gavin was slowly putting the pieces together. "We were giving him the reasons he needed not to pull the plug despite her movements."

"I'm sitting here watching the two of you have this conversation as if it's for the first time. How is that? Do you two ever hold obviously important discussions?" Sandwich abandoned, her eyes *screamed* in disbelief.

"I… I don't know. I guess not." The alcohol seemed to be stepping their intellects down a notch or two. By saying that out loud, he suddenly realized it made them appear pathetic, and he couldn't let his pride take such a big hit. "Actually," and he looked at Gavin. "We spent countless hours, day and night, scouring the data surrounding the event. We scanned for patterns based on the time of day the spike occurred. But nothing."

"We didn't really need to discuss what we knew was critically wrong. They destroyed data for seemingly no reason, and we couldn't exactly quit and walk away from our jobs."

The men locked eyes, fully comprehending the gravity of what they were saying. That's the interesting thing about alcohol. Some things become foggy, and others become crystal clear.

"Finally, when there was a no-kidding event that we knew wasn't a malfunction, we realized we needed to record it in as many places as possible to make it more difficult to erase. That's why I log everything in my notebook. Print out all the data and archive it immediately. We even incorporate an automatic save of the data to our personal files on the classified intranet."

Justin picked up where Gavin left off. "Erasing one piece of data is one thing, but there's no feasible way to erase what is happening now. As I said, I think he's a whole lot smarter than we want to give him credit for. He may not understand the scientific and medical side of all this, but he's got the strategic smarts to know when and how to manipulate information. As well as to know when he can't without us acknowledging there's something viscerally wrong."

"But you do know something's wrong," Maria stated matter-of-factly.

"Yep." Gavin took another sip from his glass and cringed. The bite wasn't as sharp now. "I think the only way we're going to find out what that 'wrong' thing is, is to make sure Calla stays alive."

Justin could feel there was still a story the two of them hadn't yet spoken of. Either way, he knew they were on the same channel. Regardless of what happens, Calla doesn't die.

# Chapter 13
## On the Road

July 31, 2029

“Does anyone else feel like we're in a movie? You know, where you have these three idiots who take on a job they know nothing about, no clue where they're going, no idea what to do when they get there, and they take it anyway because they really have nothing better to do. Then get killed doing it.” Aidan was lying across the back seat of their new Benz, tossing a Hacky Sack up and down.

“Yes, well, can't say we never took you anywhere,” Joe said, pouring over the Raven Rock Mountain Complex maps.

“Do you think this is all some weird penance for humanity being uber selfish over the last 100 years? Like, we decided dumping oil in our oceans, lighting fires in California out of boredom, and spending hours creating herniated discs in our necks to text everyone we'd ever met all day every day was more important than, ya know… farming, raising kids, not being serial killers?" Aidan was bored.

Zoey checked the rearview mirror. "Maybe?" She held the word out a few extra seconds and then turned her view to the empty road in front of them. "Or maybe another race of beings wanted to make a clear and easy path for their arrival here once we've wiped ourselves out." She smirked.

"I can see you smirking."

"Wasn't hiding it."

"Alright, kids. The Raven Rock pictures my contact sent me show little more than two bunker entrances with barbed-wire fencing around it on empty property. Not much in the way of structures on the site according to the layout, so our access points will probably be limited. I'm just having a hard time understanding why we also have blueprints of a building not located on this site." Joe was going back and forth between all the papers in his lap, trying to determine what he was missing. "The 700,000 square feet of potential space we can get lost in is underground. Since there are no blueprints for that space, I can only guess they are military-affiliated, and the Stranger didn't have access to those blueprints." Joe spoke as if he had not shared this information at least 100 times in the past few months.

"We got it… we got it… buildings, bunkers, yada yada." Aidan rolled his eyes from his lazy position in the back.

Joe had spent weeks, day and night, trying to glean any information still available out in the world about the maps they'd been given. He barely spoke for days at a time, and when he did, it was to guide them on building or troubleshooting the tech equipment they would need on their secret mission, as they now called it. He was using their drive time to drill into them every aspect of the area they were infiltrating.

"We should be there in about four hours. Plenty of time to conduct serious recon of those bunkers and building, if there even is one based on these blueprints, and ultimately avoid things like getting shot."

"Sounds like fun," Aidan said with a big smile.

# Chapter 14
## Purgatory

*I* am not *dead.*

*I'm imprisoned within my own body. They can't stop me from getting stronger, though. I can feel the energy within me. Willing me, daring me to break free of these invisible restraints.*

*The voices are so close now.* "—increase the pressurization in the unit. The vibration of her body is resisting the… no, not that high it could crush her internal organs!"

*I want you to know I'm here! I can hear you! Why won't you let me breathe?*

"I don't know if we can contain her like this for much longer. She's getting stronger."

*I can hear the tap of a pen on the glass. Tap, tap… tap,*

*tap, tap… tap, tap… tap, tap, tap.*

*What is with this guy tapping! I'm losing my mind here, and he's tapping away like it's the lobster tank at a seafood restaurant.*

*This is where I am. This is what my life is. I am trapped in my own personal Hell. Inside a box, fully aware of myself but unable to communicate. Listening to people talk about me as if I'm a child or really nothing at all. An incomprehensible thing. How did this happen? I had a purpose, didn't I? My life meant something, didn't it? Why can't I remember what it was?*

*I can't remain this way. There has to be a way out. I've tried to fight against the extreme pressure on my chest. To move my hands. Stretch my neck. Open my damn eyes!*

*Voices are getting louder. They're not in my head. I know they aren't. They are real.*

"Do you see that? She's trying to stretch her body! We need to increase the pressure!"

"We can't. It'll destroy her." *A woman's voice. She sounds angry. Voices louder still, from all sides. The pain in my belly and ribs are reducing my ability to fight but inflaming my desire to do the same.*

"If we don't, she may wake up, and what are we supposed to do then? She's… she's not even supposed to be able to do any of this!" *A distinguishably male voice that time. Angrily growling out those last words.*

"Wake up? She's already awake! We need to back off the stabilizer, or she'll die!" *She sounds scared now. Kill me? What is happening?*

*They can't kill me. I'm here. I'm alive. I'm ALIVE! I'M ALIVE!*

*Lights.*

*White blinding light everywhere. A silence so sharp it temporarily stuns my senses. I feel the air on my eyes. I can't see anything but light, but I can feel something or someone nearby.*

*Silence.*

*Complete silence around me.*

"Her eyes." *A whisper of a woman's voice so close.*

"Her eyes are open...."

# Chapter 15
## Getting Closer

Aidan was in front with the passenger seat laid all the way back. Joe was on the roof of the car on a negative ten degree rated sleeping bag. It was a chilly sixty-eight degree night for August, but he was a big man and a hot sleeper. On it, was better than in it.

A wordless blood-curdling scream reverberated through the inside of the Benz. The piercing sound had Aidan flailing awake, right arm slamming into the window, knees into the dash. Joe sat straight up from the rooftop and slid down the windshield. By the time both men were able to put eyes on Zoey, she was arched, stomach up in the backseat with her head down by the floorboard. The contortion of her body seemed impossible.

"Grab her!" Joe yelled through the windows. As he yanked the back door open, the decibel level magnified beyond any sound he'd ever heard. Her body was so rigid it wouldn't straighten out, keeping them from pulling her from the car. Aidan was half in the front seat, half in the back, with his arms around her waist, but couldn't get a good hold on her.

"What is happening," Joe said, not to be heard over Zoey. He could only watch as the intricate markings made their way up the right side of her face. With no sign or warning, the shrieking stopped, and her body slumped back to the seat, taking Aidan with her.

Aidan's arms were still around her waist, pinned beneath her when she collapsed. She was breathing but dead weight. "Joe. Joe, pull her out. I can't move." He grunted, trying to pull himself upright. As Joe pulled Zoey out, Aidan managed to break free, slid into the backseat, and then out the door.

"She's unconscious but breathing." Joe grabbed the sleeping bag from the ground in front of the car and laid it next to her. Together they grasped her shoulders and legs and hoisted her onto it. "What happened?"

"I have no idea. I was sleeping. What is happening to her?" The adventure was no longer fun for Aidan. "Look at her face. Whatever this is, it's killing her. We have to stop this!" His gritted teeth were almost to the breaking point.

"HOW?" Joe's voice boomed. Aidan fell back in shock, jarring his head as he hit the ground. Joe had his hands on his head, squeezing his hair tight. Walking back and forth next to her, it was the first time Aidan had ever witnessed him on the verge of a breakdown. After a few more paces, he stopped, and his hands fell to his sides in fists. "How? We have no way of knowing what is happening to her. Some days, I feel like we have a purpose and others… I don't know. I just feel like maybe we're crazy. Maybe she's just sick, and our dumbasses are blindly following. Agh… I—"

"—Joe." Aidan looked up from his perch next to Zoey. His eyebrows raised in a 'calm down' expression. "Even if she's sick, we have no way to help her."

"We could go back! Force her to stay in bed! Let the Doc do whatever she can to help her."

"You really think Zoey will let—"

"—We don't have to give her a choice! Just throw her in the damn car and go back. She's unconscious!"

"And I guarantee she will wake up and kick our asses for wasting her time! We're almost there! Going back would be stupid!" Aidan was standing now, and Joe was on the verge of jumping over Zoey to tackle him. "We cannot do that, and you know it. Whatever is happening… well, I believe her. Crazy as all this is, she's never led us wrong, and I actually believe this insane theory of hers. None of it makes sense, but what in the last seven years *HAS* made sense? Nothing. So we're *doing this*."

They stood, staring each other down.

"Thanks for the vote of confidence." A raspy voice came from below them.

"Zoey," both men whispered at the same time, dropping to their knees beside her. Their relief, and fear, were too much to hide on their faces.

"I just had the worst dream."

# Chapter 16
## Purgatory

August 3, 2029

*I*t's so bright.
*Painfully bright.*

*I see shadows of movement around me, but it's confusing, so I stay as still as possible, looking in one direction and hoping everything will become clearer if I just wait.*

*I don't feel anything touching me. Just an intense compression keeping my limbs and body from moving. It's hard to take in a full breath. I'm so incredibly relieved to have my eyes open that I don't care about anything else but keeping them open. I want to see!*

*My eyesight starts to clear some of the fog from lack of use. I can see people. They are standing just out of reach. It's* obvious they know my eyes are open, but they aren't moving any closer to help me.

They are just staring at me with their mouths slightly ajar. One woman, in particular, is standing in front of me, unmoving.

My breath hitches when I realize we are staring into each other's eyes. Her disbelief is palpable. I don't want to lose her! She is my first real link to another human being in so long that I'm terrified looking away would turn this moment into a dream... or a nightmare. I just need a connection to someone, anyone else, so I know that I truly exist.

Now they're yelling at each other. Frantically moving their arms. One of them I can see at a computer with fear in his eyes.

"Stop! Stop, you'll kill her!" The woman is yelling now, but the increasing compression in my ears is muffling the sound. Turning back towards me, she presses her hands against the glass. Her eyes are the lightest green. Almost crystalline green. But the color is fading. All of the light is fading. Are they turning out the lights? I'm losing her! I can't lose her! How is it becoming dark when it was so light only moments before? My chest heaves against the desperation of trying to draw breath.

I want to keep my eyes open, but they are so heavy. I don't want to leave this moment.

What if I never get it back?

# Chapter 17
## Status Update

"No amount of makeup would cover this."

"You wear makeup?" Aidan was genuinely stunned at the thought.

"Idiot." Zoey glanced in the visor mirror once more before slamming it against the car ceiling. They'd made it to the Blue Ridge Summit, but not without a few fights: *Get out of the front seat! Why did you eat all the jerky? Stop touching the maps with your greasy fingers!* And that was just what they said to Aidan.

"Zoe, you honestly look *badass* right now. Those interweaving purple snake tattoos. We'll call you Biker Z—"

"—Come on, Aidan, leave it alone," Joe said without turning around.

"It's fine. Joe, it's fine. I'm apparently making a fashion statement." She trailed her fingers along the web that stretched from cheekbone down to naval, only getting as far as her shirt collar. She never cried, at least not of her own accord. The unseen assault had taken its toll, but she wasn't about to let them see how much. It was getting harder to drag herself out of the fog every time she had an episode. Her appearance was rarely a concern, but her reflection in the mirror had shaken her. Would her face be like this forever? Would it take over her entire body? Yet, after all this time, the intricate swirls never crossed an invisible, perfect vertical line down her body. The webbing on her abdomen had never receded, only changed to a deep purple. Who would want a woman with a body like this? She never thought too much about finding that special someone, but the woman staring back at her from the mirror made the prospect of it seem bleak.

Awkward silence in the car became too much. Luckily Joe was pulling off to the side of the road. They were on Harbaugh Valley Road directly west of the southern entrance to the Raven Rock facility. Eight days here, and they had scoped out the majority of the property. It was primarily a wooded area that should have been green with life, yet looked like winter was already descending on it.

Besides security doing rounds on the perimeter, there wasn't much in the way of vehicle traffic. Foot traffic, however, was heavy. And that was solely on the other side of the fence. It seemed like these people not only worked on the compound but lived there as well. The maps they'd been given didn't do the place justice in person. Slightly more formidable than they initially believed, but overall, security didn't seem too problematic, a bit relaxed, like the place hadn't seen much confrontation in a while. It was decision time. Today was their last day of surveillance before deciding on their entry point.

"Joe, review the plan again," Zoey stated like a commanding officer.

"Uh, I've been thinking about that." He held his gaze straight-forward instead of looking at her. "I think Aidan and I should hike over to the facility to get eyes on it. Why don't you hang tight here, keeping watch 'til we get back."

Zoey stared incredulously at him while Aidan sat with eyes wide behind her, refusing to make a sound. "You want me to stay here." A statement, not a question.

He hung his head, "Zoe, you are tired. We aren't going in; we're just getting a final look-see to ensure the security and pattern of life haven't changed. If we're going in tomorrow morning, we need you rested. We don't know what will happen once we're in."

She wanted to throat punch him but also recognized the reality of what he was saying. "Okay."

If it was possible, Aidan's eyes opened even wider. "What was that?" His gaze went from one to the other. "This feels like progress. Zoey didn't even fight you!" A *Grinch-like* smile swept across his face. "Let's go!" He jumped out of the car and walked around to the trunk.

Joe's eyes held Zoey's for a moment. "We have no way of knowing when you might have another occurrence," his apologetic tone made her want to slink back into her seat, but instead, she took a deep breath and conceded.

"I know. It's fine." She opened her car door and stepped out.

He exhaled, opening his door. Aidan already had his 'snack-pack backpack' on, meaning he carried more snacks than equipment in that thing. His headlamp was attached to his forehead, the compass was out, and he was stuffing a water bottle into the side pocket of his cargo pants.

Joe grabbed his own backpack and slung it over his shoulders. He had the maps, a checklist for all the areas he wanted to make sure to assess, a penlight at the ready, a headlamp, and other essentials.

Finally, they grabbed their essential defense from the trunk. Joe holstered his sidearm, and Aidan placed his M4 over his head and across his body. Easy access. All three took a radio from the trunk and verified their signals, channels, and backup channels.

Zoey went through the communication and distress signals. "Aidan, what's the signal for *distress* but *no* assist?"

"Key-up four times."

"Joe. Distress, *need* assist."

"Key-up three times."

"Aidan. *Danger*, everyone scatter and convene at the rally point?"

"Three-second tone hold."

"And where is the rally point, Joe?"

"1840 feet, west southwest of the Helipad. If there is a

*100%* probability you will *not* make it to that rally point, your signal is….” Joe waited for Aidan's response.

“A solid tone for at least ten seconds.”

She pointed at Joe to give them their code names. “GREEN. Aidan, you're RED, and I'm BLACK.”

Customary Aidan, with his eyebrows bouncing up and down, declared, “Joe needs to be GRAY. Feast your eyes on his gloriously striped beard. That salt and pepper hair.”

“Dear Lord.” Zoey flashed her crystalline hazel eyes at Joe. “Alrighty, looks like you're GRAY. Everybody ready now?”

She held the gaze of both men for a heartbeat, then said, “Okay, boys. Bring me back a HoHo if you find one.” Aidan gave her a wink and a smile. Hoisting herself onto the front of the Mercedes, she watched them walk off into the woods. Less than thirty seconds had passed when Aidan chimed in on the radio. “Super-Hot to Super-Not come in Super-Not.”

She pressed the button on the side of her radio. “RED, this is BLACK. That was a solid fail in radio contact.” She smiled despite her misgivings. “Go ahead, RED.”

“Dead deer. I found dinner.”

“RED, keep the line clear of stupidity, over.” Joe's voice came through loud and clear.

“Roger that, GRAY.” No one needed to hear Aidan's voice to know he was laughing to himself.

“Keep the line clear, RED. One key-up every fifteen boys. OUT,” she said, asking them to click their mics every fifteen minutes as a form of check-in. Zoey's feet hit the pavement, and she walked around to the side door. Grabbing her binoculars, she put her arms through the harness. Until the Stranger, aka Rice Jahnsen, sent the box with the letter, she'd never had gear this exceptional. The harness was a *lot* more comfortable than a lanyard. Especially when you have so many other things you're hauling around. Some women liked Swarovski crystals. Zoey wanted Swarovski EL Range binoculars so she could hit a target at 1500 yards.

Everybody's got their thing.

Full-well knowing she should be resting, she instead put the lenses to her eyes and scanned their surroundings. They hadn't seen anyone the last forty miles on their way in. That wasn't unusual since the country's population had decreased by sixty-five percent. What *was* unusual, the area was completely empty. Being August, trees were green with summer life. Yet, looking towards their destination, all vegetation was black and decaying. No sign of life; plant, human, or otherwise. Except for a man peeing on a tree.

Aidan!

"Geez." Quickly she maneuvered over to Joe's location. He, too, was peeing on a tree. What the heck?

"That's a sign, Zoe," muttering under her breath. Climbing into the back seat, she left her legs dangling outside the door. She brought her pillow from their apartment because sleeping in abnormal places left her with even worse insomnia. With her eyes closed, she kept the radio sitting on her chest. Radio silence, other than the fifteen minute all-clear, lasted about two hours before it was broken. Daytime sleeping had left her cranky, and unexpected radio-static disoriented her for a few moments.

"RED, this is GRAY. Come in, over." Joe was trying to contact Aidan. "RED to GRAY, come in RED, over." It took about fifteen seconds which seemed like fifteen seconds too long.

"GRAY, this is RED. Go ahead."

"At Bunker Entrance A. Total RECON complete. Status check. Over." Joe's voice over the radio sounded off. Zoey had already sat up, but now she was listening intently.

"North of Bunker Entrance B. RECON complete," Aidan reported.

"RED, do you have eyes on B?"

"Roger. Is there something specific I should be seeing?"

"Do you see any personnel? Watchtower action? Moving vehicles?"

"Stand-by 1." There was a ten second pause before Aidan radioed back in. "GRAY, I've got nothing on my end. Sunset an hour ago. Maybe everyone left for home before we got here. Called an early day? What are you thinking? Over."

"Could be." Joe's voice over the line didn't sound convinced. "I've got eyes on the main building. Twenty stories high. Large parking lot. Significant security entrance. Over."

"Roger. The one that explicitly wasn't on the map." Aidan must've been chewing on jerky, his voice was muffled.

"Roger. I'm directly in front of the twelve-foot steel fence. Looking at windows, no visible lights pre-bedtime, and…" After an extended pause. "No security visible." Nothing about this felt right.

"GRAY, did you notice that everything on the compound feels… suspended?" Aidan was having trouble choosing words to make sense of what he was seeing.

Joe couldn't find a word for it either. It was almost more of a feeling than what they could see. "Yup. Not a soul in sight, but yet," Joe pulled his infrared goggles up to his eyes.

Zoey finally chimed in, "GRAY, this is BLACK, what is going on? Over."

"BLACK, I can see heat signatures moving inside the building. There is life in there, but something is off." Joe released his goggles back to his chest. "BLACK, need a status update on your end, over."

# Chapter 18
## Inside the Gate

Justin walked out of the bathroom, ill at ease. Pretty sure it couldn't have been dinner. Standard chicken and potatoes are always served in the cafeteria-esque restaurant on Thursday nights. Despite the apartment's kitchen, he generally opted for ready-to-eat meals. Seeing the same two faces every day had him craving the sound of others' voices. That, and Maria had already stripped his kitchen appliances for her own devices.

Not to mention, people-watching in the cafeteria did tend to make him feel like he'd won the genetic lottery.

Vain? Probably. But to Justin, it was like a walk through Wal-Mart once upon a time. He really wasn't, but he'd become more cynical as one year bled into the next.

The heaviness in the pit of his stomach woke him up that morning and had only intensified since. He'd intended to go to bed early but knew whatever was wrong in his gut would only give him heartburn if he laid down. Instead, he thought he'd head to the lab to check on Calla. After opening her eyes for just a few seconds, they had all gone a little mad with data collection. He'd momentarily believed that was it. She was awake. It was happening. Other than her eyes shifting towards him, her lids closed as uneventfully as they opened. At first, he thought she could see him. Now he wonders if there was any significance at all.

Glancing at his reflection in the small mirror next to his front door, he said, "You've made it another day, Justin. One of these days, you will wake up, and the world will be back to normal."

He said it every day, like every day was Groundhog Day. A mindless repetition, yet with a dash of hope. *Maybe tomorrow would be different.*

Opening the door, he wandered out into the hall, working on his swagger as he strolled through the empty halls trying to keep his mad sexy skills up to par. There was always a chance a new lady doctor would be brought in. Preferably one that didn't have just one thing on her mind. Work.

*Yeah. Right.*

The silence was almost tangible. And the closer he got to the lab, the heavier it felt. It was as if something was pressing on his mind—almost a fuzzy sort of force.

He couldn't explain the pull, but the sensation seemed

familiar.

Calla.

His feet raced past halls that led to different branches of the building. It felt as if the ground was tilting upward, making it harder to run. Something was wrong. It had to be her.

The last time he felt this, whatever it was, was just before the explosion. Right before Calla faced off the invisible enemy. He could see her as if it was happening again right in front of him. He watched as it seemed to unfold deep within his mind's eye.

*In an open field, about 100 yards from the building, Calla stood frozen, staring into the distance. Then she screamed. A blood-curdling scream. He ran toward her just as the building blew and threw his body backward. Rolling. Blinding. Deafening. He crawled his way back to her lifeless body through the debris and heat.*

Shaking off the vision, he threw his shoulder into the lab door and burst into the room. Shock confined him to the solid yet vibrating tiles beneath his feet.

"Dear God."

Outside the Gate  8:33 p.m.

Zoey was out of the car, strapping her weapon and backpack on as she heard Joe's request for a status update. She picked up the binoculars and scanned the area around herself as she keyed her radio. "GRAY, I've got nothing over here. What do you want me—" The pain hit her so fiercely her knees hit the ground. Sharp rocks jammed into her knees, jarring her senses enough to keep her from falling into unconsciousness. "—Joe." She could barely get his name out.

Both men swung their binos around to Zoey's position. Aidan spotted her on the ground first, then wrapped his fingers around his radio. Sprinting toward her, he held his radio button down for three seconds and released it. He counted to ten and repeated the hold. After a third hold, he stowed his radio in his side pocket and increased speed. He wasn't quite halfway back when the sound of a muffled siren had him tripping over his feet to stop. Dropping flat to the dead forest floor, he silently pulled his radio out again. Switching it to 'vibrate only,' he whispered, "GRAY, do you hear that?"

Out of breath and whispering, Joe's voice came across the radio. "I hear it. It's coming from the main building. How close are you to BLACK?"

Quietly. "About four minutes. Is that siren for us?"

"No idea. You're faster, you go. I'll watch your six and fall back to see what happens."

"GRAY, we need to rally!" Aidan bit out.

"This is no coincidence. Something is going down. *You* fought me to come here. Check on BLACK and give me two Key-Ups when you're ready for radio contact." He wanted to ensure there wouldn't be anyone listening when Aidan finally checked in. He watched Aidan through the sparse brush, saw him get to his feet, crouch down, pause to look around, then begin sprinting once again. Panning over, he saw Zoey lying still on the ground a ways ahead. Turning 180 degrees and creeping back toward the fence, Joe could still hear the siren. His head was on a swivel between Aidan to the rear and the compound to the front.

By the time he had eyes on the compound again, it was no longer deserted. Personnel were physically running alongside buildings and down perfectly manicured sidewalks. The bunker entrances were right there, but not one person entered either. Everyone was carrying a laptop or case holding some sort of tech. Coming from every angle and building were people in various stages of dress. Most were in pajamas or casual wear with jeans. Security was directing it all. It was short-lived. Maybe only four to five minutes passed in a fury of coordinated chaos racing into the building with 20 floors. The building *not* on the map. After which there was no activity at all.

# Chapter 19
## I Can Hear You

August 9, 2029 | 8:27 p.m.

*W*hite coats. White room. Lots of computers. No more darkness.

*Confusion and fear overflowing. They talk openly around me and recognize I can hear them. Whenever someone new walks into the room, I can feel everything in my body suddenly shut down, and my eyes close. Desperately, I try to open them, but I've come to the conclusion that the three of them do not want anyone to know that I'm awake. That I'm truly awake. Their faces are filled with compassion and fear. All of them, at some point, have come to the glass with a longing in their eyes that I don't understand. An apology on their lips, but yet they don't free me.*

*As if they're reading my thoughts, I feel a slight release in compression around me. My ears are clear, and I don't have to fight to open my eyes. They just open.*

*Did I will this to happen?*

*Without warning, I feel a hard, warm surface rise underneath me, or maybe I dropped down. Either way, it feels too hard on my tender muscles. Painful even, but a welcome pain. I can't remember the last time I physically felt anything. I'm suddenly aware of something touching my skin—a whisper of cloth fibers touching my legs and a loose-fitting shirt on my stomach and arms. The smoothness under me seems familiar yet so strange.*

*Turning my palms down, I slowly run my hands under me and push down to assure myself it is, in fact, real. My breath hitches in my throat as I realize I'm free of the incessant nothingness. The reality of it makes me want to jump to my feet!*

*Without thinking, my body makes an effort. Nope.*

*No leaping.*

*No leaping happening here.*

*Not even a slow sitting position is possible. My body is in absurdly slow motion. Just attempting to sit upright takes everything I have, which isn't much.*

*A searing headache follows the attempt to jump. My limbs are not in sync with the movements I envision happening in my mind. I manage to get to my knees before I'm left breathless and toppling backward into the glass. This is the first time I've been able to move in so long.*

*Confusion couples with joy that I'm really alive. I*

*momentarily forget about everything else around me until a shadow catches my periphery. Four people are outside my glass prison. Layers of emotion show on their faces. Elation, terror, shock. I don't think they expected me to physically move. Either that, or maybe they are upset. From their past comments, maybe they are confused about why I am not standing up, creating mass hysteria through telekinesis— throwing flames around the room with my mind. Ridiculous expectations, but from what I've heard over the past few months, that seems the consensus of what I'm likely to do.*

*Just outside of reach beyond the glass are her green eyes. Crystal green eyes staring into mine. It wasn't a dream. She is real. This woman who, for mere seconds, helped me comprehend that I was actually alive several days, or hours... or months ago. Here she is, standing in front of me.*

*So beautiful. There is a yearning in her eyes that I don't understand, but I want to hug her.*

*Without warning, a piercing sound shrills in my ears. I bring my hands up to cover them, but in doing so, I jerk my head forward, hitting the glass with unparalleled force.*

*A blaring voice jars my thoughts.*

*"Rose? Can you hear me?" It's so loud that a high-pitched whine echoes the man's words over and over. Cringing away from the sound and the throb in my head, I hear, "Crap, turn it down! It's too loud for her."*

*He tries muffling the audio blast to no avail. After some recovery time from the onslaught of sound, there's a dramatic drop in the noise around me. His deep timber voice becomes drastically softer.*

"My apologies. It was hard to determine how well you'd be able to hear us being in such a pressurized unit." *He seems genuinely apologetic and out of breath. Like he's not even sure what he is saying.*

*I nod to let him know I understand. My voice is nowhere to be found.*

*Another intake of breath as if he is struggling for oxygen.* "It's okay, Rose. Everything is fine. You may have difficulties speaking for a while. You've been here for," *he swallowed,* "sometime. We've been keeping you alive through the incubator. My name is Grant."

*I try to pay attention to what he's saying, but the dizziness is still subsiding along with the ringing in my ears. Out of the corner of my eye, the others catch my attention. They are arguing. Pointing at me, then at something on a screen. Something's not right. The man standing next to my glass prison is trying to keep his focus on me, but the tumultuous situation behind him is breaking his attention. Just as he's about to say something more, the door opens, and a heavy-set man with a strained shirt around his belly walks in. His words are so low I can't make them out, but the man beside me abruptly stands and spits,* "No!" *at him.*

*He raises his thick arm in my direction and speaks with subdued words. His neck and face change from pasty white to beet red almost instantly.*

"We *cannot* just end this. We've come too far, and we are finally getting useful data that could change what the world *thinks* our future might be!" *The green-eyed woman pleads with him. He's not wearing a lab coat like the others, and his quiet voice is unrecognizable. She is begging him, but I can see by his facial expression he's not entertaining it.*

"You know what you have to do." *His eyes are glazed with anger. Flashing his stare at me, I notice a sadness that seems misplaced. Pulling his focus back to the green-eyed woman, he said regretfully,* "Now," *and left the room as quickly as he entered.*

*The second man in a lab coat had stayed toward the back of the room during the exchange. As soon as the door clicks shut, he begins walking in my direction.* "We have no choice, Madison. We have to put her down." *His voice is level, but he doesn't look at her or me.*

*Her head shakes like she can't believe what he'd just said. Throwing herself between us, she yells,* "She's not a dog for Christ-sake! We've been waiting *years* for this opportunity to make a change so we can stop living in fear. After seven years of nothing. Waiting for something, *anything* to change so we can find a new way forward, and you think killing her is the best option?" *She frantically turns her head from me to him and back to me again. I can almost feel her heart beating from behind the glass.*

"It's our *only* option!" *His response is suddenly furious. They are staring each other down, waiting for the other to make a move.*

*And then it registers...*

*Seven years.*

*Seven years.*

*I've been here seven years? How is that possible? How can they think I'm such a threat? What have I done? How horrible am I?*

*I don't feel myself moving until I'm pressed right up against the glass, watching their battle. Listening. Now fully aware of his intentions and ignoring the man with the headset as he tries to draw my attention.*

"We've let this go too far! We have these regulations for a reason. She was never supposed to wake up, and now look at her! She's physically standing in the unit unaided!" *His fear is palpable.* "We only decreased the pressure by ten PSI which shouldn't have even been enough to let her lift her head, and she's standing. Staring straight at us!"

*I'm standing? Looking down, I'm not sure when I had even made it to my feet. Momentary shock takes hold as it registers that I'm upright. Confusion washes over me as to why all my muscles are screaming at me and I start to sway. I'm so weak. My legs give way.*

"Screw the regulations! Can you not see her? She's no threat. We can't keep her in a catatonic state anymore. She's fighting back against the medication keeping her that way. It's not effective anymore. *Look* at her! If you were expecting explosions and mass casualties, just look around the room *right now*. It's not happening! *Look. At. Her.* She is *no* threat!" *The green-eyed woman places her palm on the glass opposite my own, forcing the man to turn in my direction. Her face shows compassion and frustration as he shows only fear. What could*

*I have done to end up here?*

"We're ending this now." *Pushing past her, he comes toward me. Now on my knees, hands pressing against the window. I scramble away with my rigid limbs hindering my every move. He reaches the backside of my box, then lifts his arm to a lever at the top of the case. Behind him, the woman screams at him to stop and runs full throttle. The man with the booming voice in my ear drops the papers in his hands and scales the tables, nearly tackling the scared man before he can pull the lever.*

*Almost.*

*The sound of metal crunching metal causes an electric shock to snake down my spine, followed by a brief clicking sound.*

*Click one, and air pressure increases.*

*Click two, and a cloudy vapor releases inside my prison.*

*Click three, and the smell of... flowers.*

Darkness.

# Chapter 20
## The Frenzy

"**G**ood god, what is going on?" Maria's head snapped up, her cooking mojo wrecked by the thunderous sound of racing feet outside her apartment door. Lately, she only felt relaxed standing in front of her semi-adequate kitchen island with all the edible colors of the rainbow in front of her waiting to be made into a masterpiece of a meal.

And these jokers were ruining it.

Cracking open the door, she peeked out to see a ridiculous sight. Half-dressed, shoeless, bed-headed, and robed—an awkward stampede of peers.

"What is going on!" she let fly. A rhetorical question as no one bothered to stop and answer. Instead, they all raced forward, as if with tunnel vision, moving with one purpose.

And Maria was not in on the secret.

Every employee was sworn to secrecy regarding their part of the mission. Each filled a position on a compartmentalized team with its own puzzle piece in this mystery of keeping the world humming. Maria, Justin, and Gavin focused unequivocally on Calla's survival. Everyone *outside* their work area focused on the data the three of them gleaned from Calla. Not *one* team knew the entirety of the situation. They lived and worked on a compound surrounded by armed guards, electric fences, fingerprint entrances and egress', and secrets no one else on the planet had access to.

They lived in a glorified college dormitory. All meals were provided, but each doctor, engineer, technician, and janitor had his or her own micro-apartment with kitchenette, bedroom, bathroom, and living room. Families, though few, had a separate space within smaller buildings on the interior of the compound. For the most part, these families were related to the top leadership within the compound.

Sure, there were always a few Chatty-Kathys who would decide to open their mouths about what they did. And subsequent rumors painted a grim picture of their fates. But no single member was more important than their team's mission. Of course, Maria worked with Calla, the primary reason they were *all* there, whether they knew it or not.

Maria's thoughts spun as she processed the odd scene outside her door. *Untreated ADHD.* She tried medicating, but that only dulled her creative and clarifying juices.

*I need to FOCUS!*

*Has to be a fire. But a fire would've been closed off and immediately tamped down. Every room is equipped to eliminate almost any kind of threat from within.*

*Yet.*

*Wait.*

Racing back through her kitchen into her living room, she pushed her Susan Elizabeth Phillips novel off the side table revealing a pager beneath. It had gone off three times, according to the flashing red light. *Crap!* She must've been in the zone. *This thing never freaking goes off!* Frazzled, she slipped on her black sandals, grabbed her badge, and glanced at Calla's monitors on her personal link to the lab. She saw the data, but her mind couldn't process it. The readouts were five times over the maximum they had adjusted for.

After a beat, she headed for the door, quickly dashing back to turn off her oven at the last minute. A fleeting glance of sadness was offered to all the peppers *almost* perfectly caramelized. Her taste buds were going to regret the meal *that almost was* for the rest of the night.

Out the door and down the hall, she ran into a wet-haired Gavin. Hesitating, he dropped his gaze down to her sandaled toes. "Green?"

"Hey! I do what I want on my own time! And this color goes perfectly with my silky mocha skin."

Gavin's surprise fostered a hint of a smile before increasing his speed toward the elevator. He was a very serious man when she first came on board. Barely a crack in his studious demeanor back then. His smile, in a moment of questionable crisis, took her aback. A thought she tucked into the back of her mind to analyze later.

Their lab was a long three-minute, thirty-second elevator ride below the surface. At the moment, however, it was stopping at every floor on the way down. Upon exiting, they raced down long stretches of hall to the entrance to their lab. Swiping their badges and scanning their fingerprints, they finally entered. Other than Director Jones, they were the only three with access to their lab. Gavin reached the door first, walking in ahead of her though abruptly stopping, causing Maria to crash into his back.

She would not have figured his backside to be so fit if she hadn't accidentally groped him in the sudden stop.

"*What are you—*" she began to say. Peering over his shoulder, she caught a glimpse of the scene that stopped him in his tracks.

Calla was standing.

Staring.

Maria locked eyes with Calla for a brief moment, noting the agitation pulsating from her small frame. The glass surrounding her appeared to bow out. *Can't be.*

Justin was already in the room with a headset on, attempting to communicate with her. It was an eerie sight as the blue light above the door washed over them. No matter how loud he cried out to her, Calla didn't respond. Until that moment no one had witnessed Calla move more than a head twitch. And seeing her stand firm against the pressure of the chamber, they had no words.

"Any and all help would be appreciated!" Justin called out. He was directly across from her, seemingly oblivious to the power she was either reigning in or attempting to release.

Terrifying didn't do the situation justice. Justin, glancing back, noticed Maria's flight response forefront in her eyes. He also noticed her professionalism as it propelled her forward to her computer, which was dark. Looking back at Justin, she asked, "What happened? All the screens are black!"

"Do you think she's doing this?" Gavin yelled over the incredible noise filling the room. A noise they felt as much as heard. Smacking the desk, he shouted, "Why isn't this working? This is why we have backup generators isn't it? I mean, what's the point of a failsafe if it isn't going to keep us from failing? And why are the lights still on?"

Without any discernable reason, the microphone Justin had been using to connect with  Calla stopped working as well. He had been trying to get her attention when it quit, deciding to go for the more tactile approach of pounding on the glass itself.

Throwing the headset to the ground, he jumped up on the desk, put his hands on the glass in front of Calla's face, and looked directly at her, talking to her as if she was within whispering distance instead of behind soundproof glass.

"Calla, look at me. Calla. Listen to my voice. It's me, Justin. Do you remember? I *need* you to remember," he whispered, begging her to look at him. "Calla, just look this way, you can do it. Look toward me. Come on now. *Calla!*" he shouted, pounding his fists on the glass in front of her face. *"Dammit! Look at me!"*

Just standing there, enraged, her eyes slowly shifted toward him though it was clear she wasn't actually *seeing* him.

"Zuri!" he shouted. At the sound of her *proper* name, Calla's eyes seemed to focus. "Zuri, you know who I am. I need you to remember me," he said, locking eyes with her. As if no one else were in the room, her face softened from a look of rage to a gentle sorrow. She recognized him.

Her entire body language shifted from looming destruction to hopeful curiosity as Justin shared memories only she could have known.

"Do you remember the green bushes with the white flowers? What did you call them? Hydrangeas? You told me they were tolerant, strong against the harsh winds, and beautiful. They were protecting you. It's where I found you. Your dirty little toes were sticking out from the brambles of the bushes. I never told you how I almost walked right past those little toes and would never have found you if you hadn't started humming. The singing. It's what brought me to you. If it weren't for the tiny voice of an angel humming life into the flowers, I would've never turned back and seen those little toes. Those hydrangeas were bigger and brighter than any of the others surrounding them. The more you hummed, the more I could see all the vegetation, even the nearby grass around us, becoming brighter, more alive. Just the sound of your voice made everything so much more vibrant.

"That's when I looked through the leaves to see your tiny faces. She was trying to cover your mouth to keep you quiet, but she couldn't quiet your humming. She couldn't contain the beauty you were pouring into everything around you. You and Lexi, you changed my life."

Zuri's angst at the sound of Lexi's name reinvigorated the force around her. All three of them witnessed her eyes begin to glow, as if her rage was coming from something only she could see.

Without warning, all three felt a blow to their chests as the wind was knocked out of them. An intensity never felt before burst through the room in the blink of an eye and they crumpled to the floor.

No one could move or breathe. Lying there, shaking off the shock, they gathered their wits and visually scoured the room. Despite the tornadic force they had just experienced, everything was still in its place as if nothing had happened.

Justin rolled to his side, his arms shaking, trying to push himself upright. He hadn't felt this way since attempting that marathon years ago when he ended up in the same position.

As his vision re-focused, he noticed Gavin on his hands and knees slowly making his way to Maria. He watched as Gavin grasped her hand and pushed her hair back from her face, asking if she was alright. Concluding that Maria and Gavin were alright, Justin crawled to the glass enclosure and leaned against it. He was close enough to fog up the window, barely keeping his emotions in check.

"Zuri, listen to me. I need you to hear me," Justin whispered once again, the noise in the room having finally ceased. The pain in his voice caught the attention of Maria and Gavin who stopped what they were doing and watched intently. Both were still in shock from the bombshell he had just dropped. That he knew Calla more personally than either could fathom. He knew her name.

Suddenly she began to scan the room, stopping on Justin, and looking *at* him instead of *through* him. With the tension gone, she finally, with a clear mind, took note of his presence.

The light surrounding her began to dim. Tears slid down her face—the face of a twenty-two year old child.

"Save Lexi," she said softly.

# Chapter 21
## Lexi

August 9, 2029  |  8:40 p.m.

*F*lashing lights keep me blind, and the air is so thick every breath is agonizing. Reaching out, I try to grab something, anything to get oriented, but the darkness encroaches. In the shadows of my vision, I see movement. First, right next to me. Then darkness.

It's as if sparks are flying, flashes of light, disorienting me further. Everything seems so loud and bright, and the smell of burning wood, metal, and... flesh makes me gag. I make it to my knees, but the movement of lifting myself off the floor ignites vertigo that launches me into unconsciousness.

Gasping breaths bring me back to reality, and the shadow I saw before is now next to the door. I can barely keep one eye open through burning tears. When I finally open both eyes, the *shadow is gone.*

*My body is overheating. My skin feels like it's melting. I try to reach out again, but the effort takes my breath away.*

*The blackness takes over again.*

# Chapter 22
## Zuri

VISP | August 9, 2029 | 8:40 p.m.

Justin's heart jumped to his throat at the sound of her words. "Save Lexi."

But Lexi's dead. He watched her die. He'd held Zuri in his arms as she cried oceans of tears when Lexi didn't come out of the flames. Justin had held her until she was pried away from him and brought to this place. This place he spent months formulating a way into. To be part of her life. To reclaim his place as her protector.

"Zuri! Zuri! What do you mean? Where is Lexi?" His skin prickled, knowing without knowing that she was alive. How could he be so blind? All these years, how could he not know if Lexi was alive or not? Maybe Zuri didn't know. Did she even recall what happened to Lexi?

"Zuri, do you remember the fire?" She's sliding down the glass to her knees, crumpling to the floor.

"Dammit, open the tank, Gavin!" Justin wanted to run over to open it himself but was afraid to break away from her.

"But—"

"—I said, open the tank! She's not going to die. We are not letting this happen! Just do it!" Gavin didn't budge.

Through the glass, he whispered, "I'm coming, hold on." Racing around to the back he ripped the hoses off the tank. His desperation pushed Gavin to move toward the sealed hatch where he punched in the code with stiff fingers. Justin considered doing that first but didn't want anyone to lose their cool and pull the lever on the back of the tank instead. Whether or not Lexi's alive was secondary. Zuri is the priority. And he needed to get her out first.

"We don't know what will happen if we open that door," Gavin said, trying to hold onto an ounce of sanity and logic in their implausible situation. "And you know her. You called her Zuri. How is it that you know her name, Justin? Who are you?"

Staring Gavin down, Justin said, "You may not know what happens when this door opens, but I do. I've held this girl in my arms, and I know exactly what I will do if you don't open this up so I can get her out." His voice was low and menacing, a warning to Gavin if he didn't comply.

Maria, standing off to the side, watched the interchange. "Who is Lexi, Justin? How could you possibly know who Lexi is?"

"I'll tell you everything. Just open the door." He knew he

looked crazy and sounded crazier still.

With eyes twitching between Justin and Zuri, Gavin noticed the computer screens starting to boot up now that whatever was inhibiting the power had stopped. Holding his breath, he slammed his hand down on the red DO NOT PUSH button.

The door clicked and opened. Justin wasted no time yanking the handle before scrambling next to Zuri. Checking first for a pulse on her neck, he then put his ear down to her face to feel for breath. Every muscle in his body grew tense with each passing second. "I'm here, Zuri. I'm here," he said softly upon finding the heartbeat he was looking for. Delicately he scooped her up into his lap, wiped her hair from her face, then began talking to her in a quiet and settling voice.

"You don't have to worry. I'm here. We'll find Lexi. If she's alive, we will find her."

All Maria and Gavin could do was stand and watch. And wait.

The blue lights were going off up until the point they found themselves on the floor. Now they sat dark and still.

After an eternity, Justin maneuvered to his knees and carefully stood up with her still in his arms. Ducking his head through the low opening, he stepped out into the room.

All three stood facing one another. Maria and Gavin continued processing the reality that Justin was holding this petite woman in his arms who, just minutes before, was lying prone. The same girl who, for seven years, offered little more than the twitch of her eyes.

In an instant, both realized she was indeed a person. Not an enigma. Not a creature. And both wondered exactly what world they'd suddenly been transported to.

Shaking off the amazement, Gavin walked over and picked up the cot they'd been using more often than not over the past year as Zuri's enhanced energy kept them on edge. "Put her down here. Close enough to the monitors so that we can reconnect her. I want to make sure we have at least a chance of being prepared when she wakes up again."

Once Justin had her safely on the makeshift bed, he turned his wary attention back to their incredulous faces.

"Maria, Gavin, this is Zuri," he said, looking down upon her gentle face. "Apparently, she holds the fate of our existence in her hands. I couldn't honestly tell you whether that's true or not, but I know this girl." He paused to take a breath. "I mean, young lady. She holds a whole lot of power within her little frame. And we've hardly witnessed a spark of it. Where did she get it? I don't know. But many people want her capabilities for their own purposes, and by no means are any of them concerned for her well-being."

Justin didn't realize he was holding his breath, waiting for the onslaught of angry questions, until he exhaled in a long-awaited whoosh. Even then he was met with silence as neither one seemed to be able to find appropriate words. Maria opened her mouth to say something but then closed it. Instead, she turned, quickly found the cables they needed, and hooked them up to Zuri's temples, chest, and stomach. When she finished, Maria pulled Zuri's shirt back over the ECG pads and stood up, struggling to comprehend what was happening with this uniquely different human in front of her.

Justin knew they were waiting for his explanation, but there wasn't much time before security would be charging in with Jones, and he could only guess who else. Likely people with guns. Lots of guns. Wondering what they would do with her, or them, for that matter, fueled his urgency.

"I know there are many questions I have to answer for." His palms were out, gesturing in surrender. "But right now, we need to buy time before the 12th floor makes it down here. If we know, they know."

"What do you expect us to do? We aren't going to fight our way through this." Gavin gritted his teeth as he processed all the years of deception.

"No, no. Just…" Justin looked around the room. "What if we call up there and see if we can slow them down? Tell them it was an error on our part. We had a malfunction of some sort? I—"

"—I got this, Justin." Maria turned on her heels and ran to the Red Phone situated under the stilled blue light. It was a direct line to Director Jones' office. She put it to her ear. "*What?*" Tapping the hook switch several times. Turning back to Justin's curious look, in a weak voice of disbelief, she said, "There's no dial tone."

"Did the whole building lose power? That doesn't make sense. That line should work regardless," Gavin commented as if Maria must be doing something wrong.

"Well, if you feel like pushing the button *yourself*, be my guest!"

"You're right. I'm sorry," he replied, trying to reign in his rising panic. "Hold on." Gavin ran to the door and put his hand on the biometric pad. Nothing happened. "This can't be." He moved his hand off and tried again before slamming it against the pad.

"The door's not working either?" Justin's brain couldn't process what was happening quickly enough.

Gavin stood silently, shaking his head.

"Alright, just open it manually." Standing up, Justin walked away from Zuri and straight for the door.

"Nothing is happening," said Gavin, pulling a lever on the upper right side of the door designed to release a pin and allowing them to manually push the door open with the crossbar. "Dammit, what is going on!"

Justin tried to help him push but it wouldn't budge.

Maria stepped in. "Ok, let's not panic. We know there's no way that someone won't be down here soon. If they can be down here within minutes of an eye twitch, no doubt they'll be here any moment for this. So what do we do? Put her back in?"

Gavin shook his head. "We can't. We have to assume that they may already know she's out, either by our hand or hers."

"He's right, and I'm not putting her back in regardless." Justin's voice was unforgiving.

"Then what do we do?" Maria didn't sound scared. Whether motivated or just amped up on adrenaline, she was ready to act.

Justin assessed both of them, then turned and lifted the

window cover latch to glance into the hall, anticipating security, guns, or both pointing back.

Nothing.

No one.

"There's no one out there," he said, glancing back into the room at Zuri, at a loss as to what to do next.

Gavin hadn't said much, but Justin saw the expression on his face shift from furious to confused as he looked at Zuri, then back to furious. When he caught Justin watching him, he finally opened his mouth to say, "I don't know what's going on, or how you could've kept, whatever this is… this information about you… her… why?" Sucking in his breath. "You seriously have a lot to answer for, but Cal… Zuri *is* my first priority. So how do we help her? I don't know how we're going to get out of this, but the only thing we can do until these doors open is help her."

"Right now, the only way I can think of to help her, and us, is to find Lexi. If Lexi is still alive," he said as he whipped his hands through his hair. Silence engulfed the room. He waited a moment, expecting questions to fly, but neither Maria nor Gavin said a word. He exhaled loudly, then jumped in.

"Lexi was her sister. I guess you'd say she was always Zuri's, uh, guardian because Zuri, well, both of them, were so young. Lexi was killed in the power plant explosion in North Carolina with the first electric substation at the government's Harris Plant. The first of nine substations in the U.S. to explode that day, causing the grid to fail. I was there. Lexi never came out of the inferno." His intense gaze at Zuri and the pain in his face showed how well he must have known them. His feelings were palpable.

"You were there? You were at Ground Zero? But how?" stumbled Gavin, trying to analyze all the information being thrown at him, but there were just too many questions.

Pacing back and forth, Justin wasn't sure how much to share. "I…" he started several times, not knowing how to explain. Finally, he took a deep breath and decided after what they just witnessed from Zuri, they might actually believe his story.

His eyes flicked back and forth from the empty window on the door to their faces. His words came out fast. "I was only a part of their lives for a short, yet enlightening, time. Somehow Zuri has always been able to…" he swallowed the disbelief he hoped they could get past, "feel her sister's presence. Feel when she was hurt. Feel, her life force, I guess you could say. Lexi responded similarly but didn't have the same internal force level as Zuri. Or maybe she did, but it just worked in an opposing way. They worked together in unison, and Lexi provided the fail-safe that the force inside Zuri needed, so it didn't get out of hand. Without her, well, she's been in a coma since that day so I'm not sure. Now, if Zuri was able to pull herself out of the unconscious state she's been in simply because Lexi needs help—" the realization of what he was saying struck him as the words left his mouth. "—then Lexi *must* be alive. And something has happened to her that has brought her sister back."

The others remained silent, wrestling with his words. It's

not as if they weren't well-versed in the potential of the human brain. And it's not as though they hadn't witnessed these wild events with their own eyes. Yet, what could they say to show say they understood?

Justin's vision jumped from one to the other. "She can feel her sister. I know this sounds crazy, but based on what I just saw—we just saw, the only thing that makes sense is that something drastic happened to her sister, and she woke up to protect her." With pleading eyes, "We have to find Lexi."

Despite the unbelievable situation and the insanity of seeing Zuri awake, functioning, and thoroughly ticked off, Maria took the lead and jumped into action.

"What if Lexi is here? On this compound. Why *wouldn't* she be? If she's alive, then maybe just like Calla—I mean Zuri, she is encased in glass." Her mind raced as she tried to mentally break down how the building and the compound were laid out. Where the most likely locations for holding someone just like Calla might be. It's not as if they would have known she would be here, considering how every mission component was strategically isolated.

"How do you do that?" Gavin was standing only a few inches from Maria, staring at her as if she had lost her mind.

"I don't know what's happening, but I'm betting on Justin right now. There's a whole mess of a story we haven't yet been told, and if I have to find this Lexi person to get the details, by God, I'm going to do it," she said, hand on hip, full of sass, and ready to rumble.

Gavin's expression was new to Justin, and he couldn't

decide if his friend was momentarily confused or indecisive before landing on something more akin to angry determination. Justin watched as Gavin walked straight to the back office, and within seconds, files, folders, and boxes started flying out of the room. Beelining straight for the research table, he moved everything out of the way, dropping the rolled and laminated tubes on the table. He wrestled the office chair back upright after having kicked it out of the way moments earlier.

"Grab a chair because we have some old blueprint designs of the building to analyze." Gavin, beyond furious, but grasping the urgency of the situation, bit his tongue on all the expletives he wanted to say.

"Where did you find these?" Justin smacked one of the rolls against the table's edge to knock the dust off.

"They've been in the backroom for years. Apparently, we were supposed to hang them up, you know, highlighting the fire safety route in an emergency. If you had ever been in the backroom to file some of our daily paperwork, you *might* have known that." His words would've sounded sarcastic if it weren't for his understandably angry tone.

"Amazing. Thank God for your attention to detail," Justin said with a smirk. "I don't do filing. That's why I brought you in." His quip dissipated some of the tension.

"Great! Now hug and move over. Jones should've been here by now. We can't possibly have that much time left before someone tears down that door. Gavin, did you already hit the data auto-saves? I have an idea about these maps."

# Chapter 23
## Alien

Blue Ridge Mountain, PA | August 9, 2029 | 8:44 p.m.

Aidan's heart pounded irregularly as he ran through the brush. He could see Zoey on the ground, body contorted in Exorcist-like positions. *This can't be happening* he repeated over and over in his mind. Nothing made sense.

About fifty yards out, her body slumped to the ground and stopped moving. "Zoey!" He barked, too afraid to place his full force behind it, not knowing what was happening to his rear. He felt like the sound around him had been squelched and wondered if it was because his heart was beating so loudly in his ears.

Sprinting at top speed, he slid on the rocks to stop himself as he came upon her lifeless form. "Zoe. Zoey!" Knees to the ground, his hands hovered over her for a moment while he quickly assessed the situation.

"Hold on… Hold on, Zoey. Please be alive." At first, she didn't appear to be breathing. When he held his own breath to steady his gaze, he could see the air in front of her face blowing the loose dirt by her mouth. "Thank God."

Carefully he took hold of her shoulders and rolled her onto her back. As he did, she began to open her eyes. "Wait, Zoey. Wait. Let me brush the dirt off first." She followed his directions and kept them closed as he used his fingers to carefully wipe the dirt from where her face met the ground.

Pulling her upper body to rest in his lap, he said, "You're good now. Take it easy. Open your eyes when you're ready."

She took a few more steadying breaths and squinted up at him. "I think… I'm not sure, but I think someone is hurt badly."

"You're okay, Zoey. Just a few scrapes, but I don't see anything major."

"No." Her movements were a bit jerky, but she managed to put herself into a sitting position before finishing her thought. When she fully faced him, his eyes grew wide.

"Zoey?" he said, choking on his deep inhale. "Your eyes Zoey."

It's as if she didn't understand him. "No, Aidan. Not me. It's the girl. Something terrible is happening to her."

His heart skipped several beats staring straight into her eyes. She was serious.

The stomping of Joe's feet broke their trance. "Zoey!" he gruffly whispered seconds before sliding to a halt, spraying loose gravel into Aidan's lap. Hitting the ground beside her, he threw his hands up as if to hold her face, not wanting to hurt her. When his eyes landed on hers, he fell back hard on his tailbone, wincing in pain.

"What's wrong?" she asked, her voice hoarse yet stronger than moments before.

"It's… your… your eyes again, Zoe," Joe said, looking to Aidan for confirmation. All Aidan could do was nod in agreement, which irritated Zoey all the more.

Pulling out the small mirror from his kit, a tool intended to peer around objects in tight spots, Aidan handed it to her.

"I don't want to see the hideous lines," she replied, trying to shove it back at him. "I know they're there."

Gently he handed it back, saying, "No, Zoey. It's not the lines." Then slowly placed the mirror in her hand.

Closing her eyes to gather strength, she slowly raised the mirror to her face. When she opened her eyes, a shimmer reflected in the glass, causing her to drop it.

"No!" Her mouth held a small O shape in shock as she gripped Aidan's shirt with clenched fists. "How is this possible," she whispered, searching his eyes for an answer. "What's happening to me?"

Neither man had a clue as to what they should do.

Joe's mind was spinning as he stared at her in awe. "After the first big one you had back in March, your eyes were different. But this—"

"—is some serious alien sh—" Aidan's attempt at levity was cut off when he saw tears welling in her eyes. Giving in to the moment and realizing that she'd earned the right to a good cry, they sit quietly, letting the tears fall.

After a few minutes, Joe took a deep breath. "Maybe… maybe we need to stop this. Maybe we need to go home." He said this knowing she wouldn't but wishing there was any other way to save her from what was happening.

Zoey shook her head back and forth. Not really saying *no* to his advice, but more so to herself in disbelief.

Aidan carefully pulled her hands from his shirt but didn't release them. "Maybe Joe's right? Maybe this is too much. We don't know what could happen if we continue down this path. It could be getting worse because we're so close. Do you think?"

She gently picked the mirror up, careful not to bring it near her face again. Handing it to Aidan, she brushed herself off while taking stock of her body. No injuries. Just a body that's become, as Aidan put it, alien to her.

Picking her bag and gear up from the ground, she threw it over her shoulder and tilted her head back.

"No, guys. We can't. We need to follow this through. I am connected to someone that, as far as I know, I've never met. I don't know how or why, but we have to go in there and stop whatever's happening to her. I don't think distance is the problem. On the other hand, I think you will be digging my grave soon if we don't find her and help her," she proclaimed, standing there in her best Lara Croft stance. Despite the extreme pain that had just racked her body minutes before, she appeared stronger than she'd ever been. "We need to get in there. I think we're almost out of time."

Joe reached a hand out to Aidan and helped him to his feet. Both wanted to tie her up and force her into the back of the car, fully knowing they would regret it if they did.

"I want to kidnap you, Zoe, and take you far away from here," Joe said lightly. She started to protest, but he put his hand up in surrender. "But I know that won't do us any good."

Her eyes spoke volumes of love and gratitude that they wouldn't fight her on this.

Aidan, smiling a broad smile, said, "We'll follow you to the ends of the earth, kid."

# Chapter 24
## Inside the Glass

**"I**'m 100% certain there's an excellent reason, which you're going to fully explain to me, why that young woman who was enclosed in a containment unit for the past *seven* years is suddenly *not* in it!" The fire-breathing Jones entered their laboratory on a heart-attack-inducing rampage of angst and anxiety. He seemed to have no problem opening the door from the outside when the door flung open, shocking the three of them out of their seats.

"Did I miss something? Did I all of a sudden get *fired* from my position as Director of VISP, and no one thought to tell me? Has the world already ended, and no one called to give me a heads-up!" His robust walk made his abnormally large gut jiggle, stretching his shirt beyond comprehension and pushing the buttons close to the point of detonation. His neck flushed fire red, and Justin was pretty sure he was a hair's breadth away from imploding.

"Explanation? Anyone? Quickly! Before I—"

"—Where's your entourage?" No sass in her voice. Just a simple question.

"What?" Caught off guard, he didn't even say it with anger. Instead, they see a flash of guilt skirt across his features. He quickly disguised the look with fury.

If looks could kill, Maria would be six feet under.

"I have never seen you enter this room without at least five lackeys behind you. Where is everyone, *Mr.* Jones? Has something significant happened? Did it occur to you that you are, as you stated, standing in a room with a young woman that has been in a glass prison for *seven* years? Not breathing the same air as we are for fear of... of what? Being infected? Infecting her? Afraid she will harm us somehow or *'kill'* us because she's some raging alien, sorceress, or what? What, Mr. Jones? You don't seem to be running for the hills to get away from her." Cornering him, her boss didn't say a word. "It's been an hour since she woke up. One. Whole. Hour. When her eyes twitched, you were down here in minutes. As long as it took the elevator to bring you down here to the deep underground Delta 4. D4 is where *all* the cool stuff happens, yet it took you over sixty minutes. What's going on up there, huh? Because the moment things went south down here, our door was locked. From the *outside*, we were trapped. I don't recall being briefed on that part of the protocol."

Justin and Gavin do a double-take, unaware of how much time has passed after being so focused on Zuri, data, blueprints, and discussing Lexi. Maria was the only one noticing that no one from security, nor Jones himself, had bothered to show up for that length of time.

"She's right." Gavin surprised all of them with his genuine endorsement. He walked right up to mere inches from Jones' face and spoke in a low, harsh tone. "Where is everyone, Jones? Where are they?" He wasn't giving Jones even a modicum of space to try and spin a lie.

Jones sidestepped away from Gavin, heading over to where Zuri lay on the makeshift bed. He knelt on the ground right next to her—no discernable fear in his actions. After a short-lived but very intense awakening, she slept—restless, the way anyone trapped in a nightmare might be.

Justin readied himself to strike in case Jones took this opportunity to harm her. Yet, his slow, defeated movements were almost fatherly.

"I can walk in here because," his eyes lock with each of theirs before turning his vision on her, "Zuri is no threat to us. She has an extraordinary power of some intangible kind, as I can tell you have all witnessed. What just happened, what she did… it was out of some fear or threat only she was aware of. She doesn't have the control over her power to be entirely safe, but she has no malice in any bone in her body." Jones carried on, quietly talking, primarily to himself. "If anything, we are a threat to her. Hell, what am I saying? We are a threat to her."

Justin and Maria's eyes shift to Gavin. They could

physically feel his rage. So incensed with anger, through grinding teeth, he growled, "So you mean to tell me, for years we have been down here living, eating, sleeping… breathing life away? A chosen imprisonment under the belief that we were working to save lives. Save this *planet*. And it was all a lie? A cover-up? For what truth? What is the damn truth Jones! Why are we even here? Why didn't you just put her in a living containment unit and let us live our lives?" He snatched Jones from the ground and pushed him against the wall. The others gasped, shocked by his strength. Jones' shirt tore and buttons flew as the director trembled. "How could you do this? We could've had a life outside of here! At least what life there is to live out there. What have we been doing all this time!"

Attempting to lower the tension, Justin placed his hands on his partner's shoulders. "Get off me, Justin! You're part of this too! You knew who she was all these years and never gave us a clue. Your team. Your *family!*" Jones and Justin lock eyes, giving away the truth.

His eyes cut to Zuri. "Look at her!" His breath hitched in his throat. "You've stolen so much life from her too." Gavin refocused back on Jones and then Justin. "You've forced me to steal her life."

Clearing the lump in his throat, Justin said, "You're right. You're right. I should've told you, but anyone in this place could be a Breaker or worse. I couldn't take the chance. Not on her life." Gavin released Jones with a shove, pushed past Justin, and walked to the other side of the room.

"A Breaker? Did you seriously just say that to me?" The

pain in his face broke Justin's resolve. He never truly believed Gavin could be a Breaker and immediately regretted saying that to him.

"You had a purpose," Jones whispered. "All of you. Your purpose was to protect her and hopefully learn from her. Those above me have always felt that if she was contained here, we could study her brain activity in hopes of mimicking it or learning how to use it someday."

"Use it how? Against our so-called enemies?" Gavin spit out. "Who are these enemies, Jones? These ghosts of destruction. Do they even exist?" His breathing was heavy as he began to lose control of himself. "There are no armies left, or, or countries to fight against."

Jones took in a deep, but unsteady breath. "They do. There are real enemies, but we are her worst enemy." He stared into Gavin's now red eyes. "We were terrified that if she awoke, we wouldn't be able to control her capabilities without…" he paused and changed direction in what he was saying, "Those above us would rather her die than lose control of her." This last statement was said through grinding teeth.

"That's why we have such simple rules, then," said Maria. "Unreal. We've been sitting here watching endless screens of data come across our desks all this time. If you had just *told* us what you were trying to achieve, we could've been implementing other testing avenues to determine what makes her tick. Yet you fed us all of these lines of bull to keep her comatose, so we had no way of doing our jobs.

"This political garbage is just that. *Garbage*. How many

*millions* of dollars and countless hours have been wasted contriving this place, putting all these brilliant minds together, and for what? For nothing!" she yelled, casting her eyes to the floor.

Gavin took one last somber gaze at Zuri, and without acknowledging anyone else, he left through the now functioning door.

Jones dropped to his knees. Putting his face in his hands, his shoulders began trembling. When he finally looked up, he was pale and breathless.

Justin knew Zuri before the grid failed, which was why he was there. He did not, however, know the circumstances of what Jones had just shared. "So all this time, we were just pawns? Just playing the game, day in and day out. All fake. Well, Mr. Director, here's what I want to know." Squatting down next to Jones, his voice became menacingly low. "What do you get out of all this? If you knew this the entire time but said nothing to us, what is it or who is it that you did it for? And what has happened in the last hour that could be bigger than Zuri waking up?

The director's hands locked together in front of him as if in desperate prayer. Justin could see that every word out of his mouth was pained but true. "I did this for my daughter. I want her to have a better life to grow up in than the one that exists today. *They* have a plan to make things better, and I think they can do it. I did it for her." His head dropped. After a few strained breaths, he faced Zuri.

Maria didn't notice his resignation. "What does that mean?

Who are "they"? What the Hell are you talking about?" The pitch of her voice increased with every word as she rounded the table toward him. "What's going on out there?" She wanted to haul back and hit him in the face, but he didn't react whatsoever to her advance. He was looking only at Zuri. No longer paying attention to any of them. Zuri lay on the cot. Eyes closed. She was all he could focus on.

In slow progression, Jones cast his gaze around the room. Each person saw the full-throttle anguish across his face. When his eyes finally rested on the petite young lady on the cot, he exhaled the words, "I'm sorry."

He pulled out a pen from his shirt pocket. Closed his eyes. And clicked the end of the pen.

Two things occurred simultaneously. Jones dropped to the tile floor in a heap as the steel door imploded into their lab. The door crashed through the horseshoe of tables and took Maria down with it.

Violent ringing in Justin's ears disoriented him long enough to lose sight of which direction both Maria and the cot holding Zuri were flung. By the time he came to his senses, their lab was full of smoke and debris. With eyes burning, tears poured down his face attempting to clear the particles. Even with his vision impaired and hearing muffled, he could feel a change of presence in the room. As he lifted his head, his sight flashed like strobe lights within his eyes. Vertigo took over. Through the flashing images, he finally saw what he already knew.

They were not alone.

# Chapter 25
## They Meet

Zoey, Joe, and Aidan stood outside the room they'd been instructed to go to based on the blueprints. Four floors below ground, in a section labeled D4, they could hear quiet chatter interspersed with yelling behind the last door in the long hall. Until now, they'd been unable to decipher some of the handwritten information on the side of the maps Rice Jahnsen provided. D4, LR14 they suspected referenced a location but couldn't confirm it until stepping foot into the building.

Aidan was on lookout duty, but to their surprise, they hadn't encountered a single person in the building, or the compound, since they gained access.

"Something's wrong here," Aidan said, his head on a

swivel, as if waiting for a surprise assailant. "Where is everyone?"

"I don't know. Obviously, there's someone behind this door," Zoey said while holding the tubing for Joe as he set up the detonation cord to breach the door.

"All set. Ready to do this?" They nodded. No one was backing out now. They knew that blowing the door with people behind it could mean receiving gunfire. Or worse, causing casualties. It seemed like it was now or never, though. With everyone gone they had to believe the one they were looking for was still there. "Alright, let's move back to where the hallway turns. Masks and earplugs," he whispered, keeping up with them from behind.

As Joe rounded the corner, the explosive went off. The violent concussion knocked the wind out of them.

Within seconds, shaking off the shock, they moved forward to crouch in the blown-open door space, weapons ready, waiting for the smoke to clear enough to see through their masks.

Justin pulled his M9 from under his shirt and trained it on the newcomers, simultaneously scanning the room for Zuri. Disoriented from the blast, he spotted Zuri lying on the floor several feet from the cot she'd been on. Crawling toward her under cover of the vacating smoke, he shielded her with as much of his body as possible. Through the smoke, he could see two men with their weapons pointed at him and a woman just standing there.

Wild, curly, dark hair surrounded her intensely focused face. The weapon in her hand hung lifelessly at her side. Justin could see her eyes were on Zuri. She was completely ignoring Justin even as his gun leveled in her direction.

The dust was still airborne in the room as she took off her mask, revealing that half her face was covered with a unique tattoo. She cautiously moved closer. With every step she took, he could see that what at first appeared to be an elaborate tattoo no longer resembled something needled into her skin. The dark purple web snaked from the top of her shirt, ran up her neck and jawline, almost reaching her right eye.

Quietly but forcefully, she said, "Put your weapons down." Her eyes flicked to Justin. "Please. We're not going to hurt anyone here." She was entirely focused on Zuri. "It's *her*." She moved her head to the side, searching for the man with the beard. The redheaded man walked up behind her and holstered his weapon in his waistband.

Nodding at Justin, "What's up, cowboy." Justin trained his weapon on him instead, and the man immediately put his hands up, palms out. "Hey, it's totally fine. We aren't here to hurt anyone. Zoey—" He glanced her way, hoping she would say something to calm the situation, but found her attention had only one target. "—She, well we… we're here to help." He could see he wasn't making progress.

Without diverting her gaze, Zoey whispered, "It's her. This is the woman I've seen in my dreams. We found her."

Aidan could see her comments weren't helping the

in any danger. "Hey. We're sorry about your door. We were in kind of a rush. I'm Aidan, and this is Zoey. That big guy over there is Joey."

"Joe," Joe said, annoyed. He can barely tolerate Zoe calling him Joey as if he were a five-year-old, but Aidan saying it was straight-up obnoxious.

"Joe… sorry, he's a little particular about introductions," Aidan said, slowly reaching his hand toward Justin. "We came a very long way, and Zoey has been through a whole heck of a lot of… of, I guess you could say trauma, in trying to get here." When Justin showed no sign of returning the gesture, Aidan carefully walked to the other side of Zuri and leaned over. Justin was on his feet before anyone could react and had Aidan by his collar.

Stumbling back several steps, Aidan threw his hands in the air. "Whoa!"

"Wait." Zoey pleaded with him. "We're not going to hurt her. *Please.*"

Something about her eyes made Justin's lungs constrict, and without breaking contact, he released his tight grip on Aidan.

Zoey knelt down and reached to put her hand on Zuri's face. Before she touched her, she glanced up at Justin for consent. He seemed genuinely confused but nodded in approval. Carefully, she laid her fingers on the side of Zuri's face. With hope in her eyes, Zoey said, "I think it's her. Her face is…." She halted, her eyes squinting. Turning to Aidan, then Justin, and back to Zuri, her conviction wavered.

Aidan scrunched his forehead, confused, looking between the two of them for answers, then said, "Strange. I thought she'd have the marks on her. You said you felt that whatever was happening to her was happening to you? That you were in some way linked?" Aidan's voice was soft with concern.

Zoey felt disoriented, studying the young woman's face. "I did. I do. I mean, it's got to be her. She's familiar, but something is different."

Justin moved in and put a hand on Zuri's shoulder. The need to protect her was still present even as he realized there might be nothing to protect her from. At least not from anyone currently in the room. "Who are you?" Now that he was only a few feet from the woman's face, his professional curiosity was taking hold. "What has happened to you? How do you think you know Zuri?" He wanted to reach out and touch this woman's fascinating and delicate face.

Zoey remained silent.

Her hands lifted toward Zuri again. "What are you doing?" Justin wasn't angry, but the idea of a stranger touching her like an animal at a petting zoo was becoming too much.

Her eyes pleaded with him until, quietly, she said, "Please. I just need to see her eyes. I don't want to hurt her. I just need to see her eyes." Her own Hazel eyes caught Justin's, and he could see the glow in them. Not just a pleading sincerity but the bright fireworks on display within. Though her eye color was different, he knew only two other people on the planet had glimmering eyes like that, and he was momentarily stunned.

Zoey gingerly pulled the eyelid to one of Zuri's eyes back far enough for the color to show. The instant their eyes connected, Zuri's opened fully.

She sat upright so quickly it startled the others, already on edge. Both women, only inches apart, stared at one another. Out of nowhere, they grab the sides of their heads, screaming as if in excruciating pain, all the while keeping their fixed eyes on one another.

Everything in the room, even their screaming, suddenly stopped.

Silence.

It's as if the oxygen had been sucked from the room.

Seconds ticked by with no one moving. Everything was slow. Heavy.

Laboriously Joe managed to speak. "Hey." Putting a heavy foot toward them. "Hey. Zoey. *Zoe?*" He got to her side with difficulty, but the weight on his body holding him in place began to ease. "Zoey, stop. *Stop!* Hey, look at me!" He reached for her shoulders and tried pulling her away, but he could barely move her.

"Zoey! Grab her, Aidan! What's happening? Zoe? *Zoey!*" Panic began to overtake them.

"What is she doing?" Aidan said to Justin. "Grab her, man!"

Anger rose in the room as Justin placed his hands on Zuri's, which were still pushing into either side of her head like a vice. The vibration of a very low electrical current began running through his fingertips. He could tell the bearded man,

Joe, felt the same sensation by the expression on his face.

Suddenly, Joe shouted, "What color are her eyes? *What color are her eyes?*" An unmistakable hum began to fill their ears.

"They're crystal!" Justin yelled back. Every second seemed filled with chaos, and the color of her eyes was not a question he could fathom having any bearing.

"Crystal what? *What* color of crystal?" Aidan growled from a foot away.

"They're crystal! How do you explain an unexplainable color? Just… crystal!"

"Like diamonds." Maria's quietly firm voice rang out from underneath a pile of tables, chairs, documents, and other random debris hurled in the blast. Justin had practically forgotten about her with the strange guests' arrival. He scoured the room in the direction of where her voice had come from but remained near Zuri.

Maria drug herself out from underneath the wreckage just as both women dropped their arms and fell back against the men situated behind them.

"Diamonds," said Zoey, quietly clarifying, "You have diamonds in your eyes." As if in a trance, she couldn't look away.

"You're not looking for diamonds," Zuri replied. "You're searching for the ocean. The ocean is in Lexi's eyes."

# Chapter 26
## The Last Purgatory

August 9, 2029 | 10:10 p.m.

*D*iamonds.

*Her eyes are the color of diamonds.*

"Zuri!" Lexi tried to cry out, but the pain in her throat prevented anything but a gruff sound from ripping through.

*I need to get to her. I need to see her, touch her, know she is alive.* So much anger. Red was all she could see.

Blinking through her tears, the grit in her eyes left a burning sensation with every pass of her eyelids. As her vision began to focus, her brain registered pinpricks of pain all over her body. The crush of pressure was gone, but her skin felt like it was crawling with insects, itching, and shivering. The more aware she became, the more rage she felt—no control over the hate engrossing her entire being.

The ground beneath her was so unfamiliar that it momentarily curbed her volatile feelings. Every muscle ached, and she groaned with each movement.

Placing her hands on the cool surface beneath her, she pushed herself up. In every square inch of skin, she felt excruciating pain. It fueled a madness she'd never felt before.

*What is going on?*

She was losing control and realizing it didn't help her to calm down. Instead, it just kept growing.

Peering up, she saw what was once a glass case broken to shards all over the hard white surface she was sitting on.

Looking out onto the floor below, the glass particles were spread through most of the room. Lexi recognized the shape of the box she was once in. Technically, still in.

Glass. She could see and feel a million cuts on every inch of her body. Less blood than she would have thought, but that was likely because the glass was still embedded in her skin.

She'd laid in that glass prison for hours just staring, listening, and waiting. A hose nearby spewed some sort of gas. Below the hose laid two men. She could feel their life force. One draining rapidly and the other weak but slowly increasing. Crawling over the side, she reached down to the floor, catching her leg on the jagged edge of a small piece of glass. A scream erupted from her lungs as the shard sliced through her thin skin. Angry, she swiped her hand toward the piece of glass, but the glass was blown apart before her palm connected with it.

*What did I just do?*

Being able to break glass to pieces without touching it

should have terrified her.

But it didn't.

Every coherent thought was gone before she could grab hold of it, replaced by a burning sensation within her skull.

Tumbling outside the box onto the tiled floor knocked the wind out of her. So much agony. It was everywhere. Her head was ready to explode as her heart rapidly beat against her chest, causing her to shudder with every breath.

Over her shoulder, she felt, just before she saw, that the man on the floor closest to her was starting to move. As soon as he noticed Lexi on the floor beside him, his eyes grew wide and he quickly rolled over, behind a blown-over desk. Without hesitation, she reached her hand toward him and the desk flew away like nothing more than a plastic bag in a wind storm. Stunned by what she'd just done, she stared at her hand now shimmering like heat over hot asphalt. A foreign appendage.

*Did I break all that glass?*

Streaks of blood seeped through her clothes, down her arms, and onto her hands. Hands she didn't recognize. They seemed too big.

The man threw his arms out in front of him and tried yelling her name, "Rose! Rose, it's me, Grant. You know me! You've listened to my voice for a very long time now. Please! You know me!" He was on his knees, no longer backing away but shielding himself as best he could. "I would never hurt you."

Lexi couldn't understand his words but they didn't make sense. The pressure in her head was overwhelming, and everything inside of her was just so fiercely engulfed in rage. Sweat running down her face reignited the burning in her eyes. "No!" She cried out. "I don't know you!"

Her mind spun wildly as her body rebelled against its better nature, acting only in a defensive state of rage.

Something deep within her hesitated, but the compulsion to reach out and punish him was stronger. As she tried to stand, her muscles convulsed, jerking her body through the movements as she rose. Grant was now halfway across the room toward the door.

"NO!"

Before she could stop herself, a numbing feeling spread from her chest down through her arms. Blistering heat in her fingers lasted only a moment before it passed through and off their tips. Grant was instantly thrown into the white concrete wall. So unaware of herself, it didn't even register what she'd just done.

Lying there in a heap of broken glass and bones, he whispered, "Rose. Please. I can help you." His voice was strained and deep inside, Lexi understood something was off. It didn't feel right hurting someone like that. Yet she couldn't grasp her identity.

A small part of her wanted to run to him. Help him. But her unexplainable desire for violence was greater than the nagging doubt in the back of her mind.

"Please. Don't," he continued to plead.

Before giving in to this uncompromising draw to crush him with her life-ending force, she managed to reign in the growing rage long enough to address something he had said.

"Who's Rose?" Unsure if she'd said that out loud, the split-second confusion allowed her the chance to turn away from hurting him any further. In a panic, she ran toward the door, sweeping both arms in a wide arc in front of her. The doors ripped apart as she raced through them. Lost and confused, she steered her body to the right and began to scramble down the dim hallway. Terror welled up, matching her anger, as she took off through endless white walls.

"Lexi!" a woman called out from an open door not far behind her.

*Lexi.*

Somewhere inside her soul Lexi knew the woman was talking to her. She hadn't thought about her name, but she knew Rose wasn't right. Hearing Lexi didn't quite register, but it was like smelling a familiar scent from her childhood. She *knew* it but couldn't comprehend how.

Her feet slid on the smooth surface due to the blood from the cuts on her feet. The glass fragments dug deeper, but there was no pain. She turned and stared at the figure standing halfway across the threshold. Cautiously, the woman took two slow steps into the center of the hallway, letting the door close behind her. "Where are you going to go, Lexi?"

*That voice.*

Crouching like an animal ready to strike, Lexi edged her way forward. Her mind went dark. The pressure deadened her senses. Most of her body felt numb, but her *need* to break everything in her path consumed her.

"There's nowhere to go. I need you to come with me now." The woman's voice was calm but urgent.

Lexi gathered the newfound power in her arms. The light between her shoulders and fingertips shimmered and distorted.

Her demeanor showed fear, as if she knew what Lexi was about to do, even though Lexi didn't know herself. As Lexi released the energy, the woman raised her arms to block it. Instead of the woman being thrown backward, Lexi felt an incredible power collide with every inch of her body, launching her helplessly into the air and careening into the furthest wall.

As the woman moved closer, Lexi saw a spark in her eyes. A green spark. Like the woman in her dream, or was it a memory? She had green eyes, only now with anguish on her face, and yet somehow still comforting.

As the woman bent down, reaching out to touch her, Lexi lifted her hand out as well.

This time the emerald-eyed woman flew up from the ground, crashing against the wall.

*No one will ever hurt me again.*

The room went dark.

# Chapter 27
## Inside the Gate

They stared at Zuri. At twenty-two, she looked more like a fifteen-year-old, tiny and frail. Justin carefully removed his arms from around her so as not to startle her.

"Zuri? Are you hurt?" Sliding her onto the floor, he situated himself at eye level.

The familiar voice caused Zuri to look his way. Once her eyes found him, though, her confusion became discernible. Reaching her hand up, she slid her fingers down the side of his face. "Justin? I… but, you look… different." That wasn't the first response he anticipated from her.

"He's older, Zuri." Maria's soothing voice provided the answer Justin was searching for. He couldn't hide his dismay, knowing that they would have to show her just how old she was now.

"It's been kind of a while, Z, since you fell asleep." He took a deep breath. "I've been here with you the whole time, though. Waiting for you to wake up. So you wouldn't be afraid." She wasn't acting frightened, however. In fact, she no longer seemed confused either, as if she realized she should've expected to see him this way. Like she knew how much time had passed.

Seeing her with eyes open and so wide, glowing in the dim light of the room, they were in awe. Justin watched as she studied herself. Holding up her hands. Turning them back and forth. Noticing her longer and more slender fingers as opposed to the childish hands in her mind's eye. Yet, she was still quite tiny. "How long has it been?"

A quiet lull hovered over them before Justin breathed out, "Seven years." Pausing to gauge her reaction, he went on, "It has been seven years since you were fully awake."

After a moment, she said, "You kind of look like a doctor." A half-hearted smile formed on her lips but didn't reach her eyes. Putting her hand down on the edge of the cot, she attempted to stand despite the weakness in her muscles. Once upright, her gaze looked down the length of her body. "Funny, I thought I'd be taller." Tilting her head up, she observed each face in the room. Only two of them felt familiar. "I knew time was passing. It was difficult to tell how much, though," she said, recognizing the timbre of her voice carried a hint of her younger self. "Seven years? For so long, I've lived within the walls of my mind, wondering where I was, who I was, if I was.

There were many times when I thought I'd gone crazy. I couldn't imagine what I must've done to be locked in such a place." Her big round eyes looked up into Justin's. "Did I do something bad?"

"No. No, Zuri," said Justin, moving to her side, needing her to know without a doubt she did nothing to put herself in that place. "You did nothing wrong. There's noth—"

Suddenly, Zoey screamed as she was thrown across the room. Zuri reeled back at the sound, though was untouched by the invisible force that left Zoey sprawled on the floor. Aidan and Joe raced to her side, helpless as she tried to draw a breath against her compressed lungs. Maria and Justin crouched down, slowly moving around the room, trying to understand what hit her.

Maria only made it a few feet before low-level panic began to consume her. Her eyes filled with terror as she scanned the room, bracing herself for another explosion. Stumbling back, her heels hit something with a thud. She whipped around, choking at the sight of Director Jones, flat on his back with legs twisted awkwardly beneath him. His eyes were open and bloodshot with a blank stare she couldn't tear away from.

"Maria? Maria, sit down!" Justin grabbed her shoulders and helped her to the floor. "Breathe! Just breathe," he whispered gruffly, acknowledging the blank stare coming from Jones and knowing without a doubt that he was dead.

Aidan and Joe were holding their friend down as she shook violently. Her shrieks only lasted a few seconds, but the effect was impossible to comprehend.

As if in slow motion, Justin turned his head, tracking Maria's gaze. Gulping in fear, his legs reflexively launched him upright as he sensed a presence behind him.

Zuri was standing, eyes so wide it was as if she was looking straight through him. Before he could grab her, she moved toward Zoey with agility he wouldn't have thought possible.

"Lexi!" she screamed before landing beside Zoey with a quickness and gentleness that stunned them. Before they could intervene, Zuri was cradling Zoey's head in her lap. One hand on the side of her face, the other over Zoey's heart.

The purple marks on the side of Zoey's face were inflamed and inexplicably spreading past her temple into her hairline.

No one moved.

No one spoke.

They just watched.

Each one of them glued to Zuri as she said, "She is connected. To Lexi."

"How? How can they be connected?" Justin moved to her side, wanting to see what Zuri was seeing. "Where's Lexi?"

The rest of the room remained still.

"I'm not sure. But they are. These marks are Lexi's marks. I've seen them in my dreams. Someone is after her. Hurting her." Tears welled up and trickled down her face. "We need to find her, Justin." Just as he'd thought earlier, that if Lexi, her sister, was hurting, then Zuri was hurting. And somehow, this stranger on the floor was also connected, feeling her pain even more than Zuri.

Turning around to find the blueprints of their building, Justin noticed Maria had gotten there first. Tears in her own eyes, she held the blueprints out to him.

Maria's expression showed exhaustion, but her words were crisp and clear. "That young woman has... We've put her through a hell we will never know. It's time we show her some love. And make sense of this while we're at it."

# Chapter 28
## The Search

**M**aria walked toward the phone lying on the floor. Passing by Jones, now a lifeless body, a shiver ran up her spine as she picked up the phone and placed it back in its cradle.

"Maria, what are you doing?" asked Justin, watching her course through the lab.

"We need to know if someone is manning security. We need to get out of here. Somehow these three made it down here without being shot, so I'd like to know who is not paying attention."

Picking up the receiver and pressing the speed dial, she paused. Her eyebrows quickly angled downward, and her lips pursed. After a few more seconds, she hung up the receiver, then tried again and again. "The blast must've killed the wiring." She took long strides for such a small woman. Not giving up, Maria walked around the glass case to the emergency phone attached on the backside as a fail-safe.

"There's a dial tone!" she said before calling up to the Ground Floor security office. "It just keeps ringing." Gritting her teeth, she said, "What event *other* than what is happening in this room could possibly keep the security office unmanned? This is ridiculous." Replacing the receiver, she quickly jerked it up once more and dialed two—this time to the head of security for the compound.

Nothing.

Aidan raised the obvious question. "Why are you just now trying the phones? Wouldn't that have been the first thing on the list in a life-threatening situation?"

"Are you serious? Do you have any idea what our protocol is around here," said Maria incensed. "Obviously, that would make sense. However, there are alarms in the headquarters and security offices linked to this lab. When they sound, security is to arrive ahead of the Director and stand guard until released. Usually, within minutes we have a room full of suits up in our business." Maria's arms flew up in the air as she spoke. "An explosion should've brought the entire security team down here."

"Today, as you can see, that is not the case," said Justin, raising his eyebrows as he continued that thought. "We've never had to call. They just came running. Today is clearly not the standard." He looked down at the prints in his hand. "We need to check if anyone else on this floor is hurt. There should be total chaos around here right now. Particularly after you blew the doors off the room." Confusion washed over his face. "We still don't know why the only one that *did* show up was Jones," he said, looking at Jones' body on the floor. "The doors blew just as Jones… or did he…." It was all surreal. The timing was so precise. Too precise.

For the first time, he stopped. Looking at Jones, he took three long strides over to him and knelt down. It was obvious Jones was gone, but nothing hit him when the blast occurred. In his mind's eye, he saw the Director pull his pen out of his pocket, and at almost that exact moment, the door blew in, and he fell to the ground. Yet, he was falling already as it happened. Scanning his body, nothing seemed out of sorts. On seeing the pen in his hand, Justin pulled it from Jones's grasp. As he did, a needle slid out of his thumb. His breath hitched, and he dropped the pen.

"What?" Maria was behind him, looking over his shoulder.

"I… he…" muttered Justin. He couldn't believe it. Jones had done it to himself. The petechial hemorrhaging in his eyes proved that whatever toxin was in that needle killed him instantly. "He did this." His gaze met Maria's.

"Why? Why would he do that?" She shot an accusatory glance at the newcomers. "He knew you were coming. Right? Were you planning to kill him? So he did it before you could?"

"What? No!" Aidan was the first to respond. "We've never met that guy!"

Justin stood up to get in his face when Zoey put her hand

up. "Please. Please stop. We did not know him, and that's not why we're here." She took a deep breath and got up to her knees. "We only came here to rescue someone. We thought that someone was her." She nodded toward Zuri.

"Lexi," Zuri said matter-of-factly. "Lexi is who she thought she'd find." She turned to look at Justin. "We need to find her.

With Zoey and Zuri both in agreement with their purpose, everyone followed suit.

"There are several sub-floors, and they are closely monitored for safety. It's unlikely that no one is aware of what has been happening in this part of the building," Justin said.

"They might just be following blast protocol. Waiting for the all-clear?" said Maria, the voice of reason.

"But from who? No one came down to assess." Justin glanced at Jones' body on the floor. There's no time for grief. Not wanting to address it, he knew that keeping Jones in the same room with them would only cause the situation to become more dreadful than it already was. "Uh, can you assist me for a moment?" he called out, looking toward Joe and Aidan, hoping they would take the hint.

Following his lead, they gave a quick nod.

Gently they maneuvered Jones' body out to the hall and into a storage room for the time being. It felt utterly disrespectful, but it was better than leaving his body in the middle of the hallway where anyone might run into him. That, and it still wasn't clear if he was one of the good guys or the bad.

Kneeling next to him, Justin removed the Director's ever-present handkerchief along with his ID from his pocket. He intended to leave it with security on the main floor. Jones cited his daughter as the reason for his final actions, believing his actions would provide a better life for her. Now, Justin was making it a high priority to find out *what* Jones was involved in, and the two most likely candidates to start gathering information from were standing right next to him.

"Thank you." He wiped his hands on his jeans. Nothing was on them, but they felt dirty after carrying a body. It was a weird moment. He thought he should maybe say something about the man. Opening his mouth, he tried to speak, but it was too strange, and, instead, he turned his attention away. "I'm hoping Jones' last actions alive really were for a good cause. Considering he killed himself as the three of you breached our doors. The timing's a little suspicious, don't you think? Which leads me to ask: who-are-you?" Justin stood tall with hands-on-hips and legs in a power stance. He wanted them to know that his masculinity out-ranked their own at this point in the game, despite Joe's beard, Aidan's muscles, and the fact they had more tactical gear than Rangers on a raid in Kandahar.

Aidan and Joe glanced at each other. Their expressions told him they might not know precisely *who* they were either. Clearly, they had their own questions about all of this, but he was committed to getting his answers first.

"Well, brother, would you like the long or short version?"

Joe asked.

"I vote, short version," quipped Aidan, hand held high.

"Agreed. Short version while we do some recon around D4. I want to see if anyone else on the floor has been injured or knows anything has happened. Feels like a ghost town." He had walked D4 enough times to know exactly how many tiles there were in each hallway. Justin knew where each crack and scrape of paint was on the walls. However, he couldn't say what just about anyone else on his floor, or any other for that matter, did in detail. Every door was either a key card or biometric entry.

Justin's lab was tucked away in the back of a long hallway. No doors existed on either side of the hall until they reached the connection point of four different pathways leading away from their own. The underground layout was pentagon-shaped, but the above-ground portion looked like a very out-of-place twenty floor skyscraper.

Joe realized most of the significant square footage was primarily underground. Each hall had an elevator that fed up to the main floor, except for the one that held Zuri. That meant four elevators and four staircase options. A private elevator and staircase sat at the center of the building. "What's the deal with the elevator in the middle here?"

"That is... was the elevator the Director primarily used on his rare visits. For security reasons, our hall is without an elevator."

Joe tried pushing the button. When nothing happened, he opened an electrical panel near it. "That's odd. Maybe the backup generators only keep the essentials running. You'd think at least the center point elevator would be functioning."

Justin took a last look at the non-working elevator. With a sigh, they turned to assess the other four wings of D4.

Aidan started their story as they quickened their steps down the adjacent hallway. "We got into this situation by chance. Well, potentially not by chance, but definitely not by choice."

"To the point," Joe said.

"I'm trying. It's just… does anyone know what happened back there with Zoey and Zuri? I mean, I know girls are crazy, but this is just downright karay-zee sh—"

"—Yes. It's crazy. Trust me. I've been there. Focus. Tell me what brought you here," Justin pressed.

No doors open as they continued down each wing, hitting their fists on every door as they went by. They tried the intercoms outside each room, and all remained silent.

When they reached the end of the last main artery, the two men had given a semi-short version of how it all started with Zoey's nightmares, post-power grid failure.

"About a year ago, her night terrors began causing *severe* pain, and we couldn't wake her from them. There were times we were afraid she wouldn't make it through the night." Joe could feel his emotions rise but kept them from showing on his face.

"She wouldn't see the Doc. We have a doctor in our building, but Zoey is… well, she's stubborn." Aidan gave Joe a pointed look. "We would take turns staying by her side as she slept. Making sure someone was with her if she woke up not knowing who she was, where she was, or why she was filled with debilitating anguish.

"It was to the point where we would have to adamantly remind her who she was and that she *wasn't* this other woman from her dreams, who was becoming almost a part of her."

"Yeah, she kept seeing the face of a woman with green eyes. But the way she would describe it, it didn't sound as if the woman with the green eyes was the woman she could feel. The green-eyed woman was watching her." Aidan's shoulders shivered just thinking about it. "Creepy, you know?"

Joe took in a level breath avoiding Aidan's juvenile irritants. "Not long ago, she started hearing her, the one she could feel. The woman would plead with her to come rescue her. Only it wasn't just while she was sleeping. It began to happen while she was awake, too, and it would completely disengage her from reality." Joe paused to collect his thoughts.

Justin couldn't help but ask, "Did you think she was having a mental breakdown of some kind?"

Joe shook his head from side to side. "No. Of course, I realize what I'm saying would make anyone think that, but she's highly intelligent. Street smart like no one I've ever met. I don't question her sanity. Whatever's happening, it's happening *to* her."

Justin nodded. He could understand thinking about Zuri and her sister Lexi.

"Then, maybe a year ago," Aidan jumped in, "about the time Zoey's nightmares really got crazy, this man showed up at our door saying that he needed our help. 'For the greater good of our country,'" he mocked. "'To bring peace back, bring everything back. Only this time it would be even better.' At the time, we really didn't believe him, but with what was going on with Zoey and the timing of this man coming into our lives, we didn't see much of a choice. We're fairly certain he was not *giving* us a choice. Either way, we decided we had to dive in, if for no other reason than to find a way to help Zoey."

Joe flinched at the idea of saving her.

"We thought it was too big of a coincidence not to follow through. So, we took a chance. We had to figure out who was doing this to her," Aidan continued, his arm muscles contracting like he wanted to hit something.

"We were terrified." Joe's admission left his voice shaking. "Every time she went through it, feeling she was being crushed, it would cause the marks to spread further across her body." *Break down more of her soul,* he thought to himself. "She knew someone was in immense pain, and for some reason, she could feel it happening to her at the same time. She had no idea who it could be, but Zuri must look very similar to the woman in her dreams."

"We didn't know what to anticipate, but it sure as heck wasn't this." Aidan lifted his eyebrows as if to say, 'holy crap!'

"You said she told you it felt like she was being crushed?" Justin asked, processing their story as small puzzle pieces began to take shape.

"Yeah? Why?" Joe turned, forcing Justin to stop behind

him.

"I'm not sure. It's just that we've had Zuri in a pressurized glass enclosure for the past *seven* years. Keeping her alive yet comatose. Afraid she had the capability to end civilization."

"That sounds dumb." Aidan's wide eyes looked disturbed at that explanation.

"Yes. Agreed. My point is that if she ever started moving, our regulations were to increase the pressure inside the case to prevent her from doing so. We never needed to do that with Zuri, as she had never purposefully moved. At least not until today, and she didn't give us an option. She went from unconscious to standing in a matter of seconds. She had so much energy around her that the glass she was in was physically bowing outward. I'm honestly surprised the glass didn't shatter.

"What you're saying makes me believe that Lexi is in a similar place, maybe a similar chamber. Maybe she's been more coherent and functional than Zuri. If so, the doctors keeping her contained may have been using pressure to keep her still. If they were, that might explain the crushing feeling. Assuming Zoey is actually linked to her."

"That's who the young girl back in the room was talking about? Zuri?" Aidan wasn't confused. He just wasn't sure how much more his brain could handle.

"Yes. Her sister, Lexi."

"So where would Lexi be then? It's not like there are places like this just anywhere." Joe's conversational tone was gone, and he leaned in toward Justin. Feeling like the more he found out, the less he understood.

"I don't know. Until today I didn't know Lexi was alive, let alone potentially being kept in a place like Zuri all this time!" Tempers began to flare, and Justin was at his breaking point.

Shaking his head, Aidan stepped in to break the tension. "So the little redhead, Zuri, is the sister of the woman Zoey can feel?"

"Yes, Lexi is Zuri's sister."

Joe rubbed his left temple with his fingers and closed his eyes. "When Zuri said something like, you know, *the ocean in Lexi's eyes*, what did that mean?"

"Lexi's eyes are the color of the ocean. When your friend Zoey said she saw green eyes, I honestly had no clue what she meant. Zuri was telling her that the woman she was *feeling* or sensing was Lexi." He paused. "And Lexi's eyes are blue."

"And no one knows where she is," Aidan reiterated.

"No. She could be anywhere. She could be on this compound. Hell, she could be in this building. Or on the other side of the world for all we know." As Justin said those last few words, he turned around and hit the flat of his hand against the wall.

There were too many unanswered questions, and no one was knowledgeable enough to answer even one. Aidan brought them back on track. "Well, you're the doctor. Do you think she's here or not? Is there any other place in the *world* that could care for someone like… that?"

Taking a steadying breath, he replied, "It's possible there's another group out there with similar equipment that could have her. It just seems unlikely. It's not like anyone knew about them other than me back then." He stopped walking and covered his mouth before responding. "However, it's more likely that she's here. The way VISP has us all separated, she could've been right next door this entire time, and we'd likely not know it." Justin felt stupid for not knowing something so monumental.

"So then we find her. We search this building top to bottom, then move on to the rest of the compound." Aidan's feet picked up speed.

"Yes. But," Justin paused, killing Aidan's forward motion. "Before we go off half-cocked, Maria, Gavin, and..sh— Gavin!" At the sound of Gavin's name coming out of his mouth, he immediately felt a sense of hope and regret. He was going to need to find him, too, if he was still there. He was a massive part of all this, and they needed him whether he liked it or not. "We have already gone through the blueprints and maps of this area. We've narrowed it down to several locations that are the most plausible to investigate. Still, first, we need to find Gavin."

"Who?" Joe asked.

"He's part of our team."

"Do you think he's even still here? No one else is," Aidan stated as if it were already a fact.

"I don't know, but we need to find him. He's as much a part of this as any of us." Justin remembered Gavin's recently odd actions, and now would be a great time to dig deeper into his motives. There was no way he wasn't hiding some information of his own.

"I still need to know who you work for." Justin looked at the last door in the final wing. The small window was open, but there was no sign of anyone inside. No one.

When he didn't hear any response from the intercom, he turned around to see both men contemplating his posed question. "The simple answer? We don't know. When the Stranger came to see us, he told us pretty much nothing other than they were working hard to bring the world back to 'not just the way it was before, but better…' and so on. He believed the three of us could somehow help them carry out their mission."

"Military?"

"No, at least we aren't. Not sure if he is or not. His name is Rice Jahnsen. Ring a bell?" Joe asked.

"None. So you're not a military group, but you know how to blow up a door?"

"Part of the longer history. You asked for the short version. Maybe later," said Joe, abruptly ending the conversation.

Justin wondered if they could feel the skepticism oozing from him.

Aidan felt it. "Listen, apparently, the three of us have special skill sets they claim are needed to help them." He shrugged. "We still haven't figured that part out. Except for Zoey with her link to this other woman."

"Along with her innate sense to tell when a person is threatening or not." Joe's statement triggered Justin's memory of Zoey telling him to put his weapon down mere seconds after bursting into their lab. She didn't even have her own weapon up. He knew he would have shot her if he'd needed to. If she was a threat. But how did she know *he* wasn't a threat?

"You're replaying your initial meeting with her, aren't you?" Aidan smirked. "Everyone that has a run-in with her always walks away wondering what happened. You know, the classic, *I thought I was here for a fight, so how am I leaving with a fruit basket* sort of feeling? She's very persuasive."

"Which is funny because she's not the nicest person about it," Joe said, only now realizing that he hadn't previously recognized that fact before.

They hurried back to the central crossway of D4, turning in a circle to ensure every hall had been cleared, when Justin burst out, "How can there not be one person down here?! That's too many people to coordinate moving that quickly." They searched the entire floor. The elevators were out, and not a soul was standing around wondering why. No one smarting off about the lack of power and all the work they were missing. Granted, it was the middle of the night, but they didn't have standard business hours. "There's no one running up the stairs trying to get out of the building or anyone coming down to verify personnel safety. Where is security?" He turned back to the two men.

"Sadly pathetic security if you ask me. We have better security in our apartment building. I mean, we got in here—"

Justin raised his arm, effectively cutting Aidan off. "—yeah, how did you get in here *exactly*?"

"That would be part of the long story version." Joe was losing patience and wanted to get back to Zoey.

"Got it. I *will* need to hear that version eventually, but for now, we need to figure out why we are the only crew here. We need to check the rest of the building." Justin prayed they were genuine in their desire to help their friend. "Right now, I'm choosing to trust you. I have no *proof* that you're legit, but considering you are literally the only other people around right now, my options are limited."

"Gee, thanks," Aidan's faux innocent smile spread across his face.

They jogged back to the now wide-open lab doors and stepped over pieces of burned drywall and shredded electrical cables as Justin posed an important question. "Regardless of how you got in here, what was going on up there when you did?"

Maria was leaning over a desk, talking mostly to herself. She looked up from the blueprints in disgust when she heard them come in. "About time you got back. There is something shady going on around here."

Aidan couldn't resist. "You're just now feeling that, are ya?"

Zoey was sitting on the cot next to Zuri. Both had cool rags around their necks. They weren't talking, but how they sat made Justin recognize how similar they were.

Putting his question on pause, he said, "Are you alright?" Taking a step toward her, he was once again taken aback at the sight of her sitting, awake, alive. He essentially directed the question to both ladies simultaneously, and they gave a little nod.

"Alright," said Maria, focused on the blueprints, "after pouring over the compound's layout and scrutinizing this building, I've narrowed it down further to five specific areas." Her analysis was a full page of notes, but she barely glanced at them as her arms did much of the talking for her.

Suddenly she stopped, hands on the table, and said, "Do you think it's even possible that she has been so close this entire time, and we've never heard about her, Justin? I mean, yes, obviously, we all signed non-disclosure agreements, but that doesn't stop the rumor mill. I've never heard anything in relation to another person like Cal… Zuri, being here."

She shook her head and leaned back in the chair. "But, it makes sense they wouldn't want them together. Why would they want the two most likely people on the planet with the ability to *crush* our existence to be within reactionary distance?"

Justin's brain hurt just processing the myriad of directions her mind was going. "I don't have a clue. I thought the same thing. We need to devise a plan quickly here because there's no one else on this floor but us."

Maria lifted her head. "No one on the floor? What do you mean?"

"As in no one, nada, zippo," Aidan chimed in.

Aidan's quick-witted comments were grating on Justin. "We walked every hall, knocked on doors, nothing. There's no one here but us. And the elevators aren't working. We'll have to staircase it."

"Damn. Stairs," muttered Joe.

"That makes no sense. How can no one be on this floor?" Maria was shocked. "There's always at least a skeleton crew."

"For emergencies?" Aidan waggled his eyebrows.

Rolling her eyes back at him, she said, "Yes. For emergencies."

Aidan pointed in Joe's direction. "You should get *that* guy to do your security because this is sad."

They were quickly learning to ignore his responses.

Maria's eyes lit up. "Wait, what about Gavin? He left only minutes before you three got here. Did you see a man leaving the room or in the hall?"

Zoey's voice startled them when she spoke up, "No one. Could he have taken the central elevator?" On weak legs, she made her way to the table.

"Technically, no. He shouldn't have the pass-key to turn it on, but that doesn't necessarily mean he didn't have one." Maria hopped up. "Wait. Justin, did you notice if Jones still had his key when you…." Her voice trailed off, not wanting to talk about watching Jones' body being dragged out of the room.

Justin realized where she was going with it. "I didn't check, but when Gavin grabbed him and put him against the wall, maybe he took his badge? He huffed out of here. It's possible he could've gotten to the central elevator or even stairs before running into you guys." He walked toward the hallway. Once outside, he inhaled as much settling oxygen as he could before opening the storage room door. There was already an odor, causing him to take short choppy breaths. With as little contact as he could get away with, Justin searched Jones' pockets, then checked his belt loop and any other place Jones would likely have put it.

Nothing.

Closing the closet door, he walked back into the room, shaking his head. "It's not there." He hoped that meant Gavin *did* take it and was still somewhere in the building.

"I don't think there was anyone around to even run into," Aidan said ominously.

That reminded Justin. "Care to share on my last question?"

"Question?" Both Maria and Aidan said in unison.

Joe walked up to the table with the documents they received from Rice Jahnsen to compare to the ones Maria was looking at. Laying them out next to hers, he began, "The question about what was going on upstairs before we came down here."

He held down the edges so the paper wouldn't roll. "We've been surveying this compound for the past week to learn your security patterns. The plan was to make our move at 0600 tomorrow morning just as traffic was picking up."

"Foot traffic," Aidan added.

"Your nights are pretty quiet, so we wanted to use the increased movement around the compound to provide a casual distraction for the guards. Hoping they'd be less attentive to our access point. Only, plans changed. Zoey was hit with another attack during what was supposed to be our final surveillance. An audible alarm went off moments after her attack while Aidan and I were outside the gates making final preparations. By the time Aidan made it back to Zoey, the entire place was silent and empty.

"Turns out we didn't need to be sneaky. The place was a ghost town."

"Wait," said Maria, visibly trying to process Aidan's information. "What do you mean? As in, it was emptier than usual, or literally no one outside at all?"

"No one." Joe was just as genuinely confused as they were.

"What about security?"

"None," Aidan piped in.

"How could there be none?" Justin couldn't tell if they were talented liars or if they just sucked at getting to the point.

He and Maria's eyes locked. "So why didn't you bring this up when we walked the halls?" His temper was beginning to flare.

"Well, before we finally made it down here, our first going theory was the possibility that, as a military base, maybe you were working through some kind of training exercise." He took a breath. "Our second theory, however, was that whatever caused Zoey to have her episode might have come from *within* this place. There are a lot of rumors about that redhead over there. We weren't 100% sure she would be here, but if all of this turned out to be real, then somehow Zoey was actually connecting with her. Getting into the building turned out to be less challenging than we thought. And in the halls… well, we were more focused on Zoey's relationship to all this—"

"—So then," asked Maria, "how did you physically get *in* the building? You still need a fingerprint scan and a code or keycard? And *please* don't tell me you came in through the ventilation system and then down the elevator shaft."

With a blank stare, Joe said, "Well, actually, that was, in essence, granted not completely, but mostly our plan."

"That's so predictable," she muttered, staring at the two men. "Alright, Bruce Willis, so you rappelled down the elevator shaft? I seriously can't believe that was the plan. I was waiting for some high-tech Alcatraz meets Ocean's Eleven. Something with a little more pizzazz!" Shaking her head, she mouthed 'lame' before looking back at the plans in front of her.

Both men gawked in disbelief. Maria's obvious distaste for their mode of breaking into this top-secret lab, not to mention her disregard for the actual crime of breaking and entering, floored them.

"Yeah, I know. She never fails to impress, right? So back to it. You shimmied down the shaft—" Justin prodded them to keep going.

"—Ah, no." Aidan picked back up. Trying to rip his gaze away from Maria, who he might've just fallen in love with. "We didn't have to."

Justin squinted his eyes, trying to understand the turn of events when it finally hit him. "The power went out."

He looked immediately at Maria, and she turned to them. "So, was it you that cut out the power? We thought it was Zuri." More puzzle pieces. "But the power going out should have created a complete lockdown across the compound, not open it up to the public."

"We didn't knock out the power. It went out when the alarm went off. Like we said, the plan was to come in tomorrow morning before sunrise, scale the building wall to a pre-arranged entry point right after foot traffic increased. That would have provided a natural distraction. Nothing out of the norm. Ultimately, it kept us from having to come up with our diversion."

"Lexi." Zoey answered their question. "The power went out when I felt her. She was in agony. Something was happening to her."

"No."

Everyone turned to Zuri. She was standing, looking at the door, and talking to no one in particular.

"It was when I stopped her from being hurt that the lights went out."

No one knew what to say, but at that moment, they all realized Lexi was *in the building.*

After a long silence, Aidan brought them all back to the present. "Just to close the loop, we came in through the front door."

# Chapter 29
## Waking Up

Lexi felt grit in her eyes, like salt disintegrating under her lids. Rough concrete scraped skin from her legs as they drug behind her limp body.

*What is happening?*

*Pain everywhere.*

Something was pulling her left shoulder from its socket. The throbbing in her head was disorienting. Even without the headache, she couldn't focus any one of her body parts to move at will.

*Come on, eyes. Open up.*

*Focus!*

It felt like hours had passed as she tried to fight her way to full consciousness. Opening her eyes was an enormous request and only made the pain worse.

*Would be nice to know who my knight in shining armor is.*

Sarcasm in a moment like this. Her sister would say it's her most annoying trait.

*Zuri! Oh, God.*

The thought of her sister made everything else fall away, bringing her purpose back into focus. *Find Zuri.*

Lexi's endorphins skyrocketed, but that didn't make her body cooperate. There was no pressure like before, and she could open her eyes even if they were blurry. The fog in her mind cleared rapidly with the adrenaline rush, but none of her muscles would do as she asked. Someone was pulling her.

Lexi could hear a man's voice as the buzzing began to quiet.

*Who? I know that voice. No. Yes. That voice.*

"Can you hear me, Rose? Lexi? We're almost there. Just hang on. I know you're in pain, but we're almost there. I will help you. I just need you to trust me." He gasped for breath between words, grunting as he strained to pull her along.

Another voice echoed in her ears but wasn't making any sense. The sounds were coming from her and were completely unrecognizable.

*I need to get away.*

Starting to gain dexterity in her fingers, she grasped a piece of his shirt.

"Almost there. Just hang tight. I need to get some medicine in you to abate the effects of the gas exposure. Just a few seconds more and we'll be there." The more he spoke, the more confident she *knew* who he was, maybe even better than she knew herself. His familiar, almost comforting tenor helped clear her mind further as she recalled him telling stories about his life. Always there, close enough to talk to, but unable to move any inch of herself with the pressure.

Her lips were formulating sluggish, silent words. The first thing she wanted to say was his name. She needed him to know that she *knew* who he was. The urge, the *need,* to run as fast and as far as she possibly could was still there, but she instinctively knew that he wouldn't hurt her. She didn't need to run from him.

"Grant." At his name, he stopped, looked down, and sucked in half a breath that was cut short with pain. After a second glance at her, he pushed forward with renewed intent. She wanted to help him by using her legs, but they rebelled. With every passing second, Lexi could feel how difficult it was for him to carry her. Something was drastically wrong with him.

Before she could put sound to any other words, Grant yanked her through a door, propped her up against the wall, and groaned, hunching over her. Supporting his weight with one hand on the counter while the other held his ribcage, body wavering, his eyes rolled back in his head.

*He's going to fall.*

Just as his legs buckled, he blinked his eyes, shook his head, and caught himself. Inhaling slow, choppy breaths, he pushed away from the table and limped toward a wall covered in steel panels. Opening one, a white mist curled over his hand, dissipating outside of its cold storage. He removed several vials and then seized a syringe while simultaneously closing the steel door with his hip. The unexpected jolt from that small ricochet made it impossible for him to mask the agony.

Lexi could see herself going to him to help him, yet her muscle spasms immobilized her. The sight of the needle, however, shook her.

*What has happened to me? This fear.*

Her need to comfort him was replaced by a compulsion to get away from that needle. Her mind couldn't call up the memories required to answer for the urgency she felt, but she had no desire to return to whatever it was.

"Here, this should help the pain and grogginess." He pulled as deep a breath as possible, then said, "And the millions of bee stings your skin probably feels." His half-smile calmed the internal terror she felt.

After a weak breath, she nodded, knowing she couldn't get away if she tried. With a voice she never would've perceived as her own, she said, "Go for it."

He found a vein and injected the fluid into her arm. The syringe slipped from his fingers and made a pinging sound on the floor.

With effort, he sat down next to her. Lexi's fingertips slid slowly across the ground, realizing that it wasn't rough concrete but smooth flooring. Looking at her legs for the first time, she could see glass and swaths of raw blisters.

*Stinging pain. He said bee-stings.*

She now understood what he meant.

Leaning his head back, he concentrated on inhaling small pockets of oxygen without opening his lungs too far into his rib cage. Each puff of air was laced with torment.

"What happened to you, Grant?" Lexi's voice came out raspy and broken. At least it was coherent.

He took a few seconds before turning his head.

"You." He smiled.

A memory flashed through her mind.

She remembered wondering what his smile would look like if she ever got the chance to see it. Her mind's vision of him didn't compare to the man in front of her. Thin upper lip with a plump bottom one. Although that was likely her doing based on the bruising. Long blond lashes encircled one blue and one green eye—a long, rounded nose.

Not having the luxury of seeing anything clearly for so long, she got used to hearing how someone smiled, frowned, or wore their emotions. Face to face, only inches apart, he was completely different. She had only ever been able to see him in her periphery.

"I did this to you?" she said, choking up. "I hurt you?" The catch in her throat stunted her words.

*How could I have done this to him? I can't even move. Even my face will hardly move the necessary muscles to show my grief.*

His smile remained in place as her feelings of guilt deepened.

"You finally woke up." His joy was real. "I'm just so grateful I was around to see it. I knew you were ready. You've been ready for a while. I did *not*, however, realize you could pack a real punch when you wanted to. Would have been an amazing sight if it hadn't been directed at me." He winked.

"I punched you? When?" She glanced at her hands. "How?" Her throat felt dry and rusty, like an old car after years in a North Carolina junkyard. Talking caused her to cough, twisting her insides to feel like she'd also been sucker-punched.

"Not physically, no. Well, actually... I don't know how you did it. But I'm glad you didn't wake up just now in the same mood as your most recent awakening. Pretty sure I don't have the strength to fight that version of you again." With this last sentence, his face scrunched as a little moan escaped his lips. He closed his eyes and rolled his head along the wall until he was looking forward again.

A whisper escaped her, "What do you mean when I woke up the first time?"

He sighed. Reluctant to share more.

"Please. What happened?"

"Lately, you've begun showing solid signs of consciousness, as in full functionality from your brain to all of your body parts. I would tell you stories, and your eyes told me you could hear me. Even understand me."

His green-blue eyes found hers in search of confirmation, but she couldn't quite recall.

The constriction in her lungs began to ease. She thought the injection must finally be working. "I prayed every day that I would wake up from the horror I was in. There was just nothingness. Except you."

"Well..." he said, not knowing what to say. Heavy with guilt.

Lexi watched as his gaze kept traveling to the door as if waiting for someone to arrive. There was an urgency to it that even she could feel.

"There are many people that prefer you stay in that horror-filled state forever. Although I never knew you before you arrived, I guess just the thought of keeping someone in a coma for the rest of their life became something I couldn't—it just didn't seem right anymore."

*Anymore?*

"So, I began to give you more of a chance," he whispered, gurgling as if bubbles were filling his lung. Struggling through, he continued, "I medicated you less month by month. Not a noticeable amount. But even those small changes were enough to give you a chance to..." Looking for the right words, he said, "feel something. Feel alive again, I guess. Even if I couldn't let you get to the point where you were fully free." Genuine shame washed over him.

"I'm guessing I backfired on you somehow, then?" She tried to make her voice light, but remorse over hurting him was still in her heart. That and so much uncertainty. Lexi wasn't sure if she should be happy he wanted to bring her back from the darkness or angry that anyone believed it was okay to do that to her in the first place.

"In a sense, yes. Whenever I saw that you were there with me, hearing me, I wanted to give you a little more mental freedom. It backfired. You took that little foothold into the door I cracked, and you, well, you blew it wide open." Grant's grin diminished, only showing on the left side of his face.

"I think that's when I started to hear you," she said as she felt him succumbing to his injuries. Her pain, however, was dulling. He was right. The medicine was decreasing the pinpricks all over her body. The incessant need to run was receding.

"Once we saw you moving of your own accord, I would come in to sit with you, one-on-one. I guess, I thought… I started rethinking what my mission was here. That's when I started telling you stories. Things about me. Wishing I could ask questions about you. I knew you could hear me. With lesser medication, your eyes would flutter open at times. Even unopened, I could see the shift in your body from being relaxed talking about my family, or slightly strained talking about the losses the world has witnessed.

"I want you to know right here and now that I enjoyed having the opportunity to talk with you on those days. I knew a long time ago that you were important." Grant kept talking even as his lips turned blue. "I think the leaders of our dilapidated country didn't know how to make things right. They only know that there's something about *you* that makes them afraid and no longer care about anyone else. At least, that's how it seems to me."

His eyes closed despite how hard he tried to keep them open.

"Grant. Your lips are blue." Lexi felt a wave of panic.

Being so close to him, she could feel the buzz of his energy waning the same way she used to feel Zuri's vitality growing. Her heart ached. Grant needed to stay awake. She needed him to help her. Help her understand where she was at. Help find her sister. She needed him because he was the only person who knew and cared about her, even if she didn't understand why.

Getting up on her knees, she looked him over. Maneuvering her limbs was difficult but no longer impossible. The pain had dulled from the meds, but every body part still jerked.

His eyes began to roll but jolted open with renewed energy. "I didn't get into medicine to hurt people. When I started here, I thought I was truly living up to that ideal." His words quickened like he feared he wouldn't get it all out in time. "Helping to save people. When I started working here, leadership convinced me that we were saving millions of lives every day by keeping you secure. We were brought in to try and figure out how this person, *you*, lived. How you functioned. But most importantly, find out how you could use your brain, a brain unlike any other." He started to drift again.

*I will* not *lose him.*

Putting her hands on his shoulders, she shook him. His eyes barely flickered. She took his face in both her hands. "Grant, please wake up. Please listen to me." Lexi shifted her weight to lean closer to his face. "I need to know where my sister is. Can you tell me where my sister is? Please, Grant. Stay with me!" He was nearly gone. Suppressing her cry, her throat felt like she had swallowed knives.

He cracked his lids open just enough to meet hers with bloodshot eyes.

"Being here with you these past few years taught me a couple things."

She could hear more gurgling in his lungs.

"First, you have a mind the rest of us could only ever dream of having. Our lack of understanding has led to some stupid decisions." Blood was now trickling out of the corner of his mouth. "The second is that once I gave you more wiggle room to use that amazing mind of yours, you gave us ten-fold the amount of information we'd had up 'til then." He sounded like he was breathing in water. Drowning.

She didn't know what to say or make of his rambling.

*Heal him. Heal him so he can help me.*

"Grant, you have to tell me what's wrong with you. What can I do?" Her body staggered as she stood up on legs that did not feel her own. Once at the medicine cabinet, she said, "Which one? Which one of these will help you?" Frantic, she'd never seen any of those words before—unpronounceable medical terms.

*Why can't it just say painkiller?*

Grant's voice was so quiet behind her that she almost didn't hear him. "You have so much to give us. So much to teach us. To teach me." He looked up with wet, red eyes. Larger than she'd seen them since they came into the room. The raspy rattling of his airways intensified. "You were getting stronger all the time. Keeping you in a coma became futile." Tears blurred his vision, but he continued, "I want you to know

I'm sorry." Voice-breaking, he started to choke.

*I don't understand.*

"Sorry? What does that mean? Why are you sorry?" Lexi's strength was failing. All of the vials of fluids looked the same. Confusion swept over her as her knees buckled. Crawling to him, an onslaught of memory fragments flashed through her mind.

"I wanted you to wake up so badly, but not everyone wanted that. To keep you still, we had to increase the pressure in the unit. Every time it increased, it would crush you a little more. It was torture. I tried to stop it but didn't try hard enough." His voice was so weak. Trying to get past his emotions, he coughed up more blood, but it didn't stop him. "At least not until today. I just couldn't let them hurt you anymore. All that pain, but your body was just so still."

She braced herself on the floor, hardly listening to him as her mind raced through all those moments when the air was pressed out of her lungs. Her ears and eyes had felt like they were going to explode. Trapped in an ever-tightening vice.

*It really happened.*

*It almost killed me.*

Her voice came out in a whisper. "All that pressure. All that pain. That was to keep me from moving?" She put her hands on his arms. Fingers dug in hard enough to keep Grant alert and talking.

"Yes. It was the only method to keep you immobile. They *couldn't* know how far you'd come."

"They?" She breathed out the word. Grant continued

without noticing.

"We tried drugging you, but that didn't stop you from dreaming or eventually moving." His lids closed tightly as his chest spasmed. Lexi was now holding his body upright. "You were able to control the functions of your body on your own again. I knew… I knew if given a chance, you'd be up and walking around. It was killing me not letting you do that. The risk was too great."

His lungs struggled. Everything seemed so unreal, almost unimaginable. Lexi had so many questions running through her mind, but only one mattered at that moment.

"Grant, we need to keep you conscious. What can we use?" With that, she forced herself back to her feet. Using the same table he had used to hold himself up, she felt strength regain in her arms now that she'd released him from her anxious grip. On shaky legs, like a toddler, she managed to rise.

His eyebrows lifted in surprise. After everything he had just told her, she was still going to help him.

Taking a deep breath, Lexi pushed down everything unsettling in her heart and answered his unspoken words. "I realize I can act one of two ways after hearing that story, Grant, though I'm certain I haven't heard half of it. I can either be angry. And kill you." Her eyebrows lifted. "From the looks of it, it wouldn't be hard. But I can sense that's not what I'm meant to do. So you don't have to look at me like that."

"Or?" His eyes closed.

"Help you. Because once you're feeling better," she said, her heart racing, "I'm going to need you to tell me what is happening and where I can find my sister."

He started to say something, but only a gurgling sigh came out. Once again, she pulled vials out, and he nodded or shook his head with each one as his face drained of color.

*What am I doing? I've never given anyone shots before. How hard can it be? His chest is barely rising with each shallow breath. His eyes are barely open.*

"Grant, just hold on. We can do this. You're not going anywhere." She was talking as much for herself as she was for him.

Sliding the needle in his arm, she prayed it was even remotely close to where it was supposed to go. His body tipped further over to the side. Without thinking, she threw her knee around him and caught his head before it hit the ground. *There's gotta be something I can do.*

With her sister, it was automatic. She didn't know how they did it, but it was… natural. Bowing her head over his in despair, she wanted to cry. The only person who knew anything about her was dying in her lap.

*Please don't die. Please don't die. Please don't die.*

With her forehead on his, a warming sensation began behind her eyes, releasing a pressure she didn't realize was even there. Through her next breath, she felt her body tingling. Immediately, Grant's body shuddered.

Lexi's eyes flashed open to see him staring at her. Snapping her head back away from him, a smile crossed his face. She'd never been able to do anything like this with anyone other than Zuri.

"That must've been the good stuff," he whispered, his voice as raspy as hers. "The medicine."

She'd already forgotten she had given it to him.

*He's right. It must've been the medicine.*

His humor caused her to snort a laugh. Tears began falling, but laughter, though excruciating, bubbled up and felt great in her broken soul.

Grant shook his head, not making any attempt to sit up.

"Are you still with me?" she asked, watching him smile as his face relaxed. "Figures. I didn't receive the same jolly side effects when you gave *me* that shot."

"Because the one I gave you was an antidote for a toxin along with some pain medicine." He took shallow breaths, now obvious he was babying a few broken ribs. Lexi decided not to mention the tingling sensation. When his eyes opened, he realized where he was.

Head in Lexi's lap.

His eyes tracked up to her ocean-blue ones and locked in understanding for a moment. He had saved her life, and now she had saved his.

Groggy and sedated, he snuggled deeper into her lap. *Men.* None too gently, she moved back and let his head fall to the floor with a soft thud, sending him into a coughing fit.

"Do you remember… the last thing that happened before I pulled you down the hallway… into this room?" Grant said softly, breathing shallow breaths.

"I don't," she said, knowing that what he was about to say would be bad.

"We were in the lab, and you were still inside the glass case. You'd woken up and were coherent. I attempted to talk to you through the intercom system, but Madison and Gray were fighting behind me." He winced. "You began focusing on what they were saying about, about—"

Her memory became clear. Slowly, she took over where his breath gave out.. "—About how I shouldn't be able to move, let alone be awake and aware. He—Gray? Got mad. He was yelling at the woman with emerald eyes. I remember thinking how much I wanted to thank her. She was the first person to really and truly acknowledge my existence. Not just a thing. A non-entity." Her memory of that was clear because it was the moment Lexi finally knew she was still alive. "Then, you fought him?" She looked down at him, covering her mouth as she realized what had happened. "He ran toward me and flipped a switch on the case I was in. I remember the sound of crunching metal. And flowers. There was a scent of flowers."

"Yes. The gasses used as a fail-safe were made from a toxic flower called Calla Lily. It was supposed to put you to sleep, and then the toxicity within the flower would... kill you. I'm so sorry, Lexi."

She kind of chuckled under her breath, which threw him off guard. "Calla Lily. Pretty name for a deadly weapon. Obviously, it didn't kill me." Her expression pressed him to continue.

"Ah, well. You fell asleep to the initial reaction, which is how it starts," he said, words flowing a little easier. "Once it got into your system, though, it didn't kill you. You're right. It also may not have had the chance. The glass around you shattered as soon as I saw your head hit the floor. I have no idea how. After that, it was mostly chaos. I think the toxicity may have amplified the amount of energy you had running through your system. It was crazy. It was a heck of a sight to see. Pretty sure I got knocked out when the glass shattered."

He took a deep breath and then released, clenching his jaw. His pupils dilated as they locked on hers. "When I came to, I realized you were awake. I wanted to come to you. To help you. But when I saw..." his head shook back and forth. He couldn't explain it. "There was something in your expression. I knew there was something wrong. Then you moved your arms like you were throwing something at me. I didn't understand until I felt my backside hit the wall." He touched his side. "Where I cracked these ribs and possibly a few other things." A crooked smile passed across his lips.

"Gray was killed in the process. He was a doctor who'd been with us for about two years," he said, looking toward the ground.

*Did I kill someone? Why? How? Why would I have possibly done that?*

"Remember, he tried to kill you first," he stated firmly, attempting to help justify her fight for survival. It didn't diminish Lexi's fear. Fear of herself.

*Is this why I was in that cage to begin with? Is this why I was tortured? How could I have no memory of something like that?*

"Hey. Listen, it's okay." He lifted his hand toward her.

"No. It's not okay. And I still don't understand how I ended up in this room with you."

He pulled his hand back to his chest, trying to hold the bones together so they wouldn't stretch when he inhaled. "By the time I got to my senses, I realized you were gone. I followed the most likely path you would have taken, and eventually, I saw you on the floor at the end of the hall. You and Madison, actually. I'm not sure what happened. You both lay on the floor like you'd been thrown there. Based on how each of you landed, I think you attacked her. The way you attacked me."

"I wouldn't have done that." *I couldn't have.* The words barely escaped her lips.

"It's just, what doesn't make sense is your own injuries and how you were lying. It was as if she—" His words faltered. "You were sprawled out on the hallway floor just like she was. I think, I just, I don't know. The same way I ended up blown against the wall in the lab was how you looked sprawled out in the hallway." Even as Grant said the words, he couldn't believe what he was thinking. Somehow the idea of Madison having the ability to do something like that was even more incomprehensible than having watched Lexi do it.

Overcome with emotion, Lexi hit the ground in disbelief that she would harm the woman who wanted to protect her.

*Did she really want to help me? Or was she trying to stop me? Or worse, kill me?*

"Don't worry. She was still alive and breathing when I found you. I needed to get you out of there. After your glass case blew apart, Madison took off. I thought she would get help from security or, at the very least, save her own skin if you had decided to kill us. Fortunately for me, you were unable to get rid of me, and I'm hoping to keep it that way." His last words were a cross between a statement and a question.

"Lexi, Madison has been in your corner since the day she started working here. Do you remember seeing her in the hallway?" Grant was trying to be gentle. "Do you think you tried to attack her? Or maybe out of fear, she tried to stop you? I'm sure she didn't want to risk you getting off the compound in your state, afraid you might hurt someone. A legitimate fear," he said, stumbling over his words. "You were pretty much wild and unchained at that point." His breathing was leveling out, but she could see his eyes getting heavy.

"I'm having a hard time grasping all this," she said under her breath, her mind racing.

*I couldn't have done something like that. How? Zuri had that power. Power? That sounds stupid. She could heal things. People. Grow life. Open hearts when they were closed. The only thing I've ever been able to do was temper Zuri when she would become too overwhelmed by her own gifts. Basically, take in some of what she was putting out to diffuse her.*

"I'm a diffuser," Lexi said, laughing to herself so she wouldn't cry. Grant didn't say anything.

*Could what he's saying be real? That there's someone else out there like us? Someone hiding in plain sight? Why would she want to hurt me?*

Lexi's head ached as she dug the heels of her hands into

her eyes, hoping to release some pressure.

Taking stock of the room, she realized she didn't even know *where* she was. Grant's eyes had closed as she sat there, lost in thought. When she finally refocused, she could tell he had officially passed out. Sitting and waiting for him to awaken wasn't going to benefit either of them.

Groaning, she hoisted herself up and moved toward the door. Pain still wracked her body, and she willed her nerves to calm and her courage to rise. She needed answers.

"Oh!" The sound left her lips before she could stop it, dropping to her knees.

A woman was standing right outside the door. No telling how long she'd been there.

*In and out, just breathe, in and out.*

Slowly rising, ignoring the aches, she peeked back into the glass. The woman's movement mimicked her own. Taking a step closer, this woman stared back at her with eyes like a shimmering ocean. Lexi's lungs constricted, recognizing those eyes. Eyes she hadn't seen in a long time. They were beautiful, yet her face was unfamiliar. Deep purple and red lines spread out from her left eye down the left side of her face, crossing her jawline and down the left side of her neck like a spiderweb of something painful.

As Lexi reached her hand up to her face, the woman did the same.

It wasn't another woman in the window.

It was her reflection.

*This is my face.*

# Chapter 30
## She's a Witch

"So, she's a witch?"

"No, Aidan. That's not what I'm saying," said Justin, placing his hands on the desk in front of him and shaking his head.

"Dude, you just said that Lexi and Zuri have heightened senses. That they can see what we can't. They can change things like plants around them, the world, you, and me. They are capable of so much more than we are," Aidan replied, laying on a thick dose of mockery.

Hearing his own words back at him in that ridiculous melancholic romantic voice, Justin shot back, "That's not what I said!"

Aidan drew in a slow breath, then said, "So, you agree.

She's a witch."

"Ugh."

"Is he always this frustrating?" Maria whispered to Zoey.

Zoey's smile spoke volumes.

Justin stretched his arms behind his head and interlaced his fingers, effectively ending the conversation. He walked over to Zuri. She had spent most of the time since her awakening asleep, and he couldn't help but check that she was still alive. After years of machines doing most of her daily functioning for her, watching her out in the open was like a dream and also a bit of a nightmare at the same time. He feared her body might shut down any minute.

Maria walked up next to him as he shook his head back and forth in awe. "You know Justin, she did go from zero to sixty in a heartbeat. She hasn't exactly been up on her cardio these past few years, so I'd imagine she's a little smoked. Not to mention the wild show she put on earlier. God only *knows* how Zuri did that, let alone what it took out of her."

"I know, but it's not that. It's just... I have waited so long to see her live free, stretch, speak. Now she's here, but yet, she's not really here. It's as if she's watching everything around her but not actually a part of it. Almost like she hasn't yet realized she's awake."

Zoey maneuvered slowly over as they spoke, listening to their worries. "I know it's not my place, but I thought you should know that she doesn't know."

"Know what?" Dropping his hands from his face, Justin turned toward her.

"She's not fully here. As I sat with her for a while, she held my hand and touched the left side of my face as if she was following the lines on the *right* side. I know this sounds insane, not that this day has been a ball of sanity, but I don't think she was looking at *me*. It's as if she was seeing someone else. When she spoke, she was talking to herself. Not really to me." She glanced at Zuri before continuing. "I think she has a sense of what's happening around her, but primarily her focus is somewhere else entirely."

Her face was scrunched up as she slept. As if in distress. Like she *was* living a nightmare.

"Found what I could of food and fluids on this floor." Everyone jumped at Joe's voice breaking the spell. "The primary power is still out, which includes the elevators up to the ground floor. Aidan and I have devised a plan, but Justin, we'll need your expertise on how this building operates and what security may do."

"If there's any security," Maria said under her breath.

"The plan is simple. We take the stairs." Aidan threw out the obvious.

Joe's voice softened when he asked Zoey, "You think you can make it?"

"Have I ever not?" she shot back, eyebrows lifted high.

Zuri woke up as Joe came into the room. Sitting up, she wiped her eyes. Justin went to her and crouched down. "Are *you* fine to walk?"

Her beautiful crystal irises glinted in the fluorescent light when she settled her vision on him. "Have I ever not?"

Surprised by her witty reply, everyone chuckled. Even Joe gave a small grunt of appreciation. "She's feisty. That's familiar."

With a firm wink, Aidan chimed in, "Right, let's go then."

Aidan's skin had been crawling for the past couple of hours, bouncing on his toes as if ready to roll into a boxing ring.

"I think maybe these ladies should stay here until we know it's safe up on the main floor." Joe barely finished that sentence when Maria's cackle echoed through the room.

"Not without me, you're not." Her sass went a long way within the compound, but Joe and Aidan weren't familiar with her brand of it and didn't recognize her conviction.

"I'm not sure that's a good id—" Aidan began.

"If you think I'm spending even one more minute in this dungeon, you can forget it! If anyone knows this place better, I can guarantee it's not you, Red." Her eyes darted between the two of them. "So let's skip all the *buts* and get to it. I have been studying these maps for hours. Comparing them to what I currently know about this building and the surrounding area, not to mention the maps you all brought, there are a few things that don't jive. So before we head out, we need to create an exit plan in case we get to one of these points and can't go further or get stopped by security, if there is any." Aidan and Joe raised brows in unison, unsure of how to respond.

"Yes, she's serious." Justin intervened. "I've made many trips round and round this place over the years. I can get us through those sticky points. We can also spread out on each floor to cover more ground."

"No." Zoey stood up from her perch next to Zuri. "Aidan needs to stay here." She put her hand up to stop him from his onslaught of complaints. "Joe is the better option. If there is an electrical or technical jam, he is the guy you want to have in your pocket. Aidan, we are going to need you here. With Zuri and me. Once the floors are cleared, then we'll follow. We can make it up the stairs just fine, but neither of us is in decent enough condition to handle major problems. If, for some reason, you don't come back," she turned to Aidan directly. "I'm going to need your help getting her out of here. You are the best option for a quick getaway."

Aidan hung his head like a teenager. He knew she was right but hated every second of it.

"Alright then," said Justin, knowing there was no outside help on the way. "Maria, what do you think?"

"I think we need to clear the top three floors above us before we hit the Ground Floor. Whatever's going on up there isn't going on down here. I guess I'm not sure if it's because something so bad is going on up there that we're not on their radar or they think whatever's going on down here is so bad that we've been closed off for further assessment. We just never got the memo." Tilting her head to the ceiling, she hoped for the latter option. The former would mean more trouble. Like the rest, she had no desire to crack open another can of trouble.

"That's a good point." Justin nodded, thinking through the scenarios. "Maybe they don't realize that everything is alright down here. They've just closed us off because they don't know what the implications of Zuri being out of the glass will do."

"Will do?" Joe and Zoey echoed.

"Calla Lily," Aidan spoke up from his position against the arm of the couch. Arms crossed in front of him, sulking. He glanced at Zuri. "Calla Lily is the name the world gave her, but Zuri is her real name. *She is the end-all-be-all. She's the reason we're alive. She's the reason we'll perish.* At least those are the rumors circulating. When the grid failed, she was supposedly there." He looked at Justin for confirmation but received none. "Her power caused the first explosion, as the story goes.

"She probably has the power to cause a world-crumbling, universal explosion. That said, she probably has the power to bring the grid back and banish the Breakers too. Personally, I'd kinda like to see her as our first woman President."

They all stopped what they were doing and stared at him.

"What? I told you. I know things." Aidan turned around and sat on the couch. He stretched his legs in front of him and crossed his ankles nonchalantly—the defiance of a twelve year old boy with an expression to match.

"Oookay," said Maria, drawing out the word in exasperation. "From what I've seen today, that story may hold some truth. I'd just like to get the heck out of here in one piece, so let's focus on that. Cool?"

# Chapter 31
## Is This Me?

*How can that be me? My face?*

Lexi backed as far away from her reflection as the room allowed. Inspecting the rest of her body, she saw that her face wasn't the only target of those winding, deep maroon, purple, and red veins stretched across her skin. Ripping off her shirt, she couldn't comprehend what her eyes saw. The entire left side of her chest and torso had crisscrossing lines. They snaked to a point left of her belly button where the color was almost black.

Tracing them with her fingers, they felt slightly lifted as if tattooed on her body.

Didn't hurt.

She scratched at the twisting ridges on her arm and chest.

Then harder and more frantic as her mind spun with muddled understanding. Searching the room for anything that might help, she ran to the case with all the little vials of clear and cloudy medical mixes. Manically searching the shelves for anything, but nothing made sense—so many names. The medications may as well be in Norwegian.

Racing for the door, she caught Grant's form in her peripheral vision. She almost didn't stop, but something about him made her pause. His eyes were open. Frozen. His body wasn't moving.

*NO!*

"Grant!" Lexi croaked, throat dry and scratchy. *He can't be.* "Grant!" No movement. He didn't blink. "Grant, no, no, no, Grant!"

Clutching his shirt in her fists, she pulled him toward her and buried her face in his neck. Tears streamed down her face soaking his collar as her mind screamed.

*Why? Why is this happening?*

A burning sensation touched her fingers, but the pain in her heart overwhelmed her.

Without thinking, Lexi stood up, tucked her chin, and launched herself into the door, causing a shower of debris to spray down the hallway. The very empty hallway. Flashes of memory came back. Visions of herself delirious, out of control, running down a desolate hallway just like this. This time, however, she wouldn't run blindly. Instead, Lexi searched every passing door, but nothing opened. Sealed.

No one came out.

Her memories kept emerging. Trapped inside glass. Crushing agony squeezing the air out of her lungs. Glass shattering. She didn't remember breaking the glass, but at the swipe of her hand, tables and chairs flung out of her way with an invisible force she didn't ever remember possessing.

It scared her to her core. She knew she threw Grant against a wall. The memory of it hurt. Stumbling down the never-ending hallway, trying to shake off the guilt, she was fully aware that she did these things, yet her brain couldn't process how.

*I'm not capable of all this.*

Madison's image came back to her. The look of hate. *Hate? Was it?* As she stood face-to-face with Lexi. *Daring me. Daring me to do what? Her eyes. Those emerald crystals. Like fireworks.*

The only other eyes she'd ever witnessed like that were her sister's and her own. The thought made her stumble again. Her legs were so weak.

Finding the elevator, she pressed her palm on the *down* button unsuccessfully. The lights in the elevator weren't on. Slamming already red hands against the metal walls until they stung didn't make the elevator open. Lexi leaned back against the cool steel. It felt surprisingly nice against bare skin, though she wished she hadn't thrown her shirt aside, leaving her in only a black sports bra.

*What does it matter at this point?*

"Hello?" she screamed, her scratchy voice catching a sob in her throat. "*Anyone!*"

Nothing.

Pushing away from the elevator, she turned and then raced down *every* hallway, banging on doors, fear welling inside her. No one was there. She felt no human energy.

There was no one anywhere, just emptiness.

Finally, a door that didn't require a badge opened, causing her to fly through it uncontrolled. Barely having enough time to avoid careening over a side railing and down a stairwell, for the first time, she felt hope. A way out. With nothing but a ceiling above her, she was at the top level with an abyss of steps below.

*What's that?*

Moving closer to the wall, she spotted an out-of-place notch high on the right side. Her fingers traced the indention. She couldn't tell if it was just a hole in the wall or a pseudo handle. She tried pulling, then pushing, but nothing.

Giving up, she turned to the stairs and started skipping down them two at a time. Her legs ached and wanted to give out, but that same urgency to run had taken over. At every floor, Lexi pushed through the entrance door and yelled down the hallway with what little voice she had left. No response. No sign of anyone.

Three staircases down, she was already breathing hard. Looking over the banister at circle upon circle of stairs below, vertigo hit. Struggling to focus on the steps directly in front of her, she could feel her legs giving way when her ankle buckled. Screaming out in agony, Lexi reached for the railing only to catch air. Upon hitting the stairs, her arms folded beneath her body weight, failing to protect her head before it hit the concrete treads. The pain from her ear pinched between her head and the edge of a step sent an electric shock through the length of her body.

Darkness closed in.

Lexi tumbled the last ten steps in the stairwell before landing in a heap on the platform. Limbs twisted. Blood began to pool around her face. Vision came in and out of focus for mere seconds, just enough to see a faded number sixteen on the door in front of her.

Without a sound, a figure appeared through the door on the stairs above. Lexi's breathing was shallow, and her eyes were just thin slits. In and out of consciousness. Two boots stood by her face. She knew. Without seeing, she knew. That person had green crystal eyes.

Just before she fully succumbed to the darkness, she felt a blinding pain at the back of her head.

Before passing out cold, she heard, "It's done."

# Chapter 32
## Sixteen

Mumbling.

Zuri was mumbling in her sleep. Aidan watched as sadness came over her like a mask. Within seconds her arms began flailing back and forth. "Night terror," he said under his breath as he leaped from his rolling office chair. Not knowing what to do, he knelt beside her and touched the side of her face. It was similar to what Zoey had been going through, except Zuri didn't seem to be in pain the way Zoey's night terrors left her.

Everyone else had left except for the three of them: Zoey, Zuri, and Aidan. It was quiet until a few minutes ago. Without warning, Zoey crashed to her knees behind him, and a second later, Zuri sat upright. "Sixteen! *We have to go to sixteen!*" she yelled, pleading with Aidan, who was completely at a loss. Zoey was barely holding herself up, gripping a chair. She wasn't unconscious or screaming in pain this time, and he was torn between running to her and trying to understand Zuri's hysteria.

"What's sixteen? Who's at sixteen? Zuri, look at me." Aidan had one hand on the side of her mottled face and the other on her shoulder. Her eyes were unfocused as if she was looking through him. "Zuri. *Zuri.* Hey, look at me. Sixteen what? You need to tell me," he yelled as Zuri's entire body began to convulse while Zoey screamed behind him.

He wrapped one arm around Zuri, and football carried her across the floor, hoping to grab Zoey around the waist before her face got personal with the tile floor.

Sitting there, a woman in each arm, and trying to keep them both from shaking their teeth loose, he had a flashback to the day the grid failed.

Teenager. Dirty face. Running around the house playing tag when what felt like an earthquake knocked his feet right out from under him. He heard the sound of a freight train barreling toward him before his eyes focused on what it was.

"Aidan?"

He blinked.

"Aidan? Can you release the death grip?" Swiveling from one woman to the other, he shook his head. Releasing fists full of bunched clothing, he cleared his throat and wiggled his aching fingers. Zoey's concerned face caught him off-guard since he should be the one concerned.

"Sorry, what happened? You both went down at the same time. Zoey, what happened?" he asked, hiding a sadness from the flashback.

Zuri was as lucid as Zoey, finally looking at them and not through them. Although confused, it was at least simply in-the-moment confusion.

"Zuri, are you alright?" He gently moved her from his lap to the floor. Then turned to sit in front of her.

"How did we get over here?"

"Well, you started to fall, and I caught you. My question is, what made you fall? Both of you. At the same time. I mean, there's nothing going on in this room." He glanced around to be sure he was telling the truth about that. It happened so fast.

"It's Lexi. Just now. I could feel her," Zoey hesitated, "as if she was right here in this room." She raised her eyes in an I don't believe it either fashion. "I couldn't actually see her, but I could feel her emotions. Like I could feel what is, or was, going on with her? Does that make sense?" Aidan shook his head with a resounding no.

"I don't know how to explain it, but I didn't realize how much a part of me she'd become until just a moment ago when it felt like she was ripped out of me." Zoey's loss was unmistakable. "I can't feel her anymore."

Zuri's eyes were wide with fear. Standing up and turning around in a circle, she swept the room as if truly perceiving it for the first time. With one last look at Aidan and Zoey, she took a deep breath.

"She's here."

Zoey's eyes bore into hers. "What? Where?"

Without another word, Zuri turned for the door and took off in a sprint.

Aidan grabbed Zoey's hand and yanked her to her feet, already in motion. There was no discussion. There was no plan. Just the way Aidan liked it.

They had to stay with her.

Zuri was the key.

Justin halted walking up the stairs as a burst of sound came from Joe's backside, which happened to be right in front of his face.

"What is that?" he asked, just as he realized it was Joe's two-way radio. Joe reached back and pulled it out of his pocket as a never-ending stream of obscenities interspersed with unintelligible verbiage sprang from it.

"Aidan. Repeat your last, over." Joe backed down the stairs pausing on the landing they had just passed.

"Where you guys at?" Aidan yelled, short of breath. "Zuri took off at a dead sprint, and we are trying to follow her, but those little legs are fast! I think she's coming up the stairs behind you, so *pay attention!*" His voice broke over the radio as he ran.

"Aidan, where's Zoey? Where's Zoey, Aidan?" Joe sounded calm, but his body language gave away his panic. As Joe tried to get Aidan to reply, Justin's attention was drawn over the railing to the stairs below. The sound of distant thunder was getting closer. Maria and he both caught a glimpse of Aidan's red hair bounding up the stairs from below.

"Joe, Zoey is right behind him. I can see her." Just as Maria spoke, Justin felt a wave of air push up against him. Reacting before thinking, he thrust his arm out, snagging Zuri as she tore past him, silent and strong as an ocean breeze, nearly pulling his arm out of the socket as he yanked her into his chest.

Maria, caught off guard, started to yell out as Joe clamped his hand over her mouth. Justin did the same to Zuri as she shrieked, "Let go of me! Let go of me, Justin! *I have to go get her!*" He tried to keep her quiet, but she was in high gear. Before it registered what was happening, he flailed backward over the railing as the wind got knocked out of him. Blind-sided, Zuri had slammed her elbow into his chest, providing enough lift for him to stagger over the side.

Before Justin's body took the plunge, her tiny hand grabbed his shirt and pulled him back to the safe side of the long drop. Zuri's hand was still grasping his shirt as she stared into his eyes. Recognition. He could see that her eyes were clear and focused. Aware of where she was.

"I almost killed you," she said, matter-of-fact.

White knuckle hands braced the railing as he whispered, "Z, you can't go through that door. We don't know what's on the other side of it yet."

"Lexi's up there, Justin." Her voice was solid but scared. "She was there, and now she's gone. I have to get up there and find her." She leaned away from him and turned back toward the stairs, but Joe stepped in front of her path. "Move!"

Joe looked to Justin for his next move and said, "Zuri, we can't save her if we die before we get there."

Justin gently placed his hand on her arm. "He's right, Z. We need to stay together."

"She's here? In this building?" Maria questioned in a loud whisper. Zuri's expression made the answer obvious. "I knew it!"

Zoey and Aidan were out of breath when they reached the landing. "She's telling the truth. I felt it. She's here, or she was only a few minutes ago. Lexi has to be here somewhere," said Zoey, her sense of urgency palpable.

"She's here." Justin's breath came out in a rush. "We need to move—"

Joe's voice stopped them all. "—no one moves from this landing." Eyes deadly. "We are going to find out what's on the ground floor before any of you," he stared pointedly at the women, "move any further up these stairs. In fact, you are going to stand behind this door." He grasped the D1 door handle and opened it. "Keep the door cracked. If you hear gunshots, you find an unlocked door on this floor and put yourselves behind it. We'll find you if that happens."

Zoey wanted to be mad but honestly had very little left to give. Every limb felt weighted with concrete. She figured of the three of them, she may be the only one who knew how to take care of herself under assault, so staying with Zuri and Maria was probably not a bad idea. Although, for Zuri, that thought might be far from the truth.

"Go!" commanded Joe, not waiting for approval.

Shockingly, even Maria didn't argue.

Zuri wrapped her arms around Justin quickly, then turned away. It was so quick he questioned whether it happened at all. Before he could return the hug, she was walking through the doorway. He wanted to say something, but even if he had the words, he would be telling them to the empty air she no longer occupied.

Zoey gave Aidan and Joe a quick nod and walked in after Zuri.

She wasn't a hugger.

"Well, good luck, boys. I'm not hugging anyone because we are leaving this place together. If you don't come back, know I will find you, and mama won't be happy when she does." With that, Maria took the radio out of Aidan's hand and put it in her pocket. She spun around and walked through the door Zoey was holding open. They pulled it almost closed behind them together.

"If Lexi is up there, or they thought she was, and now all of a sudden she's not, then this building isn't empty," said Aidan, standing with his foot on the railing and gun in hand.

Glancing up to the door ahead of them, Joe exhaled, "Nope." Flicking off his radio to maintain silence until they determined it was safe, and pulling a pistol out from behind his back, he said, "There's a good chance it's probably not."

Turning on his heel, Justin gazed up the stairwell, grabbing hold of his bullet launcher. "I'll go through first just in case, by some miracle, the world is normal behind that door. The two of you look like a B-Rated apocalyptic war movie. You may scare the natives. Besides, I'm more likely to be recognized if someone is there." With that, he took the last few steps to the Ground Floor door. Inhaling the stale air, he said to no one in particular, "Here we go."

# Chapter 33
## At Their Limit

Rice Jahnsen stood next to his computer with his hands on the back of his head as if by squeezing his neck he could make the past twenty-four hours start over. Years of working toward this end, to get the right people in the right places, preparing for every angle, and they're left in the dark.

"Why haven't they contacted us?" Jahnsen's second in command, Phil, was stressing out. Loyal to a fault and typically laid back, he was the voice of reason, the one that stepped outside the storm to keep the big picture front and center. If he was pinging, it wasn't good. "They went in over four hours ago. They should've been out by now with a status update." He was on the radio every two minutes, asking for confirmation whether their special three-man team had obtained the target.

Phil was starting to question Jahnsen's belief that Zoey's skill sets were as valuable as they initially thought.

Jahnsen put his hands on his hips, breathed, and said, "They're still in the building. That's the only answer."

"Or they've gone rogue. Or maybe they're dead." Phil remained in his seat, eyes on the giant screen above their heads. They had access to Remotely Piloted Aircraft imagery. It could stay airborne for upwards of twenty-four hours. However, with the scarcity of fuel sources, they were limited to the length of an average mission, usually two, maybe three hours. Jahnsen had anticipated the difficulty of obtaining this particular target, but the start time occurred almost eight hours too early. When they saw Zoey's group moving in, they had a bird up in the air at only half a tank.

In total, they planned a 145-minute operation to procure Calla Lily and bring her back in one piece just before sunrise.

Sunrise was still several hours away.

"We would have seen them leave the building. They have no reason to go rogue."

"They have no reason not to!" shouted Phil, his patience wearing thin.

"What could they possibly gain from running away from us?" Jahnsen shot back, unwilling to let that thought poison the operation.

"Are you kidding me? We gave them no reason to stay. You told them nothing! They just risked their lives going in there to find and retrieve a young woman they knew nothing about. From everything I have seen, they went in there to save

Zoey, not Calla Lily. We just gave them the means and pointed them in the right direction." He stood up and glared into Jahnsen's eyes. "This isn't the way it should have gone down. We should have brought them in sooner. Gave them the understanding they needed to realize what they were doing all this for."

"Phil," said Jahnsen, trying to reason through the chaos, "some people need more info to base their decisions on. To own their purpose. Some people? Less is more."

"Oh, and you think these three need less information? Somehow I do not think that's the case. They just have a different agenda," yelled Phil, emphasizing keywords to get his point across.

"They do. But that plan aligned with our own as it turned out."

"Not if they don't know that. Seriously, what if they're dead? I mean, there hasn't been anyone moving around in that building since thirty minutes before they got in there. There was a mass entrance of personnel before they went in, and they had to move up their timeline by eight hours. At least five times the normal amount of people came in at that time last night, and then they all just disappeared. Dis-a-ppeared. There hasn't been an ounce of building-to-building foot traffic, either. Yet nothing has changed anywhere else globally that I can see. What's going on behind those doors?"

Jahnsen stared Phil down a few beats, then realized he couldn't win. Phil was right. He grunted and looked away. Phil had a good point, but he's not about to acknowledge it. "We know their procedures. We knew if, more likely when, those three were noticed compromising security that the compound would go on lockdown, and it did. And they still made it in." Jahnsen was usually the anxiety-ridden one. The one that threw his emotions and passion into whatever operation they were on. Yet, at this moment, he was composed.

His composure was infuriating Phil. They spent every minute planning for this mission, and for once, Jahnsen was too calm.

Phil snatched his hat and slammed it on his head. "I'll be back. Call me if anything comes up." He leveled his eyes at Jahnsen and walked out the door. Walking up three flights of stairs onto the broken cement patio, he pulled a pack of crushed Camel Menthols out of his pocket. Inside the pack was a row of cigarettes. Behind them was a thin cell phone and battery. He placed the battery in the phone, pressed the power button, pulled out a cigarette, and watched as the orange flame engaged the tobacco in a fire dance. After a long inhalation, he exhaled a cloud of smoke, relaxed before dialing out to the only saved contact, and then placed the phone to his ear.

"It's Phil. No word. It's a ghost town." He bowed his head and listened for a few moments. "I'm almost certain she's awake. What else would make them all go comms silent? I'll update when I know more." He put it back in the pack and pulled out another smoke. Lighting it, he shifted his gaze to the sky. The sun had a few hours before it crested the horizon and brought daylight with it. They knew the risks. Infiltrating a top-secret location, likely the most top-secret location in the country, with only three untrained non-special forces personnel, was a ludicrous idea. They had entire squads of military-trained operators. Why they were only being used as a backup was blowing his mind. It was insane they even got this far. Obviously, the conditions of this operation were far from what their own guys were used to, but how could they have believed that these three inexperienced civilians would get in and out with a target like this without issues?

Not only have they lost their ability to communicate with them, but the entire compound population has gone missing.

Phil's nerves were rattled.

*Please let them be alive.*

By some miracle, Jahnsen kept calm despite his heart palpitations when he watched Phil walk out the door. They knew this would be extraordinarily risky no matter who went in, and they'd planned it out with multiple courses of action. The most significant factor was getting Zoey within range of Calla Lily.

A mission was only as successful as the intel used to plan it. Honestly, they had not been 100% certain they would even make it onto the compound, let alone into the building. They did, though, and that minor miracle gave him hope. Now it's a matter of what they find and whether they will come back alive.

His best-trained operators were on standby a quarter mile out from the compound, waiting for the word. Their job was to retrieve the target and three operators, Zoey, Joe, and Aidan, once they left the compound. They slept in short shifts. Jahnsen thought they would only be waiting for forty-five to sixty minutes tops. It had been too many hours. They couldn't wait much longer. Even now, if he were to put them on that compound, it could be detrimental. After all, they had no idea what had transpired behind those walls.

Granted, from what he could see, there was no one there to fight. He had already waited too long, but he couldn't open his mouth. He wasn't ready for plan B.

"Boss?" said the littlest lady in the room, locking eyes with him. She had short, straight, blackish-blue hair and big black glasses with rhinestones on the sides.

"Yes, Jilly?"

"Sir," said Jilly seeming uncomfortable, "even with all communications down, and no visual confirmation of physical movem—"

"—Today Jilly." Jahnsen's patience was fading fast, shuffling forms on his desk and barely engaging in the conversation.

"Something is happening out there." The room silenced at her words.

Head snapping up, Jahnsen tuned back into what she was saying. "What? Where?" He said as he pulled up the feeds on his monitor, searching for anything out of place.

"There have been random bursts of electromagnetic energy spikes on our operators' radios and radar equipment. Initially, I thought it was just our equipment receiving interference. After analyzing the energy levels, there is no chance it can be random. Something is creating that energy, and we are feeling it. Maybe we need to send in our men?"

He knew better than to second-guess Jilly's suggestions and slammed his hand down on the "talk" radio button. "Main to Stingray, look alive out there. Target analyst says something's happening inside the compound."

# Chapter 34
## Emptiness

Filling the doorway with his body, Justin pulled his weapon back to his side. No one. There was absolutely no one.

The stillness muffled his hearing. The void of all movement: no electrical current carrying energy to every electronic piece of equipment, the lack of shoes on the ceramic tiles, no swish of clothing or bustling chatter.

Just silence.

Aidan and Joe walked out behind him and past his frozen feet. Their shock was not as sweeping as his.

"Geez, we knew it was quiet around here, but this seems a little overkill." Aidan didn't wait for a response. He ran up to the front doors and tried to push them open. Nothing.

"Everything's electronic," said Joe, searching the room.

"They must've done a complete lockdown. In this case, once locked down, they killed the power, killing the capability to open anything back up."

"Wait. Hold on," said Aidan, visibly agitated. "We walked through the *unlocked* and *open* front door." He stood pointing at the now sealed metal door in his path. "How are they closed?"

"It must've been the explosion. When the door blew downstairs, it must've triggered the auto-lockdown." Without ever looking up, Joe continued his search like a hound on a hunt.

"But wouldn't there be a fail-safe somewhere? What if there was a fire after the lockdown? Everyone just dies or what?" Aidan's claustrophobia was beginning to show, as evidenced by the beads of sweat on his forehead.

Justin was good at reading people, and Aidan needed to refocus. "Come with me. We need to check out the stairwell to the upper floors first. See if we can hear anything." Justin was already jogging toward the door on the left side of the foyer. Upon reaching it, he slowly turned the handle attempting to make as little noise as possible.

He first listened through the crack. Silence. Continuing to open it slowly, he stuck his head in. After several quiet seconds, he pulled the door open and walked in, looking up the tower of stairs. Both men stood there momentarily, waiting for a sign of life. When none came, Aidan headed up the stairs, checking every vantage point for anything out of the ordinary.

"Think we should go up to sixteen?" Aidan asked, itching

to go.

With a quick nod, Justin took the stairs two at a time. Every couple of floors, they stopped to listen.

Nothing but silence.

As they got to the fourteenth floor, they stopped again.

Nothing.

"Honestly, I think it's unlikely she's still here. If Zuri can't feel her sister," he gulped, "she's not here... or worse." He didn't have to explain the worst.

Aidan cringed at the unspoken words. "Let's see what we see, okay? It hasn't been that long since Zuri felt her presence," he said, trying to wrap his mind around his next thought. "Could she have gotten down to the main floor in that amount of time? If she did, where would she go? She'd be as locked in as we are."

They crept up the last two staircases to number sixteen. "Blood," Aidan whispered.

"No." Justin's face turned pale at the sight of smeared blood on the floor. He ripped open the door and raced the length of the hall, checking every passing door for any indication as to which room she might be in.

"I don't see anything, Justin." Aidan was right behind doing the same sweep.

"She has to be here!" Justin shouted, pulling on every handle. Some locked, some unlocked, all empty and quiet. Others stood open from what must have been a hasty retreat. None showed evidence of the blood found in the stairwell. "This doesn't make any sense!"

Aidan stopped and scouted one end to the other one more time. "Did you see any blood leading *into* this floor?"

After a moment's thought, he said, "No. I don't think so."

"Maybe they didn't come in here?" Both men grunted in frustration and took off at a sprint back to the stairwell. Through quick hand motions, they decided who went where. Aidan moved downstairs while Justin continued up.

They searched several floors on either side, searching for evidence of an injured person. Nothing. Had Justin looked at the wall directly across from the top-floor stairwell door, he would not have missed the faint smear of blood on the small indent in the wall.

From below, Aidan could hear Justin's expletive. They met back by the puddle of wet blood.

"You think this is hers? It could be someone else. Maybe someone fell coming down the stairs when we saw that mass movement of people?"

Justin shook his head. "That was hours ago. The blood would be much tackier." He took a few heavy breaths to calm down. "Okay, let's go back. Maybe something has changed."

Maneuvering down the stairwell faster than usual but slower than their ascent, Aidan couldn't help but share a thought he'd been stewing on. "You seem to know them pretty well."

Justin wanted to forgo this conversation as he knew he was likely to have it many more times. Deciding to get the first wave of explanations over with, he said, "I knew them before all of this. I became a doctor to try and learn how they do what they do. At the time I knew them, they always had an indescribable bond. Like they say about twins sometimes. They could always sense one another no matter where they were or how far apart. Like, sense when the other was hurt. I had never known them not to be aware of each other regardless of how far apart they were. It's not like I ever had the chance to test the theory, though, so I'm not sure."

"Sounds like there's more to it, though," replied Aidan, pushing him to keep talking.

"Yeah, well. There is," said Justin, explaining it would take a lot more effort than he had to give right now. Feeling his heart pound against his chest, he began choking up. Thankfully they were single file heading down the stairs, so Aidan couldn't see him. He was more than happy to keep the conversation shallow. In fact, the only thought he could manage was how he never caught wind that Lexi was here. *Have I been this close all along just to lose her now?*

Aidan could tell he wasn't going to get much more. "Let's get the girls. They are going to want to see for themselves."

As they passed through the main floor, Joe looked in their direction and lifted his eyebrows, silently inquiring about their search.

"Blood," Aidan said.

"Blood?" Joe's hands stilled.

"It was recent, but there wasn't anyone we could find." Justin was so frustrated he wanted to throw something.

"Or a trail leading us anywhere," added Aidan, just as frustrated. He was in need of some action before he became claustrophobic.

Joe nods apologetically and starts back in as if they'd never left. "A building like this probably has several options for fire safety and egress for personnel. Justin, you work here. What are the regulations?" Both men turned to him.

"Yes. There is a fire safety plan. However, I never paid much attention to it." Aidan and Joe stared at him. "In my defense, we were told it didn't matter much because we could never leave Zuri's side." Not to mention he would never have left her even if the building came crashing down. "And, we had numerous sprinkler systems in place for fire protection. Plus, we were four floors below the surface. The only way out is up. Trust me, that much I know. I've walked every hall on every floor below ground for years. No matter what happened, I would've had to get her up here to get out of the building."

Joe glared at him, unable to decide if Justin was so intelligent that he was a fool or just plain idiotic. "Come take a look at this."

Rather than head to the stairs to get the girls, Justin and Aidan followed him around the large granite check-in center. The chest-high counter sat in front of a room dedicated to security operations. "Anything seem strange to either of you?"

"There is usually a larger-than-average human sitting in this seat based on the butt impressions," said Aidan with a smirk.

Joe's eyes flicked to Aidan as if to say, 'no, you moron.' "There are no computers. No radios. Nothing but the docking stations for the laptops to sit on. These stations," he said, pointing at the black rectangular boxes on the eight-foot-long countertop, "allow employees to take their laptops anywhere they want and dock them for power."

Justin maneuvered farther around the counter and into the security office. "Same thing in here."

Joe's brain was on hyperdrive. "So the good news is this isn't a repeat of Roanoke, where an entire colony vanished, never to be found. This security team had a destination in mind, and they took their toys with them."

"Actually," said Aidan, "some think that the islanders did have a backup plan, and some even say that...."

Justin and Joe simultaneously groaned, nipping Aidan's history lesson in the bud before checking every office space on the main floor.

"Everything is here except the people and important electronics. Oh! Poptarts," cheered Aidan, breaking off a piece and popping it in his mouth while talking. "Who leaves without their shoes?" He kicked the boring two-inch woman's heel further under a desk.

Justin was disgusted watching Aidan finish off God-knows-who's leftover strawberry *chalk*-tart. Joe didn't even notice. Clearly, this was not out of character.

"So we are trapped here with no way to communicate with the outside world and no knowledge of whether this is an isolated disappearing act or a large-scale, worldwide alien abduction." Joe's eyebrows lifted as if the other two men might have another suggestion. "I did find some remaining radios in one of the cabinets." He pulled them from his bag. "We should be able to link all of ours so that most of us have one."

"I think we need to fully check the floors above. Maybe from a higher vantage point we'll see something worthwhile outside." Aidan's suggestion was good, even if his true goal was to avoid panic.

"The only decent windows are from the offices at the top levels," Justin shared as the three of them huddled inside the security office.

"Wait." Something that had been forming in Justin's mind finally took shape. "You guys are working for someone, right? Don't you have contact with them? If the point of you being here is to get Zuri, how are you supposed to tell them you have her?" Distrust started seeping in.

"Yeah. My thoughts exactly," whispered Aidan, giving Joe a look that made it seem like this was not a new question.

"Uh, well, when we agreed to do this," stammered Joe, "one of the messages we received said that they wouldn't make contact with us until we'd picked her up and were leaving the compound." He cleared his throat. "It's one of the reasons we told Zoey multiple times that we shouldn't do this. We didn't know what we were really going to find in here, and it was clear if something went wrong, we likely wouldn't have backup. I can only assume they didn't want anyone here to be able to link us back to them."

"Well, actually," Aidan said slowly, "they did give us a cell phone."

"What? Why haven't you used it? What are you waiting for?" Justin asked, really starting to feel like an idiot for relying on them so heavily.

"No, wait. Not exactly. Aidan, Jesus. Yes, they gave us a phone, but I've already worked my magic on it, and it doesn't work while we're in this building. There's one number on it, but I can't call it until we get out of here. And it's not like 911 is an option."

Justin scrutinized Joe's explanation. Everything he said made sense, but he was tired of all the surprises. "Is there anything else you'd like to share with me?"

They shook their heads simultaneously.

"Okay, so as far as you know, they could be out there waiting for you right now in hopes that you have Zuri. Or, they could have no idea you've even made it this far." This time they nod. "And you're doing all this to save your friend, Zoey." Again they nod. Justin didn't have a hard time understanding why they would take the risk as his mind drifted to Zuri. "Okay, I get it."

Aidan leaned backward, exclaiming, "Wait, what? Just like that?"

"Yeah, just like that. I know what it's like to need to do anything in your power for someone you care about. To protect them." He glanced between the two of them. "I can tell that's how you are with Zoey." He gave them a half-smile and nodded toward Joe to continue.

Joe blinked a few times and then gave an appreciative half-smile back. Then began spelling out in common-sense fashion the plan. He would stay in the security room and work on opening the doors. The girls, along with Justin and Aidan, would search for food, medical supplies, possible weapons, and anyone that might have been left behind on the floors above.

"There are *twenty* floors above us," said Justin, matter-of-fact, implying the obvious that it would take hours to clear.

"With any luck, you'll find someone with a clue before you make it that far, or I'll get these doors open, and we can go out and see for ourselves," Joe added earnestly. Though Justin sensed a pinch of humor tucked into the options.

Justin made his way back down to D1 while Aidan searched for snacks in the breakroom. Justin's mind was whirling with thoughts regarding the inconceivable events, including the possibility that every single person in this building, potentially the entire compound, had gone missing. Without vehicles? Air transportation? The only place to go within the building was down, but they had just come from that direction.

Standing outside the door to D1, he could hear them talking. It was hard to make out, and eavesdropping wasn't his style, but he also knew that Zuri had too many silent years up until now. If she was opening up about anything, he needed to give her that moment.

*"You said you could hear everything going on the entire time you were under?"* said Maria, completely astonished.

Justin's heart began to race. All those years, he could've spent more time talking to her. Reassuring her that one day he would find a way to free her. Suddenly a word crashed his conscience, nearly knocking him off his feet. His chest constricted so painfully he thought he might pass out.

*Torture.*

# Chapter 35
## It's Not Zuri



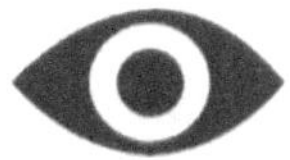

*W*e tortured her.

*She lay there completely still for seven years. Not moving. Not seeing. Not feeling. Just... listening. How she managed to survive that long under those conditions seems impossible.*

*What had he done?*

Breathing deep with a heavy chest, Justin pushed open the door to find the business end of two guns pointing at two essential parts of his body. Throwing his hands up in surrender, Maria and Zoey shifted back and lowered their weapons.

Maria's eyes were glossy and red. No question she'd been crying. He could relate and locked eyes with her in empathy.

Zuri started talking as if she knew he was walking in before he did. "There's no one up there, is there? I should've just run right past you. Maybe I could've gotten to her before—"

"—Zuri, we had no idea what was going on up there. To run up to the ground floor without knowing what was there could've been suicide. Waiting was the right call at that moment." He placed his hands on her shoulders. After a few seconds, she looked up at him, noting her youthful face truly belied the age of the woman she'd become.

*She'd become in silence,* Justin said to himself.

She was a wise child, and her lost years wouldn't hold her back. Living with open ears while her body was shut down had caused her to mature in ways none of them could imagine.

"Let's go up. The three of you need to see what's going on. Maybe you'll pick up on something we haven't so far," said Justin, inviting them up. They walked up the stairwell with an emotional heaviness weighing them down. Even though Justin knew what was on the other side of the door, he still found himself holding his breath as the three women opened it.

Maria followed the same path Aidan had. She headed straight to the front door and swiped her ID on the pad. With no response, she tried pulling on it, slamming her hands against the door in a mini rage and swearing up a storm.

Zuri stood stone still for several seconds, focusing on the door with stern determination. Zoey watched as Zuri's eyes fluttered close. Her body swayed. She couldn't tell what Zuri was doing, but something was off.

"I found these radios on the top shelf in the security room. Extra batteries were in the small fridge underneath the entranceway desk," said Joe, cutting the silence, not recognizing the moment with Zuri.

Standing in a circle in the middle of the main floor, they each took a radio. Ensuring they all worked, each person palmed enough batteries to last three days or more with minimal use. They didn't find any other weapons, so they settled in with what they had.

Just then, something Joe and Aidan had said earlier clarified itself within Justin's cloudy mind. They said there was a significant influx of people from the main compound into this building, followed by silence, allowing them to infiltrate the gates earlier than they'd planned.

"Joe," Justin said, gentle and slow, "you said before that when you were watching the compound, everyone came into the building at once." He glanced up to see Joe stop what he was doing and nod yes. "So we're not just saying the folks on duty last night got up and disappeared. We're saying *all* personnel on the compound rushed to work, then vanished. All at the same time with their laptops, tablets, phones, and whatever equipment they typically use. Except us." He looked to Maria as if she could confirm his thinking. "I know I'm slow, but this isn't possible. Is it?"

"So wait, what now? All personnel came in *here*? To this building. Grabbed their gear and went where? Are you saying they left us?" The pitch of Maria's voice rose with each question.

"Joe?" said Justin, his wheels still turning. "What time *exactly* did that happen?"

"Uh, standby." He pulled a notepad from his chest pocket. "Looks like 8:33 p.m."

"That's when Zoey collapsed. It all happened at once," said Aidan, practically dancing as it seemed they were beginning to solve the puzzle.

Justin walked away from them, head down, trying to remember what had been happening at that time. After a few seconds, he looked up and said, "So, that would've been before Zuri woke up. I remember. I remember I was just leaving my room to head back down to the lab. Something felt off, but I couldn't put my finger on it. So what if—"

"—What if this all started with her sister? Not with Zuri at all!" Aidan couldn't contain himself.

"Seriously, Aidan?" said Joe, disregarding him as usual.

"He's right. No, he's right." Justin turned back in their direction. "I don't think this started with Zuri at all."

A small voice came from the side of the room. "It started with Lexi." Zuri was listening to him intently explain something she already knew. "She had already woken up. They tried to kill her." She stood staring blankly across the room. "I couldn't let them."

No one spoke. They just stood there watching her take small steps around the foyer in a big circle. "It's just so empty," she said, her voice echoing off the barren cement walls. "I don't feel anything."

Zuri tried reaching out beyond herself, but the attempt shut her body down in exhaustion for a moment. When she came to, she was standing still in the middle of the room, slightly off balance. Breathing erratically, she tried to take stock of what had just happened.

Aidan's gentle voice of curiosity cut in a few feet from her. "What are you doing, Zuri?" He joined her, side by side, walking in stride with her smaller steps as she began moving again.

She was surprised he noticed what she was doing, and her footsteps faltered. Aidan placed his hand gently on her back and gave her his full attention. Raising her diamond eyes at him, she quietly replied, "I'm not sure how to describe it exactly. I guess I'm kind of trying to," she paused, searching for the right words, "feel around me?" When he said nothing, she continued,

"Every living thing produces energy at different levels of intensity. Not only is the intensity different, but the feel of it differs from person to person. My sister's energy is very familiar to me. I've felt it since the day I was born. Even hers changes based on how she's feeling moment to moment, but it's still recognizable. Like a signature. People, in general, give off a type of energy that is different from plants or animals."

"So you're saying that even if you couldn't see any of us in this room or hear us, you'd still know we were there?" Aidan's footsteps falter. Her description reflected what he remembered of his own family. He remembered coming home and sprawling out on his old living room couch. After a few moments of silence, although he couldn't hear or see her, he knew his sister was hiding behind the couch. She had probably been there forever, just waiting for him. By the time she jumped out to scare him, he had already planned to *pretend* to be scared.

Suddenly aware of the energy in the room, Aidan shook off his nostalgia. The group was staring at the two of them, offering their full attention. What she was saying made sense. They all agreed in their own way and continued to stand there quietly, watching and listening. Even Joe stopped what he was doing to hear what they were saying.

"Yes, and now that I've spent a little time with you and felt your energies at their most heightened, they are… um…"

"Like fingerprints?" Justin suggested.

Zuri, showing gratitude that he was near, said, "Yes. I think that makes sense." Scanning the room, she said, "I know that as long as you're alive, I'll be able to feel you. Or at least I assumed that's how it works." Her eyes glossed over as she struggled to breathe. They all knew she was thinking about her sister, Lexi. That particular fingerprint fading in and out.

"How far away can you feel someone?" Aidan's unexpected comfort toward Zuri was surprising to everyone but Zoey. He had taken that gentle tone with her many mornings after waking up from her nightmares.

Justin felt a twinge of jealousy watching them walk next to one another. He should be the one asking these questions, walking beside her. But his guilt was too heavy. Thinking of the part he'd played in her life all these years made him feel as though everything he did now only hurt her more.

"I don't really know. It depends on a lot of things. If I know you, then the bond stretches further. If you are someone I've never met, I can just feel a presence, I guess. If there's strong emotion occurring, I can feel that even more. I'm not very good at measuring distances," she said, looking into his eyes and noting that he seemed to understand, at least a little. Distance was not something she had a grasp of, having spent so much of her young life closed off from the world.

From a few steps away, Justin said, "We'll find her, Zuri. She's not gone. If she could survive what the two of you have been through, she can survive whatever is happening to her now." Justin shoved the guilt down inside him and walked over to hug her while her tears fell. He felt her relax momentarily, but then she took a deep breath and stood up straighter in his arms. He pushed her slightly back to see her face. Something was wrong.

Before he could ask, Maria piped in. "Time to get the heck out of here, ladies and gents. I'm assuming you," she pointed at Joe, "are going to continue to *break and exit* as it were?" He moved toward the electrical panel as his answer. "Zuri, Zoey, will you go to the dining hall and the medical office to grab as much long-lasting food and medical supplies as we can carry?"

"We have a good size SUV about two miles outside the gates that we can fill up. Or I'm assuming we still do," Aidan pointed out.

"Good, then how about you, Justin, and I canvas the floors and see what we find?" Maria moved quickly while saying, "I need more than flip-flops. Everyone has their radio, so call if anything of interest comes up. And Joe, if you could get the elevators working again, you will be permanently added to my Christmas card list." She grabbed the snickers from Aidan's hand and made a beeline for the stairwell door.

"I love a woman in charge," Aidan muttered, following right behind her.

"What floor is medical and dining on?" asked Zoey, her voice echoing as the stairwell door closed.

"Don't worry. Every floor has a medical station," Zuri answered, clipping her radio to her scrub pants. The weight of it pulled heavy on the waistband. Attempting to tighten her beltline with the skinny string did little for support.

"How do you know that, sleeping beauty?" Zoey raised her left eyebrow.

"I saw the directory on the desk." Common sense. It's not lost. Zuri paused before going up the stairs to open a candy bar Aidan had slipped into her hand. She then held it out to Zoey. "Here, you might want to eat this. You're almost as pale as me."

They both made their way up the stairwell to the second floor. Hearing the other three above them, Zoey thought it odd how little time it took to check out the second floor for people. When they walked in, they understood why. It was a vast restaurant-style open room with two swinging doors in the back, likely leading to the kitchen. "I'm surprised Aidan's not still here eating everything in sight," said Zoey, her sarcasm oozing through her faint smile.

They moved forward on a food mission—each one lost in

their thoughts without voicing them out loud.

Aidan caught Justin as they climbed from floor five to six. "I'm just throwing this out there. How is it that Zuri could do all those things downstairs, run as fast as she did, and yet," he paused, trying to wrap his head around his thoughts, "how are the ground floor doors stopping her?"

"To be honest? I have no idea. I've known Zuri for a long time, but before all this, I'd never seen her move things or be able to open doors or stop a full-grown man from falling over a railing. I have undeniably witnessed some interesting things from her and her sister, but nothing like this."

Maria's voice from half a flight up interrupted their discussion.

"We've checked six floors now, and nothing. I say we just skip the rest, run to our rooms, grab some things and get out of this building." Maria, though willing to take charge, was on edge. With every door that opened, she imagined someone jumping out with an Uzi, action-movie style.

"I know, but maybe in their haste, someone fell and twisted an ankle. Just waiting for help." Aidan's idea seemed plausible.

"Ugh! I can't stand this!"

"Maria, let's let Aidan finish checking these few floors below the apartment levels. How about you and I grab some essentials from our rooms? Aidan, you good with that?" Justin turned his head toward the redheaded Delta Force wannabe.

"I don't think that's—" Maria started.

"—I got it!" Aidan mumbled around a mouthful of who knows what.

"Just radio in after you clear each floor so we know where you're at. If you see anything, *anything*, suspicious, do *not* be a hero." Justin's laser-like stare was lost on Aidan as he shrugged and offered a placating smile.

Taking off up the stairs, they slowed and halted on the eighth floor. "This is the first apartment floor. Think we should take a look first?" Nodding in agreement, they opened the door quietly. There was no sound and no one moving, however, it was obvious something had transpired on that floor. The only things noticeably disturbed on the floors below were missing laptops and other electronic devices. Up here, there was a tornado of clothing, shoes, and other random personal items scattered everywhere. "I think this clinches it. They didn't just vanish, and techie terrorists didn't take them hostage. They left with purpose," said Maria, engulfed with sadness. Not the anger she'd been trying to tamp down since all of this began, but true heartache.

*They left. Without us. Did they know they were leaving us behind? They had to. Zuri wakes up, and everyone goes missing except the people with her.*

"How could we not have known where they were going? Or what the plan was if Calla woke up? I mean Zuri." She shook her head, holding her chest as if to help control her breathing.

"Not yet, Maria," said Justin, touching her shoulder. "Hold

it together a little longer. We need to get through this and out of here to somewhere safe before we let it all out." Catching her eyes, he tried to reassure her, offering a dose of strength for the time being. If only he were like Zuri, maybe he could actually do that.

"What if the only safe place is here?" Stepping away and taking a deep breath, a myriad of thoughts ran through her mind, but she didn't say anything further. "Let's go."

Leg muscles burning, they moved up the next two platforms to the floor their personal apartments were on, giving a cursory check behind each of the stairwell doors in between.

"All this mess is from when our pagers went off, and everyone ran out of their rooms to their offices," Maria said, trying to recall that memory. "Had to be, right?"

"I don't know. Maybe. The halls were empty when I ran down to the lab." Justin assessed the litter on the floor, mostly personal items.

"You ran?"

"Yes, I felt… something wasn't right," he said, reflecting on the feeling.

"Hmm, that's interesting. And strange. But as I've learned first-hand today, I need to give weird feelings a little more credit." The memory of being knocked off her feet in the lab by some unseen force only moments after Zuri stood upright made her shudder. "Well, when I left my room, it was chaos, but no one was carrying anything. Mostly half-dressed. Seems likely they were racing to their offices to grab what they needed?"

Walking the length of the hallway in silence, she finally blurted out, "What if Gavin's up here?"

Justin hesitated but kept walking. Seeing how upset she was, he thought he understood why but didn't say. He had only ever noticed a hint of flirtation between them. Nothing serious enough for the look she had on her face now. He also knew that it didn't make the loss any less painful.

"He might be," he replied, taking stock of her concern before asking, "but why would he still be here when the rest are gone?"

"I don't know," she replied, puffing out her chest and stirring up some courage. "But I've got to check." She walked down the hallway none too quietly and pulled the handle to Gavin's apartment. It was unlocked.

# Chapter 36
## Time on Target

LIMIT | August 10, 2029 | 2:53 a.m.

"Main, this is Stingray. We're holding a quarter mile out from the target, but the RECCE team just reported they are picking up something from inside the building. Positive it's radio chatter, but no indication on source." The team leader's voice rang out across the intercom for the whole operations cell to hear.

"Copy Stingray. Push into the compound walls. Do not enter the target building without confirmation from Main," said Jahnsen, his emotions ramping up. Finally, they were getting somewhere. They were so close, and now they knew, at the very least, someone was alive in that building.

Phil walked up behind him. "'Bout time," he declared, slamming his hand down on the desk.

"That's not the only good news," a female voice stated from behind the two of them.

They both turn to see the emerald eyes of their inside source.

# Chapter 37
## Open the Doors

Zoey and Zuri felt it at the same time. Severe pain from their temples wrapped around their heads. "What the—"

Zuri's knees buckled when it hit her. "Lexi!"

"Green eyes. It's her. I saw her eyes," said Zoey, holding herself up on a cafeteria table. The connection was weak, but it was there.

"We need to go get her!" groaned Zuri, grinding her teeth together from the pressure in her head. Her desire to run out the door hindered by her sudden energy drain.

This episode only lasted fifteen seconds or so but was a double-edged sword. Lexi was still alive, they were certain of it. But currently too exhausted and dizzy from the vision to get very far.

"You need to eat," said Zoey, reaching out and grabbing her wrist.

"We'll lose her again!" Pulling back, Zuri couldn't get her arm free.

"I know, but we won't make it twenty steps if we don't stop the blackouts."

Zuri stopped cold and asked, "How did you know?"

"That you were blacking out?"

Zuri nodded.

"Because I can feel it. You just shut down for a moment, like when you tried to reach out and find Lexi. You disappeared from my senses, from my ability to read your energy for a moment. Like how Lexi keeps disappearing."

Zuri felt defeated. Sliding down the wall, she sat on the floor and lay her head on her arms, slowly breathing. "This feels like a dream. A terrible, terrible dream," she whispered, lifting her head with a pleading look painted on her face.

"You know," Zoey said, rooting in her bag, "I have always eaten more food than Joe and Aidan combined." She let out a small laugh. "I think I now understand why." A smile crossed her face trying to ease Zuri's anxiety. "It's hard work being as awesome as you," she said, leaning sideways and bumping her shoulder into Zuri's. This little touch of friendliness gave Zuri the space to relax, softening her expression and giving in to a subtle smile. "I think your fuel level is currently on E. Let's eat something, what do you say? After all, we might have a long road ahead of us." Eyebrows lifted in question waiting for Zuri to agree.

Taking a deep breath in, Zuri knew she was right.

Zoey pulled out a can of mandarin oranges from her bag. It would have to do for now.

She then pulled out some granola bars she had snagged from the kitchen. Both used plastic forks as they shared the fruit but quickly realized they were more famished than they first thought and used their fingers instead. After finishing off the can, they grabbed a second. Lucky for them, there was more food than they could handle and didn't feel guilty about popping open another.

Halfway through, Zuri found the wherewithal to ask a few questions. Not having spoken in years and finally having real energy to draw from, her questions started spilling out. "Who are you? How do you have eyes like me? How can you feel all of these things? My sister and I are the only people I've ever known with eyes like yours." She started to reach out to touch Zoey's face but pulled her hand back, embarrassed at the last second.

"I wish I could say I had a clue, but I don't. My eyes haven't always been like this. It just happened. For years I could feel all this pain crushing me in my dreams… nightmares. All I could see in my mind were bright green glinting eyes.

"At first, I thought it was me being crushed. Then, it became clear that it wasn't me, at least not literally. I was just feeling what someone else was going through.

"Earlier this year, during one of the worst episodes, I discovered that the person I could feel was not the same person

I was seeing—the woman with green eyes. Instead, as I felt my body being crushed, I could also see her. I saw her eyes as she spoke to me," Zoey shared, as if back in her room, watching it unfold all over again. "Her eyes were blue. When I first saw you, I wasn't sure which person I was looking at. Was it your pain I was feeling? Or the woman that watched you?

"I honestly didn't know what to expect when we walked in there." Taking another bite, Zoey went on, "Once I saw your eyes, though, I knew it wasn't you. But obviously, we're still connected somehow."

Zuri listened intently. Quietly.

"So, maybe there's four of us?" Zuri wondered.

Zoey took a deep breath. "Could be." Then looked into Zuri's eyes before saying, "Zuri, do you know why you were brought here?"

After a few moments of contemplation, she said, "The last thing I remember is an explosion. And my sister being inside of it." Cringing at the memory, she continued, "I remember feeling her fear and shock, and then nothing. She was just gone. All that was left was darkness." Her eyes drifted away from the conversation.

"Kind of like how you've felt her at different times tonight? And then it just disappears?" Zoey's mind was working on something, but she couldn't quite grasp what it could mean.

Their eyes connected. "Yes, I think so."

"Did you," she started, without accusation or judgment, "make the explosion?" Knowing very little of what really happened the day the world went dark, Zoey was pretty sure that Zuri knew even less.

Zuri's eyes cast downward, more in thought than an expression of guilt. "I don't think so. I mean, I don't know how I could have or why I would have."

Neither of them knew how to proceed, but they both continued to feel Lexi's pull. Everything would just have to come in time. "Let's get out of here."

Helping each other up, they walked toward the stairwell door. Zoey yanked out her radio to check in. Before she could speak, another wave of searing pain hit her. Her radio dropped to the floor, breaking into pieces. "What is happening!" she yelled before collapsing to the ground, her hands gripping either side of her head.

This time though, Zuri didn't collapse with her. She stood taller than she had all day. At first, she prepared to fight but immediately realized the threat wasn't in the room. Briefly, she placed her fingertips on Zoey's face, then, without a word, sprinted for the door. Her radio's weight caused it to fly off her flimsy waistband. Somehow Zoey managed to get ahold of it before it hit the ground, grateful it hadn't shattered like hers. She squeezed the call button through the pain, grunting into it, "Joe! Zuri's on her way down, and she's moving quick." Pulling herself up from the floor, she grabbed their bags and headed for the door.

Aidan's voice came across the line but was immediately cut off by Justin's. "What's going on? Where is she going?"

"She's going after Lexi," Zoey barked. "Stop her! She

can't go out alone!"

Upstairs, Maria's ears perked as she heard the radio chatter while checking the last rooms in Gavin's apartment. "Dammit!" She turned to dart out the front door when she nearly collided with someone.

"Gavin!" It wasn't a yell but more of an inhaled exclamation as she jerked back, losing her balance.

"Maria?" He lunged forward and wrapped his arms around her.

Startled at seeing another human, she clawed and pushed at him before realizing that he was simply embracing her.

"Where the hell have you been!"

Joe had his personal laptop, along with some other gadgets, hooked up to the panels next to the entrance. He cracked through the coded web keeping the doors sealed, when the stairwell door flew open. Zuri came bounding through it in a bee-line for the front door.

The door was half-open, and he couldn't reverse it in time. Lunging forward, his fingertips barely grazed her shirttail as she slipped outside. Zoey emerged just behind her, attempting to follow, only this time, Joe's fingers didn't miss.

"What are you doing? We can't go out there yet!" he bellowed as Zoey tried to peel away from his grasp. "Zoey! Stop!"

"Let go of me, Joe! I need to stay with her. She doesn't even have her radio. She doesn't know where she is. *Let me go!*" Her strength was more than he anticipated, and, unable to keep his hold on her, she took off. His first reaction was to run after her, but caution kicked in. Quickly, he ran back to the main desk to snatch the rest of his gear.

He was able to get the radio system's primary control functioning, so someone would need to stay there to ensure it stayed running by changing out battery packs consistently and adjusting channel settings as necessary. He roared in frustration debating whether to run out the door or wait for everyone to get downstairs first. "Where are you guys?" he growled, barely able to spit the words into his radio.

Aidan's voice came through first. "On the third floor. Almost there."

Justin's right behind. "Looking for Maria. I can't get her on the radio. Go! We'll catch up."

"Copy. I'll update you on directions. Zoey followed Zuri out the main door. Zuri doesn't have a radio, and I don't think she's stopping until she gets where she's going." As he sped past the door, he quickly snagged his laptop from the floor along with the cords hanging from the panel box. Immediately the doors started shutting. There was no time to decide if he'd just permanently sealed the other three in, only to lock himself, Zuri, and Zoey out.

Aidan hit the ground floor and watched helplessly as the entrance door closed with a hiss. Bounding up to it, he threw his entire body into the unforgiving metal. His fists assaulted the door without mercy. "Open you, son of—" he swore, as the last punch provided no progress. Looking through a small window on the door, not big enough to squeeze his arm through, he could see Joe's oversized silhouette dart around vehicles and race toward the gate. The girls were nowhere in sight. *Where the heck is Justin?*

He jammed his radio's talk button. "What's going on, man? Justin, where are you? Maria?"

"Gavin—" Maria started to say.

"—Gavin?" Justin cut her off as he entered the apartment and stopped cold when Gavin's face came into view.

Between them was a kitchen island where a box sat open. Maria hadn't noticed it at first, but it seemed important.

Gavin saw her eyeing it. "It was my mother's. She gave it to me before she died. There are letters and pictures in it. Pictures of a girl I've never met." He let the pause between them sit for a second. "Pictures of my sister."

Without really understanding, just a gut feeling, Justin knew this was one of those important pieces of Gavin's story he had yet to hear.

"We don't have time. We need to go!" called Justin, infuriated at the sight of Gavin, unharmed and calm. How could he have been here all this time and not come back to see if they were all right? Or let them know what was going on up here? *What had he been doing?*

Maria knew she needed to follow Justin but felt

overwhelmed. "I, uh," she looked toward the door, then back to Gavin, and made a rapid decision. "Grab your crap and move it." She touched Justin's shoulder as she moved past, ignoring all the obvious questions. Instead, she asked Justin, "How'd they even get out of the building?"

Still boring holes into Gavin's eyes, he said, "Joe must've gotten the door open." He keyed his radio again. "We're coming, Aidan. We found someone."

Aidan's voice rang through in surprise. "You found someone? Holy—" and his radio cut off.

When he came back on, they all heard the strain in his voice. "—the door is shut again, and I can't open it! Joe made it out and is after the girls, but I can't get this damn thing to open."

With no further hesitation, Justin took the lead in front of Maria and yelled to both of them, "We have to go. Now!"

"Who's Joe? Where's Calla… Zuri? And Jones?" Gavin was confused, but no answers were forthcoming. Just reacting, he took off after them.

Racing down the hall, Maria's head swam as she tried to remember the last thing Gavin would have witnessed. He walked out of the lab before Jones killed himself. He wasn't there for the explosion that brought in Joe, Zoey, and Aidan or any of the crazy facts that have come to light since.

They took the stairs two and three at a time. Despite their fury of movement, Maria could still get out some angsty comments. "Well, kind of a lot has happened since we last saw you. Maybe you should start by telling us where *every last person* in this building has gone before we get into the rest."

Instead of answering, Gavin stopped short and pivoted back, yelling, "I'm right behind you! I forgot my bag!"

Maria, leering at him, shouted, "We are not waiting!"

"I swear I'll be right behind you!" He paused for only a moment hoping she caught his authenticity. "I promise." With that, he thundered back up the stairs.

In his room, his hand caught the side of the door, frantically trying to recall where he'd left his duffle. He had everything packed and ready to go just moments before he had heard someone enter his apartment. Not knowing it was Maria, he hid. At the time, he could tell someone was moving through each room frantically, but from his position in the hall closet, he couldn't get a view of who it was. When she passed him on her way into his room, he slipped out and stayed behind the wall in the living room. It wasn't until her radio went off and he'd heard her voice that he recognized who it was. His heart skipped a beat at the realization Maria was okay, alive, and hadn't vanished like the rest. Her shock and anger surprised him even more, as he only felt relief.

Grabbing his bag, he turned to run out the door when his mom's box caught in his periphery. He shoved everything back in it and tucked it under his arm. His mission here was far from over, and he had no idea what he might need from this box or what clues he had yet to figure out.

On his way to the front door, he caught something moving outside the window. In the distance, he could make out several people running. One lagged quite a bit behind two others. Even more concerning were the numerous individuals and several vehicles they were running toward on the other side of Satellite Hill.

The lack of movement everywhere else outside the building was extremely troubling. There was usually a bevy of folks moving from place to place, even before dawn. He wasn't sure if the three on the ground were purposely moving toward the team or were about to get a big surprise.

Unable to inform Justin or Maria, he turned and sprinted to catch up.

"Oh!" Maria sucked in air as she rounded the fifth-floor platform. Stumbling down several steps, her ankle cracked before Justin could grasp her arm to steady her.

She held her breath for what seemed like hours as the pain shot up her leg and into her toes. Clenching her teeth, a groan finally escaped her lips.

"Come on—" Justin used the words as a swear as he lowered her to the floor.

Trying to lift her leg gently and set it on his knee, she reached for his hands. "Don't move it! Don't move it! Oh… G… God bless America. I can't—"

"—Easy, Maria, take a breath."

"I. Am. *Breathing!*" She snarled. "It's broken. I know it is. I felt the crack."

Justin wished he'd been able to catch her sooner. While he wanted Maria to be safe, he was still clamoring to get down the stairs, frustrated that he had let Zuri out of his sight to begin with. Now she was outside and he was completely out of reach.

*How much can I possibly keep screwing up after all these years!*

"Hey! Are you guys down there?" Gavin's voice came from a few staircases above. "There are people out there!"

"We know! That's why we're trying to get out there." Justin's nerves were shot.

"No, I know. That's not what I mean." His voice boomed as he got closer to their position. "There are *many* people on the inside of the wall just in front of the gatehouse. I could see three people moving toward a whole group, and I get the sense they're in for a real surprise." He bounded down the last few steps and saw Maria sitting on the floor with her foot propped up on Justin's knee. "What happened?" His hand moved to touch her leg, but she swatted it away.

"Wait, there are more people? Like our people?" Justin jumped to his feet, forgetting Maria's leg.

"Aagghhh!" she yelled, eyes wide and fists clenched.

"No. Like people with guns. *Lots* of people with guns."

"How many?" Maria said, choking back both the shock of Gavin's information and the agony of her ankle thudding on the floor.

"I couldn't tell. Maybe twenty or thirty? They're moving *toward* our building, but I don't think the three out there can see them. They're on the backside of Satellite Hill, and you know it's lower on that side."

Eyes pleading, Justin looked at Maria, then Gavin. "I have to go, Maria." She nodded as tears streamed. He turned to their partner, "Gavin, I don't know *what* you've been doing all this time, but I need to know, can I trust you to take care of Maria? She can't make it. Her ankle's done for."

Instantly defensive, he replied, "Of course! You're acting as if I would hurt her."

Justin gently took Maria's hand and put her radio in it. "Keep it nearby and get to the ground floor. See what Joe was able to set up for communications." Then he said pointedly at Gavin, "Stay with her and keep her safe." He clutched the man's shirt and stared him in the eye. "Dammit, Gavin, you better be on the right side of all this."

Gavin didn't say anything. He just looked into his eyes with a fervor that seemed to satisfy him. Justin took off down the remaining steps. Within minutes they heard the stairway door crash open as Justin threw his whole body into it without slowing down.

"You have a lot of explaining to do, mister." The excruciating pain from her ankle did not take away from the hurt she felt as a result of his unexplainable abandonment. As far as she was concerned, Gavin had some serious ground to make up.

# Chapter 38
## Purgatory Ends

LIMIT | August 10, 2029 | 4:00 a.m.

Even with her eyes closed, Lexi knew she was no longer in the strange building she awoke in. She fought the urge to open her eyes, hoping to hear what she could before they noticed she was aware of their conversation. Their voices were muffled, but she could still make out their words. Trying to clear her head without moving was impossible.

*My skin, it's so... so itchy I could scream!*

"What happened to her? Why does she have all these marks on her?"

"And only on the left side of her body? How is that even possible?"

*I can't do this anymore. I can't wait another minute.*

*Just questions.*

*No answers.*

"I can't believe you got her out! I need to tell our men to stand down, regroup, and return to base camp."

"Rice, we just found out someone's in the building. Shouldn't we figure out who?" *It's a young woman's voice.*

"She's coming round." *Another woman's voice.*

Lexi couldn't control the muscle spasms but continued to clinch her eyes shut.

"We need to get her hooked up to the monitors. Here, put this on her arm."

*I can't hold it together any longer.*

Lexi's eyes flashed open. Everyone sucked in their breath as they jumped away from her. Silence engulfed the room as four people stepped back toward the walls. Even Lexi couldn't seem to take a breath.

"Lexi?"

It was her. The woman with the green eyes, only they seemed different. Not as bright, yet Lexi *knew* it was the same woman. The one that saved her. The one that almost killed her. That memory was fuzzy, but it triggered another, *Grant.* Lexi's chest hurt just thinking about him. Everyone's eyes darted from Lexi to the woman when someone behind Lexi said under their breath, "I thought her name was *Rose?* Or, *Calla Lily?*"

The man behind the green-eyed woman spun her around. "Lexi? I thought we were going after Rose. Who is this? Dammit!" His initial joy at her being here rapidly turned sour.

"Rose and Lexi, they are the same person." She pulled away from him and moved toward Lexi. "Rose is the name she is known by in our lab. Lexi is her actual name." The man's reactions are spastic, as though he wasn't up to speed on anything. Then she dropped the bomb. "Calla Lily is her sister." Her eyes were wide with emotion. "There are two."

The silence was deafening.

"What—how—you only gave us intel on Rose. I thought Rose and Calla Lily were the same person?"

Her response was quick and harsh. "I know. Me too. We all did. We are the only ones who know she's a real person, which is how it's supposed to be to avoid being attacked by Breakers. Or anyone else with a need for power. Honestly, I didn't know there were two until today." She could feel their incredulous glares at this admission. Disbelief was etched on their faces.

The man who must be in charge raised his voice a notch. "Where did the name, Lexi, come from, then?" Something wasn't adding up with what Green Eyes was saying, and everyone in the room, including Lexi, could feel it.

Lexi's quiet words cut through everyone's thoughts as she said, "So, only *you* know my name?"

"I…" Her voice choked in her throat as everyone stepped back in shock.

"How do you know my name?" Lexi could feel the woman's alarm increase along with her pulse. No one else seemed to notice.

"How could you possibly know my name?"

Her teardrop eyes seemed to plead with Lexi. "I heard you say it. When you started to come out of your coma."

Confused, Lexi thought, *that can't be right. Why would I say my own name?*

"And when I tried to stop you from running away, I called out that name." The woman's muted crystalline eyes bore into hers. "When I said it. You stopped."

"What happened in the hallway between us?" Lexi asked, her mind cluttered with bits and pieces of all that had happened. Whatever her answer, she recognized in her face that she wasn't planning on sharing any further information. At least not with a room full of people.

Clearing her throat, the pressure in the room decreased. "Let's start with this. My name is Madison. I was with you in the lab. I have been with you for several years, actually. Watching over you. Making sure you were safe. As safe as could be anyway." A flash of regret washed over her that only Lexi detected. "I know you may not understand this right now, but we are here to help you. To protect you." Lexi wanted to believe her, but nothing about this felt safe.

Several people in scrubs started moving toward her, but she wasn't ready to end the conversation. "I think you tried to kill me."

Instant silence.

"No. No, Lexi, I can promise you that's not true." She put her hands up, genuinely shocked at the notion.

"Where's my sister? Where am I?" As she spoke, a memory of her reflection made her pause. Frantically, she tried to stand, but her brain moved faster than her body could handle. This time everyone pressed their backs against the walls, and someone behind Lexi said, "Don't."

She froze. Whispers all around.

Vertigo overwhelmed her, and she started to sway. Even so, she could still make out what they were saying: *"Who tried to kill her?" "What is she talking about?"*

The man in charge raised his voice a few decibels beyond what was necessary for the small space. "Wait! Put your gun down!"

*Gun? Who has a gun?* Lexi thought he was looking at her until she noticed movement behind her.

The world spun as her knees hit the ground, jarring her brain into a wild display of flickering lights. Heavy hands grabbed her shoulders.

"Stop." Madison's voice was quiet, yet deadly, and not directed at her.

The heavy hands were replaced by Madison's gentler ones with her calm voice in Lexi's ear. "Don't try and stand up. You're still too weak." Then whispered above my head, "Get that gun out of here." Her hands were under Lexi's arms, guiding her to a sitting position on the floor. "I had to medicate you to get you out of the building, and the effects are still wearing off."

Reaching for the prickling at the back of her neck, she found several decent-sized lumps. "I remember now. On the stairs. I felt a—" shaking her head to find the right words, "—

a sting or burning on my neck." Lexi could see the touch of regret once again on Madison's face.

"I'm sorry about that. The neutralizer injection I used works best when injected at the base of the skull. Hurts like hell, but since we weren't entirely sure how long it would last in your system, I needed to make sure you stayed out cold during transport."

Carefully touching the injection site, the jolt of pain came back. "Yeah, well, remind me to return the favor."

One of the men in the room started to fidget significantly, and Lexi could tell he was growing impatient. She felt the same. Her voice came out a little harsher than intended. "Who are you people? Where am I." No one said anything. "I'm not a mind reader. Tell me what's going on," she demanded, wanting to sound angry but coming across as defeated and tired.

Madison leaned back. "We know." A sigh escaped her lips. "Why don't we get you cleaned up and—"

"—No! Enough. Just tell me what's going on. What's happened to me?" The rage was building. She'd never been an angry person, and yet she could feel this internal pressure building uncontrollably inside her. Sound stifled in her ears. Just as Lexi's stress seemed unbearable, she felt a slight release of calm in her chest. Cutting her eyes to Madison, Lexi knew she was somehow responsible for the slight sense of peace. She started to address it before catching Madison's nearly imperceptible head shake, which gave her pause.

The calm cleared Lexi's head.

"This is Rice Jahnsen," Madison said, shifting the focus. "The director and leader of LIMIT. Phil is his next in command, and the rest are doctors. To help you. You are an extraordinary woman. There are many people out there who are searching for you. Or rather, want to use you, and your capabilities."

"What do you mean? Use me? For what?" The headache she woke up with was worsening. It was as if her brain was being electrocuted, intensifying with pain at the sound of every aggravating word.

"Your mind, it's unlike anyone else's out there. Do you remember anything from before you were taken?" asked Jahnsen.

Lexi tried to focus on him and his question, but the electricity behind her eyes flashed like lightning. "I don't remember anything. Just my sister," she whispered, her head aching all the more as she pictured Zuri, causing her to fall back as if in slow motion.

Gentle hands grabbed her shoulders and lowered her softly onto a pillow.

"That's enough. We need to let her rest," declared a doctor at the back of the room.

Like a whining child, Jahnsen pointed at Madison. "You owe me some answers. Like how you got her out of the building and all the way here when I have men on the ground that've been waiting for hours. I could've ordered them to leave by now." Rice began to turn away when Madison caught his shoulder and pulled him back.

"Her sister is still in there. If I'd told you I had Rose, your men wouldn't be out there now, poised to pick her up." Madison stood with her back straight, eyes piercing.

"Trust me. I definitely caught that part."

A man in scrubs cut off Lexi's line of sight. He barked orders at a young woman tentatively squatting next to her. "She needs food first. Get an IV in her with fluids and some medication to dull the pain."

"No! No more drugs!" Lexi begged, grabbing at her head. There was so much she needed to know but was fading quickly.

"No drugs. Alright?" said Madison, comforting Lexi. "No drugs. However, you do need food. Now." When she spoke, the room disappeared from view. As she stared into Lexi's eyes, Lexi could see the hint of a glimmer.

Small, but it was there.

She knew how to take care of her. Because they were the same.

# Chapter 39
## Running

"**J**oe. Do you read me, Joe? You need to stop the girls. You gotta stop them *now!*" Justin was in panic mode as he threw his body at the stairway door, bursting into the lobby. Aidan was at the panels next to the main entrance, frustrated and lashing out like an agitated gorilla hopping from foot to foot.

"What took you so long?"

"We found Gavin."

Aidan stopped dead.

"I told you, Gavin is my," Justin grunted as he pushed up against the main door, "partner in the lab. He took off just before the three of you dropped in." Another grunt as he tried again and again. "We thought—"

"—Obviously, I've already tried brute force, man." Aidan oozed contempt.

"We thought he disappeared with everyone else, but apparently, he was up in his room doing who knows what this entire time."

Aidan's face said it all, but he threw out an expletive anyway. "Seriously? For that many hours? He never bothered to come check on you?"

They both tried pulling at the center seam of the doors.

"So, where is he now?"

"With Maria. She might have broken her ankle on the stairs on our way down."

"Are you kidding me? And you left her with him? Can you trust him?"

"Right now, it's the only option. We need to get Zuri back."

"And Zoey," Aidan added. Both had the same purpose for getting the doors open. Stepping back for a second, they assessed the immovable door in front of them.

Aidan's eyes zipped over at Justin. He did a double-take. A second later, Aidan tackled and attempted to strangle him.

"What the—" Ripping the badge from Justin's neck, Aidan turned and took a giant step to the door. Immediately, Justin realized what an idiot he'd been. Aidan was not attacking him, although he probably should have. He smashed Justin's badge on the black pad next to the door. The doors slowly slid open, letting the cool of the early morning air breeze over their skin. Sunlight was on the horizon.

As Justin muttered, both took off at a sprint. "I can't believe I didn't notice the little red LED on the box was lit."

A half-step ahead, Aidan yelled over his shoulder, "Joe must've fed power to the door. I didn't register the light either until I saw the badge hanging around your neck."

"None of the lights came back on, though."

"Maybe he found some sort of secondary power supply? Or a different circuit." Justin's mind raced through so many things all at once: where were Joe and the girls? Was Maria okay? Where had Gavin been all this time? Unsurprisingly, power to the building had been the least of his worries.

"We'll ask him when we catch up to him," said Aidan, pulling out his radio with no break in speed. "Joe? We're out of the building. Where are you?"

At first, only a static buzz could be heard.

"Joe. Joe, can you hear me? You need to stop the girls. Zoey, can you hear this? There's a group out ahead of you. You're running right to them!"

Justin was about to call into his radio when someone tackled him from the side. His cheekbone contacted hard dirt and gravel as he realized the boulder that crashed into him was actually a tiny person with sunlit hair. "Zuri?"

Her eyes widened as she whispered, "They know we're here."

Zoey and Joe followed behind, driving everyone to get down. To hid.

All five of them crawled in the dirt to the nearest brush and sat huddled together. They could hear voices and the sound of vehicles moving from over the hill. Several satellite dishes sat interspersed nearby.

"I could sense them up ahead, but I was only focused on following what I could feel of Lexi. I lost her again, though, and when I did, I realized we were running towards—"

"—an Ambush," Aidan chimed in.

"Yes. I'm pretty sure they're here for us." They all crouched in silence, trying to listen.

"They haven't fired any shots, but they definitely have us in their sights if they're paying attention," said Joe.

"Who are they?" Justin asked.

Gavin helped Maria hobble across the ground floor. Voices came from the security office, though no one else should be in there at this point. Alarmed, they dropped to the floor. Maria cried out from biting pain, and Gavin put his hand over her mouth, dragging her to the front of the entranceway desk for cover. Her jaw was so tight she thought she must have cracked a few teeth.

The sound was too muffled to understand. They both thought, *where would people have come from? Everyone else is outside at this point.*

Using hand motions and short whispers, Gavin communicated he would move around the desk to check out the security room. Her fingers reached for his arm, but he moved too quickly, and she only found air. Her eyes transitioned from pleading to flaming mad. She mouthed,

"Don't go," but he had already turned away.

Low crawling to just outside the door, he peeked around the corner. Nothing. No one. Voices rang out again, and he pressed himself against the wall. The heartbeat in his ears was so loud he could barely hear through the pressure. One of the voices sounded familiar. Justin maybe?

Taking a second glance around the corner, he saw without question that the room was entirely empty. Carefully maneuvering inside, Gavin followed the voices. "It's a radio!" he shouted, grabbing it from the counter next to a console with numerous switches and channels.

Gathering her strength, she grasped the countertop and pulled herself upright. Making her way around the desk, she held onto the doorframe of the security office. Face pale, she used all her effort to remain standing. "Maria!" he called out, hustling to her side and practically lifting her over to a chair next to a workbench. When he got her settled, he didn't immediately remove his hands from hers.

At one time, she might've welcomed his physical support, but she was still so torn on what his motives were for not just walking away but failing to come back to find them. However, being that she had been up over twenty-four hours, was hungry, and with her mind on maximum overload, she didn't have it in her to push him away. She needed him. Even if just for a moment.

Finally, they turned their focus to the debris scattered on the bench. "This must be what Joe was working on before he started messing with the door. Seems like maybe there were more radios, but who is talking? I don't recognize the voices," said Maria, picking up the hand-held in front of her and turning up the volume.

"I don't know. Keep listening. Maybe something they say will be familiar."

Maria stared at the radio, willing it to make a sound. Give them a clue. She didn't realize it at first, but Gavin was standing next to her, paying attention, just not to the radio.

She was startled as she picked up on what he was gazing at. Their eyes locked, and she tried to say something but couldn't make a sound.

Maria recognized that intensity. She'd witnessed it many times in their lab. Yet, now he was directing that fervor at her.

She tried again to speak, but too many thoughts jumbled together for anything coherent.

His breathing turned shallow. "Maria, from the moment you arrived, I have put up wall after wall, trying to keep myself protected and safe. Not that I'd ever think a woman like you would ever want to be with a monumental fool like me. The walls haven't been for you. They were for me, so that I wouldn't begin feeling anything just to have it all ripped away someday. Again, not that you would..." he faltered, stammering over his words.

"Maria, I don't know what's going on. But I'm realizing now more than ever that if I don't take those walls down now, I never will."

"Gavin," she whispered, shaking her head as he began to blush, feeling like a child. "Baby, you are an idiot." She put one hand on either side of his face, pulled him in close, and kissed him.

Her lips were so full and soft that he felt like he was melting into them. For a moment, he forgot where they were or that he was even standing until she broke away, causing him to fall forward on top of her.

"Oh!" she cried as the chair rolled back, catching them both off guard and sending him tumbling into the wall. Maria barely held onto the desk with a few fingers to steady her.

"Well, that totally went as planned," Gavin asserted as he made his way up from the floor with a sheepish grin.

"Are you guys there?" came a breathy voice from a radio. He turned in a half-circle before realizing it was Maria's two-way clipped to his waistband.

"Justin?" he answered, ripping the radio off his belt as Maria attempted to push herself with her one good leg across the floor toward him. Hurrying to her side, he put the radio between them.

"Yeah. We have a serious problem out here," he said, out of breath. "They know where we're at. We're hiding behind some brush but pretty much out in the open. We could use one of your brilliant ideas, Gavin." If Justin was asking for Gavin's help, there was, without a doubt, a problem. "We have maybe five minutes before they're on top of us."

"Nothing like giving us a heads up," said Maria, with as much sass as ever.

"Okay, Justin. Like a diversion, you mean?" Gavin's eyes were already floating around the room in search of something.

"Diversion, distraction, directions to somewhere we can hide and get our bearings."

"Got it, one minute."

"That's all we have. Make it count!" he said in a rush.

Maria put her hand on Gavin's. "You are so not out of the woods, FYI."

Jahnsen and Phil stood outside the room where Lexi was cleaning up, eating, and resting. Jahnsen couldn't say for sure, but it was as if he could feel her angst from the other side of the door. Phil's frustration broke the spell.

"How are there two? How did we not know there were two in that building?" Phil thought he might be having an anxiety attack. "Madison worked in the building. Do you really believe she just now found out that Rose, or Lexi, whatever her name is, that her sister was there?"

Jahnsen shook his head unknowingly, but before responding, Jilly came running down the hall toward them.

"Sir, they're waiting on your go-ahead," she stated. Jahnsen whipped around, jogging toward the doorway as she followed suit, continuing to update him. "They've got a lock on at least three individuals. Two women, one man. Fairly certain they've identified two of the three on our Target Team: Zoey and Joseph. But there's another female in scrubs running well ahead of Zoey. We think it's her!"

Under his breath, Jahnsen muttered, "So the three of them did find her." Then louder, he questioned, "The sister?" He glanced at Phil. "And you're saying she's running *from* our team?" Phil just lifted his hands at a loss.

Jilly nodded.

As he rounded the corner into the operations cell, he yelled, "Tell our guys to stop moving forward and let her come to them!"

Phil was on the edge of his seat. "This is incredible! An hour ago, I thought we'd lost our opportunity to get Rose. Now we have her, *and* we're about to pick up her sister. Unbelievable!" He wasn't known for getting excited, but even he couldn't deny how miraculously all of this was coming together.

Jahnsen and Phil rushed to their desks at the center of the room. The nervousness among the support team was palpable as all their years of work were about to pay off.

The voice on the other end of Jahnsen's headset responded quickly. "Sir, there are *five* of them sitting out there now. Two more men ran from the building three minutes after the first three. All five are together. They stopped suddenly, and we lost visual. There isn't much cover, so we know where the group is located within the brush. They have the high ground near the second satellite dish."

Jahnsen reached over the radio controller's shoulder and flipped the ON switch to talk to the ground commander. "Full Status Report, Stingray."

"We have them about two hundred yards to our one o'clock and five hundred yards from the building. No other persons visible within range. Next move?"

Jahnsen stood motionless. His head swiveled to Phil. "There's still no security from the compound out there? How is that possible? We've never once witnessed this compound without a security detail."

Jilly's voice rang out from somewhere behind him. "Boss. I've assessed that the five out there don't pose a threat to us, but *they* don't know that we aren't a danger to them,"

Jahnsen almost forgot they hadn't had any communication with Zoey's group. "Their radios. We pre-programmed their frequencies before giving them their radios. Why aren't we in contact with them now that they're out of the building?"

"The ones we programmed aren't connecting. We're checking other frequencies now."

"What about the cell phone? If they're outside the building, they should have a signal."

# Chapter 40
## Out of Moves

"**G**avin, take this radio, go up to the third floor and tell me what you see." Maria had gone from zero to sixty in half a second. Their romantic moment had passed, replaced with action. "You should have a better visual from that level."

"First, we need a plan," he said, ripping the map off the wall. It was a layout of the compound and the surrounding area.

The radio on the workbench continued to share conversations, presumably from the others out there. Only this time, Gavin and Maria were prepared to listen. Gavin's eyes opened wide in alarm. "Whoever they are, they know exactly where Justin and the rest of them are sitting. They aren't leaving without them."

Maria jumped into fight mode. "You need to get up there

so we can see what's going on! We need to give them some intel."

"Justin said he could hear them from their ground location. They know where they are. We need to find them somewhere to hide." She knew he was right, that intel without a strategy wouldn't be much help to them.

Their radio burst with the sound of static, followed by Justin whispering, "They've stopped. The hum of their vehicles hasn't come any closer, and their voices have died off, but they aren't going back either."

Joe's voice immediately followed. "They're waiting for something. We have to move."

Gavin keyed his radio, shouting, "Wait! Hold on! I think I've found something."

"What did you find?" cried Maria, sliding out of her seat and immediately reminded by her ankle that she couldn't stand. Gavin's hands were around her before she realized it. He set her down quickly before turning his nose back to the map.

Keeping his finger on where the five were roughly located, he pointed to a spot about one hundred yards east, then a second location another three hundred yards west.

"What are those?" Maria asked, noticing that the locations he was pointing to both had a small open circle annotated on the map. "Satellites," she breathed out in recognition.

"That's their way out." His eyes lit up like fire.

Covered in dirt and scrapes, Justin was starting to feel the burn where his face met the dirt from Zuri's tackle. Time moved painfully slow waiting for Gavin to give them something to work with.

"We can't just sit here," said Aidan, shaking with the need to do anything other than remain targets.

"Gavin will have something for us." Justin's eyes scanned left to right, searching for a way out of their mess. Something about the Satellites bothered him, a memory maybe, whatever it was, he couldn't place it.

"Oh really? The guy that hid out for *hours* while an entire compound of people disappeared?"

"What are you talking about?" asked Joe. "Who's Gavin?"

"He works with Maria and me in the lab. He left right before you blew in. We found him in his room. He's with Maria. That's who I was talking to on the radio."

"You mean the guy that left you all to die—"

"—*Enough!*" Zoey wasn't interested in a word battle. "Listen, we came here ultimately as a team for Jahnsen. Although they gave us minimal information to track Zuri down, there's no way they wouldn't have people waiting for us after we picked her up. Logically, the people on the other side of that hill are probably his people." She looked to Aidan and Joe for confirmation. "Don't you think? It's the only thing that makes sense. They haven't shot at us, and it doesn't seem like they're connected to this place."

All of their eyes met, trying to decide if this was the most plausible scenario. No one argued, but they weren't jumping up and shouting for attention either.

Zoey sucked in a breath. "Joe! Where's the cell phone?"

He knew as soon as she inhaled what she was about to say and reached into his pocket. Holding it up, they watched as his face fell. He turned the screen around for them to see. "I must've fallen on it when I dove into the brush here."

Aidan and Zoey both released a few expletives. "Come on! Can't we get one thing right today?" Aidan moaned, growing more and more impatient as they kneeled in the dirt. Waiting.

Zuri cleared her throat, and just that little sound had them all paying attention. "I don't know who they are, but I can tell you that I don't think they want to hurt us. I don't *feel* as though they want to hurt us."

"Are you guys ready to run?" Gavin's voice interrupted their discussion. "Justin! Guys, do you see the Satellite dishes to your left and right?"

Silence.

"Hey! Anyone? *Are you there?* Do you read me?"

Justin lifted his radio to his lips, "Gavin, we may not need—"

"—Wait!" Aidan put his hand up to stop Justin. "Just wait. If we go with them or let them take Zuri, we may not figure out what's happening to Zoey." He locked eyes with her. "They may even take her." Facing Zuri, his voice anxious, "I've only known you for a minute, but I'm not sure letting you walk into their open arms is the best idea for you either. To be honest, we don't know anything about them. We only started this mission because we thought we could help Zoey. What if we're saving you from one devil only to give you to the next?"

Justin cringed at that description.

Joe blinked a few times before uttering, "I agree."

Eyes shifting from one to the other, Justin said, "So what's our move then?"

"*Hey! Justin? Can you hear me?*" Gavin said, clearly concerned.

"I think we need to get back to the building," Joe said, calm and clear. "At least in there, we have supplies, and we can establish communication with Jahnsen's team on the off-chance that's *not* them."

Everyone nodded in agreement though Zoey interjected one practical concern. "Can we make it that far?"

Justin looked back at the building and then at her, put his hand on her shoulder, squeezed it, and nodded. "We can do this. Gavin, tell us where to go."

"Directly east of your position, about one hundred yards, there's a manhole cover directly behind and below the Satellite dish. Three hundred yards west, the same position to that dish, there's another. East is closer, but it also closes the distance between you and the mob. West is a longer run, but further from them as well. Understand, I do *not* know where those manholes will lead you... but I'll find out. Also, those covers are gonna be a beast to open."

"Roger, Gavin. We copy." Justin peered into the faces in front of him. Some new, some known. None he wanted to lose. "What do you want to do?"

Zoey and Zuri grasped hands, then looked at Justin. He

watched both sets glimmer with a crystalline shine. In unison, they said what everyone was thinking. "We run."

Joe didn't wait for a second opinion. "Let's move. Go west. If you say true, they don't want to kill us, just capture us. If you're fast, run your ass off and try to lift the cover. The rest of us, God willing, will help if you're still working on it when we reach you," he said, looking directly at Zuri. They all knew how fast she was. "I'll bring up the rear. I have a full clip if I need it." Immediately, thinking, *please don't let me need it!*

Justin keyed the radio on and said, "Gavin, we're making the run west. Keep the doors to the building closed. We'll link back up with you as soon as you find us a direction down there. Until then, we'll take any path that looks like it's heading back to the main building."

"Roger. Searching now. Justin, be safe."

"You too."

"Jilly! Where's that frequency? Call that cell number *now*." The whole operations cell was standing by. "Phil, what are they doing out there?"

"No idea, but we need to contact them fast. They've been sitting too long, and we don't want anyone to make a rash decision!"

"Stingray, this is Main. What is happening out there."

"Sir, we've got no movement. If they are with us, why aren't they coming forward? This would be the easy part if we could only talk directly to them. There are no combatives out here," said the team leader, just as confused as the rest of them.

"We're working on the frequencies. Maintain your position. Should not need to take by force. We're arranging contact. Standby."

"On the count of three. Everybody ready?" Joe's decisiveness and confidence dampened their fear.

"One, two…" Everyone took a deep breath at the same moment and pushed off from the balls of their feet. "Three!"

Dust kicked up, making them invisible for the first few seconds, giving them the head start they needed. Zuri took the lead, with Zoey only half a step behind. Their graceful run was not lost on the rest.

Justin, Aidan, and Joe had their weapons drawn, alternately turning back to provide necessary cover should they take fire.

Deep within Joe's pocket, he could feel a vibration. Caught off guard, he mistook it for something else and raised his weapon.

Maria and Gavin grabbed hold of each other for a brief moment. "They'll make it," he assured her with a kiss. Turning, he sprinted up three flights of stairs to the closest window facing them.

He locked onto the group just as a dust cloud billowed around them. They sprinted forward and closed in on the dish, but before he could blink, something horrible unfolded.

"NOOO!" He banged his fists on the window, but the sound only echoed within.

"Main! We've got movement to the west. Weapons drawn!"

Jahnsen yelled into his mic, "Do. *Not.* Fire. Retrieve them unharmed. Repeat, do not open f—"

All speakers in the room rang out. "—Shots fired! Shots fired!"

There was no stopping it.

Regardless of who opened fire first, gunfire was all that could be heard echoing around the room.

"Cease fire! Cease fire!" Jahnsen continued to yell into the mic. "Repeat. Stingray, cease fire!" His voice was drowned out by a loud hum coming from somewhere behind him.

All five were under a cloud of dust. The view from the reconnaissance aircraft hovering overhead showed five unmoving heat signatures on the ground.

Jahnsen refused to look at the screens on the wall. He stood motionless, with his back to the terrifying images.

Lexi stood only twenty feet away in the doorway. Hair wild, eyes bright, and an energy field coming from her so intense, Jahnsen's entire body quivered like an electrical current.

*"Zuri!"* she screamed.

# Chapter 41
## The Fallout

August 10, 2029 | 5:12 a.m.

*Zuri. No—Not again—Zuri. Zuri! Oh my God. No! I'm in the dark. How is this possible? It wasn't a dream. It was real, right? My sister is alive. This cannot be happening again. I can't—*

Light. A lot of light.

The room was familiar. She was not being crushed or tied down. She could feel the cold floor beneath her. Tilting her head back, she could see others nearby on their knees, breathing heavily.

Someone touched Lexi's forearm, and she could feel who it was without looking. Madison.

"Is she gone?" She heard herself say the words but didn't recognize the sound of her own voice—too surreal. Too much pain.

Hot tears streamed down her face. "Is she? Is she dead?"

She felt others begin to stand up and come closer. Her eyes pleaded with Madison.

Justin's lungs were filled with dirt kicked into the air, and his ears rang from the gunfire. He looked around, hearing labored breathing and a few manly groans. The one person he intently tried to listen for remained silent. Her golden-red wisps of hair were tossed lightly by the dusty breeze beside him. She was nearby, yet he couldn't see through the watery grit in his eyes well enough to determine if she was breathing. His heart beat loudly in his ears as he slowly crawled to her.

*Please, God.*

*Please.*

His hand reached for her.

Streaks glistened down Madison's face showing proof of emotion despite the intensity of her emerald gaze. "Lexi, you are not alone."

# Chapter 42
## Do You Copy?

August 10, 2029 | 5:14 a.m.

"Justin?" Gavin gripped the radio so tightly that his hand turned white. He could see his friend lying in the dirt—a cloud of dust surrounding him. "Justin! Are you ok? Are you alive?" Practically roaring into the receiver, he couldn't believe what was happening. Less than twenty-four hours ago, he had been seated at his computer contemplating Zuri's life and the possibility of asking Maria on a date in the cafeteria.

But now....

*Damn it.* "Damn it!" he shouted, pounding his fists on the third-floor window. He had watched everything as if in slow motion. The men in fatigues had come closer. They drew their weapons just as the five of them dashed from behind a few scraggly bushes out into the open. On his word. According to his plan.

Now all of them were on the ground. Did he just kill five people? His only real friend? A girl who finally woke up from a forced sleep in a glass box *he* helped *keep* her in?

Bracing himself on the window, he stared out in silence. He watched as the dust cleared, and a group of about 20 military types began fanning around them. He could see all five of them on the ground, motionless.

Holding the radio to his face, his voice shook, "Justin, please hear me. Please respond. Be alive. Come on, man! *Respond!*"

Slamming his hand against the window, he used the momentum to push himself back and away, sprinting toward the main floor. Three stairs at a time, past the point where Maria had broken her ankle and eventually launching himself through the ground floor door.

He could hear Maria yelling for him from the backroom. "Gavin! What's happening!" she screamed, pulling herself from the chair.

"They've been shot," he growled through clenched teeth.

"What—" she gasped, inhaling so quickly she became light-headed.

"They've been shot. No one is responding on the radio, and those men are surrounding them right now."

"But—"

"I killed them, Maria! I f—" He tried to speak, but couldn't find the air to pull into his lungs.

Grabbing hold of him as he stumbled closer, she said,

"They *can't* be dead. What did you see? How do you know?" Panic overtook her usually sassy responses. Tears began to well up as her fingers dug into his arms.

"I don't know. *I don't know!*"

Gavin snatched a broken radio from the table and pulled his arm back to throw it against the wall.

"Gavin. Stop!" Maria's voice cut through the thumping in his ears.

She gripped his bicep and pulled herself to him, wrapping her arms around his tense body. "Stop—Just stop—"

At first, he didn't even realize she was there, but her warmth slowly seeped in. Turning toward her, he held her back for a brief moment before she pushed him away. "Do you know? Do you know for sure they're…" she couldn't say the word.

He looked into her eyes to get a hold of himself. "No. No, I don't know." He took a halting breath. "They… they weren't moving."

"We need to get out there. Gavin, we need to go!"

"We can't."

"Yes. We can. Open the doors." It was a command, not a request.

"There is a large group with guns surrounding them. Those are just the ones I can see. There could be more, and Justin won't answer the radio. If we go out there, we might be killed too, Maria."

A static sound startled them both away from the table.

"The radio. Grab it!" Maria tried to lunge for it, but pain

shot up her leg, forcing her to the floor.

"Maria!" Gavin took hold of her forearm, and in one smooth motion, both sat her in a chair and seized the radio.

"Justin. Justin, can you hear me? Justin!"

"Where's the manhole?" Justin's voice broke through static, clearly in pain.

Almost dropping the radio, Gavin replied, "Oh, thank God. You're alive."

"Gavin. Manhole. Now."

Gavin's mind's eye brought him back to the upstairs window and the scene he'd never forget. He didn't need to be in front of it to see the picture. Mentally calculating the distance, he answered, "About twelve feet from you. Make a one hundred eighty degree turn from where your head is pointing, then go twelve feet." He released the button and hung his head, listening intently.

"Justin. Do you copy?"

Silence.

"Justin."

"Got it." The strain was evident.

Gavin cast his eyes at the doorway before focusing back on Maria. "I need to run back up to see what's going on. Take this." He handed her the broken radio. "You can't call out on this one, but you can flip through channels. See if you can pick up anyone else's communications. Maybe we'll get lucky, and you'll hear something useful from whoever those guys are out there. If you do, radio me over this one." He put the functioning one in front of her on the table. "You'll be able to keep track of us, but only use it if you hear something that might help. I want to keep the line free if he needs me."

His eyes glistened with adrenaline and anxiety as he stared at her. Quickly but forcefully, he kissed her.

Without hesitation, he turned and ran out of the room.

Maria's hands shook uncontrollably, and she desperately wanted to work out a good cry. "Get it together!" she finally said, scolding herself, convinced that now was not the time to lose it.

Focusing on the radio, she started praying she would hear anything that might help Gavin save Justin, Zuri, and the others.

The radio crackled.

"Justin, they're moving in. They're almost on top of you." Gavin's voice came through loud and clear on the radio.

Maria concentrated on the static.

"Justin, move. *Move!* You're almost there. You guys can do this."

Her heart beat hard against her chest as she listened intently to the action.

Breaking in and out, she heard, "How do I open it?" Justin's strain made her heart stop.

"I don't know! There should be a latch to lift. Justin, they're—No!" Gavin's voice stopped coming through the radio, but far off in the building she could hear the faint yelling of a man who knew he could do nothing more to stop whatever horror he was witnessing.

Then she heard something else. Someone else.

"Commander." It was a man she didn't recognize. "Target has been reached."

# Chapter 43
## Dying in the Dirt

LIMIT | August 10, 2029 | 5:16 a.m.

Coughing up a cloud of dirt, with mud-spittle oozing from his lips, Joe struggled to open his watering eyes. He knew he'd been hit, maybe more than once, but he also knew he wasn't dead. Yet. Opening his lids against the burn, he watched as the blurry silhouettes of the operatives moved in. His eyelids flickered as the shrill ring in his ears grew with each muddy cough and wheeze.

They were on top of her. Though Zoey lay only inches from his grasp, he felt helpless as they began to beat her. Like a wild animal coming to its senses and feeling the steel of his pistol in his hand, he arced the weapon toward the men. "Stop!" Joe growled with all the energy he could muster.

"Get off of her now," he demanded under his breath through coughs and spit.

Another operative, just out of sight, kicked the weapon from his hand before wrenching his arm behind his back. The pain rocked him from his singular focus.

"We're trying to save her life. Let us do our job! We're not going to hurt you. Not any of you," the gritty, though not unkind voice, attempted to reason.

"CPR?" he grunted in horror as tears cleared the muck from his eyes, suddenly realizing that they weren't hurting her. They were trying to save her. "Okay, okay! I'm good, please. Let go!"

The man holding Joe released his grip. Though cautious, he allowed Joe to push himself up on his bruised forearms. Creeping sideways, he pulled himself close enough to grasp Zoey's cold hand, expecting the worst.

The moment their skin touched, however, Zoey lurched upward, gasping for air. Violent coughs increased the blood gushing from the wound in her abdomen. Falling back to the dirt, she muttered, "Joe? Aidan?" Their names didn't pass easily through her lips as she grabbed the shoulder of the stranger crushing her midsection.

"Ma'am, you're gonna have to stop. I can't let go. Can you hear me, ma'am? Stop pushing! I've got to keep pressure on your wound." His voice grew muffled as darkness began to blur her peripheral vision.

At the sound of her voice, Aidan began to choke, gasping for breath nearby, startling both Joe and Zoey.

"Aidan? No!" Zoey yelled in a gruff whisper before her eyes rolled back and her body went limp.

"Rich, we got two in the right leg, but stable," called out the man still standing over Joe.

"This one's a through and through," Rich responded, continuing to compress the wound on Zoey's stomach.

"This one's back," shouted the operative checking Aidan's pulse. "We don't have much time. We need a helo, *now!*"

Rich nodded before relaying the message through his earpiece to an unknown source. "We need an evac, now." Circling his hand in silence as if trying to speed up time, he waited for a reply. "Roger!" he soon shouted, looking back to the others. "Evac's five miles out. Keep pressure!"

Joe sat up, shook his head a bit, then applied pressure to his leg. He saw Justin further out from the group surrounding him. He had only spent a second contemplating how Justin had separated from them before recognizing who was in his arms. "Zuri!" he coughed, wincing in pain.

As her name left his lips, he heard the armed man hovering over Zuri say into his earpiece, "We need the chopper *now. Right now!*" Trying to remain conscious, Joe strained to hear the man now muttering to himself, clearly in shock at the sight of the young girl. "How are so many bullets in her? As if she was a magnet."

"Did she... did she do that for us?" Joe groaned under his breath. Terrified at the thought of what Zuri might have sacrificed to save them, he collapsed to the ground, releasing pressure from his leg and reaching out for Zoey once more.

# Chapter 44
## More of Us

LIMIT | August 10, 2029 | 5:17 a.m.

"Zuri? Can you hear me? Can she hear me?" Lexi looked back at Madison's pensive expression, which provided no answer. "Zuri, I'm right here." Her left hand rested on her sister's while her right gently touched the side of her face. She was so different now. Her skin was much paler than the alabaster it once was. Although she's grown, she was still quite tiny. Her face somewhat sunken in. Lexi could almost touch thumb-to-finger around her biceps. Like she'd been starved for years.

Lexi's eyes shift to assess her own limbs. Skinny. Too skinny. Unused for too long. Looking up into the cabinet's glass in front of her, she saw the purple spiderwebs twisting across her cheek and around her eye, touching her eyelids as they weaved into her hair. She supposed she would be worse off than Zuri if it weren't for the bullet holes. There were so many, yet somehow she was still there. More tears slid down Lexi's face leaving a warm trail in their wake.

Kissing her forehead, Lexi followed by resting her head on Zuri's. Everyone remained quiet. No one in the room spoke as if they all felt the same anguish she did.

Lexi couldn't see Madison but could tell she was moving closer. Her presence now a constant thing she could feel. When her hand settled on the back of Lexi's neck, she wasn't surprised at the action. Instead, her touch pushed a calm through her that seemed to pass into Zuri.

A flash of light caused Lexi to open her eyes, only to find Zuri staring into them.

"Zuri!" It was a whisper and a prayer all at once. Lexi's gaze flickered back and forth between Zuri's eyes as they became more focused on her face.

"Lexi?"

Startled at the unexpected sound of her voice, Lexi breathed deeply and said, "Zuri. Oh my…."

Tears pooled in Zuri's eyes and began to flow down the side of her face. Her grateful smile turned to sobs as she strained to lift her arm to hug Lexi. Without words, Lexi pushed her arms back down and held her close as years of tears fell between them.

"I'm right here. I'm right here, and I'm not going anywhere. I promise you. I promise you," Lexi repeated, sometimes as a whisper, sometimes with no sound at all.

Curling up on the bed next to her, she pulled Zuri delicately into her arms, careful not to cause further injury or anguish. "Nothing will separate us ever again," she said, holding her tight and promising—a promise not just with words but with her whole being. *No one will ever hurt my sister again.*

As she held Zuri, images flashed through her mind of the room she'd been trapped in. Glass shattering. Running through hallways. Pain and rage all rolled into one nightmare she couldn't yet see clearly, but would never forget.

Madison draped a blanket over them and asked everyone to leave the room. Once the door was closed, she pulled a chair up to the bedside and watched both women for quite some time. Every now and then, a tear would begin to fall, and she would wipe it away as quickly as it formed.

Lexi couldn't comprehend how the three of them were so similar. So many questions saturated her mind, yet not one was she able to focus on. Madison seemed older, but not by much. A few years, maybe. She had a darker skin tone and beautiful features, though not in a conventional way. And her eyes. They were like muted, emerald crystals. The green tones were speckled with deep evergreens broken up by the lightest glow of a coral reef—something she'd only seen in picture books as a young girl. There was something strange about them, though. Something prevalent currently hidden behind the grayish green that seemed to be covering them.

"Why…" Lexi started, not knowing how to ask. "How— your eyes?" she stammered, feeling like an idiot. Clearing her throat, she tried again. "Your eyes look very green. Kind of like mine, only not as bright." It was a question, sort of, though she couldn't quite figure out how to address it.

A small smile spread across Madison's face. Bending forward and leaning her head down a little, she placed a finger in one eye.

"Oh!" Madison's right eye was suddenly brighter than she could've anticipated and so beautiful.

"Contacts," Madison smiled. "I found many years ago that it helped keep people from staring and asking too many questions."

"Wow. Those really do tame the color!" Hearing herself laugh seemed odd, almost out of place. A few moments passed before she stated the obvious. "It seems like we have a lot to talk about."

Madison nodded slowly but affectionately. "We do. But, I think we all need some recovery time too. Especially her," nodding toward Zuri. "I have so many questions myself, but it's probably best to save the heavy stuff for when we can all talk together."

Glancing down, Lexi felt the warmth of Zuri's breath on her arm as she lay beside her, unconscious again. She was peaceful and needed all the rest she could get. Just having Zuri tucked into her arms was like the weight of the world had been eased. Whatever rage had taken harbor in Lexi's body had finally subsided, and she was hopeful it wouldn't return.

"Do you think…."

"Yes, I will be back with something to eat and a pitcher of water," Madison said, finishing Lexi's thought.

Grateful, she closed her eyes, leaned her cheek against Zuri's hair, and wondered who Madison might be. A sister? A relative they'd never met? They never knew their own family or where they had come from. Snippets of memories from their youngest years were of being transferred to different homes, adults that kept getting rid of them, from one family to the next. They'd never hurt anyone or done anything wrong. Yet, each foster parent, even the good-hearted ones, would inevitably send them off, claiming something just wasn't right. The last family simply abandoned them. In the middle of nowhere, dropped them off. She thought her tears had all dried up, but another few found their way out as she revisited her past.

Justin. He was the one that saved them. His whole family, really, but he was the one all those years ago.

Only having seen him for mere seconds before they took him into surgery, her heart bounded and immediately broke at the sight of him on a gurney, clothes black with blood and dirt. Unconscious from his injuries.

Hearing the door creak open, she saw Madison returning with a tray. Quietly, she placed it on the table next to Lexi, where she could easily reach it with her one free hand. It was obvious Madison was happy to see them, but it didn't quite show in her eyes. The crinkles to the sides gave away a concern she was trying to hide.

"Is everything ok?"

Seeming surprised at Lexi's question, she said, "Of course. Yes, everything is fine now." She smiled again.

Lexi thought she should leave it alone, but her mouth

wouldn't follow suit, saying, "I know that I don't know you, but... I can... *feel* that something isn't right."

Her breath hitched just a little, but she knew neither of them needed to hide anything. They were the same. Different, but the same. *How* was a bigger question, but there was no confusion that they were meant to be here. Together.

"No, there's nothing wrong. I'm just, really, I don't know if I have the words," she said softly with a sadness that laced her words. "You are more than I imagined you would be. And to have your sister here too. I didn't even know she was on the compound."

Lexi stayed silent, knowing that giving Madison the time to process her thoughts would help her say what was bothering her.

"It's just," she continued, taking another deep breath, "I have these dreams from when I was a little girl. There's a dark room that I'm in. It's terrifying, but I'm not alone. There are people there, kids... like me. But there are others hurting us." Her head shook slightly as if trying to recall it from some deep place. "We hold onto each other to keep warm, keep safe. When I try to picture it, I can't really see everything clearly, but I can almost... feel..." she paused, "It's like I can feel the others even though I can't see them in the dark."

Lexi's chest began to ache as she started to picture exactly what Madison was describing. As if Madison had somehow glimpsed her own dreams.

"As a little girl, I couldn't have explained it, but now." Madison's eyes find hers. "As soon as I was able to put my hand on you, the feeling I had within those dreams amplified."

She paused.

"I don't think they were dreams. I think they were more like—"

"Memories," Lexi breathed out.

Nodding yes, she said, "And I think there may be more of us."

# GLASS
# PRISON

# Epilogue:
## On Three…

Afghanistan | November 23, 2011 | 5:17 a.m.

"**O**n three, move in slowly and silently—no sudden moves. Just get them and get out," Doc said. She was the only one without her weapon ready, instead choosing to keep her hands free for the task ahead. It wasn't likely they would need weapons. At least not on the way in.

Captain Jahnsen was still skeptical about this operation, and it showed as he gruffly whispered, "Seven? You're sure there are seven in there?" Bending his head down, he muttered, "They even still alive?"

"Yes. Seven," she said in a low voice. Ignoring his attitude, she focused on her team. "Do not fire unless there is *no* other option. We can't risk drawing attention, or we'll never make it out of here with all of them. You grab the first one you come into contact with, then exit, covering everyone else as you go. Make sure to use the injection before you pick them up. It'll induce a temporary coma to avoid traumatization."

"Like they aren't already traumatized—"

"—Shut it." Though a whisper, her words felt like a slap across the face.

"We leave none of them behind. No matter what," Doc said, eyes wide with readiness and a touch of fear. "There can be no mistakes, gentlemen."

Each of the ten men surrounding her nodded. Doc looked to Jahnsen, the team lead, and nodded. "Time to go."

Their special operations team was located outside a cinderblock wall that surrounded an Afghani compound. These compounds were built surprisingly well despite the lack of available resources in desert areas like the Helmand Province they were currently deployed to. Jahnsen's interpreters came across chatter by the locals about a compound housing multiple children that they believed were being experimented on. After weeks of intelligence collection, they were 95% certain they'd found them. And anything less than 95% in the military meant *no* mission. Most recent chatter led them to believe they were in grave danger. Sometimes children were used as weapons, fitted with bombs to distract and kill unsuspecting military teams.

Doc's team was not going to let that happen.

Crouching low, protected by the perimeter wall, the eleven moved to the corner closest to the opening they planned to infiltrate. They knew there should only be one or two Military

Age Males (MAM) walking within the compound at this time of night, providing security.

"Stingray, there's one MAM four feet to your three o'clock. Thermals show no movement. Prone positions of fifteen adults thirty feet back. You're clear." The voice on the other end of the radio came from a military operations base fifty miles north of their position. The unmanned aerial vehicle, one thousand feet overhead, saw everything.

"Copy that, Main. Time 'til the storm starts?" asked Jahnsen, knowing the Main operations center was tracking a dust storm coming their way. They wanted to get in and out before being trapped inside for days by the blinding sand.

"Forty minutes, Stingray," said a familiar voice. "The helos won't make the rally point if you aren't there in thirty-seven minutes." There was a pause over the radio before she said, "Move fast."

To himself, he muttered, "Don't have to tell me twice." A breeze of a prayer crossed his thoughts before replying, "Copy, MJ. Give us the heads up when the dust is fifteen minutes out."

Nodding to the frontman, he lifted his hand and gave him a two-finger wave forward, signaling him to move ahead and take down the lone MAM guarding the compound.

With practiced silence, his longtime teammate, and friend, Phil, moved around the corner to subdue their first opposition. Seconds later, Phil gave them the all-clear.

No shots fired.

Good sign.

The next five men followed and split up, moving inside the

compound to the largest stone structure that sat dead center. Once they made it, they signaled for the remaining three and Doc to move in. Silence was vital as there was no room for error.

Doc rounded the corner to see the bare feet of the man Phil had taken down. He was likely dead, but the thought didn't phase her.

One by one, they entered the space where a door once stood. There were no windows and only a partial roof on the building. Any semblance of protective doors or windows was blasted to rubble long ago.

"Eyes on target," Phil whispered.

As she entered the pitch-dark room, her night vision goggles began to illuminate the small bodies of children. Several were already being injected and lifted into her teammate's arms. Quickly making her way toward two children on the far left side of the room, she saw them start to stir and sit up. Although trained not to panic, her stomach turned, knowing they would never make it off the compound in time if the children began to cry. "Move! Now! Grab them before they make a sound."

The operators' footsteps grew louder, trying to reach the children before fear made their little voices cry out.

But they didn't.

Five children were now in the arms of their saviors and silenced from the injections, but two remained. Sitting against the furthest wall in the room, their eyes were wide with fear. Despite the dark, Doc could see glimmering in their eyes through her NVGs. So strange. *There must be a sliver of moonlight coming into the room somewhere.* She was only distracted for half a second. That was all it took.

The sound that came next jolted her body into action. "Move, move, *move!*" Jahnsen's voice came over her headset at the same moment shots rang out in the silence of the night.

She threw herself to the ground, low-crawling to the two that remained. They sat unmoving, unfazed by the sound of gunfire. Grabbing them around their waists, she said in their ears, "Hold on. Tight as you can, okay?" They both nodded. She didn't expect them to understand her English, but they did.

Crouched and waiting for the signal, another operator finally waved her to the doorway. Once the spray of bullets subsided, he grabbed her with one hand and yanked her behind him. Using his body to shield them, he gritted his teeth and said, "Run! Do not stop running until you get to the rally point." His eyes burned into hers, and she nodded in acknowledgment.

Everything happened so quickly, but she watched it as if in slow motion.

The operator's body jerked backward, causing Doc to lose balance. She managed not to fall as he was hit a second time, pushing his body away from her. That one brought him and the little one he carried to the ground. She wanted to drop down and cover him, but there was no time. Not with the two she held in her own arms. Her feet raced across the soft dirt, creating a cloud of moon dust in her wake. She never looked back.

Outside the compound walls, she made no effort to search for her team. They knew their mission, and she had to trust they were protecting the other children in their care.

More shots rang out across the night, and she could hear moaning in her ears through the radio. Men had taken fire and now called for a medic.

She was the medic. She couldn't go back.

Doc tried to stay focused on putting one step in front of the other, but her mind wouldn't stop asking, *are their deaths worth it? For these children?*

She knew the answer, but it did not decrease the pain in her chest. These men were her family.

It took her twenty minutes to get to the rally point, and all but one child was there when she arrived with her two. "Where is the seventh?" Doc looked around in circles. The trek carrying both girls had strained every muscle in her body. "Where?" Yelling out to the operators.

"She's not here," said Jahnsen solemnly.

Her eyes cut to his face. Instead of responding to his answer, she asked, "No one grabbed her?"

He just shook his head.

There was no time to go back. Several members failed to make it to the rally point, and she knew they weren't going to.

"How far out is our bird?" The whirring of the helicopter could be faintly heard in the distance.

"Six minutes."

"Will they make it in time?" she asked, already starting to feel the grit of sand hitting her face. The dust storm was close.

"They'll make it." His voice was certain, but his eyes gave away his concern.

Doc looked at the two girls huddled together on the ground at her feet. They couldn't have been more than maybe three or four years old. The littlest one had her face buried in the other's chest. All she could see were red tendrils of hair whirling up into the older girl's face. A round cherub engulfed in her own white-blond hair, blown back from the wind, and wide eyes that stared directly up at her. There was a knowing look in her eye. She wasn't afraid.

The sand in the air thickened. Looking back at Jahnsen, Doc said, "This isn't good. The bird won't be able to fly into this."

"They will, Doc! They're almost here."

Their headsets began to squawk, "Stingray, this is Blu-Jay. Thirty seconds out from your rally point. Visibility is dropping fast. We may not have the capability to land. Be ready."

Doc's gaze dropped to see their little bodies rocking gently in the wind, and she silently mouthed the words, "Please, please, please, get here." At that moment, the little red-haired girl raised her head. Her eyes, so bright in the darkness it didn't seem possible. Doc watched her take in a deep breath and slowly release it. The beginning light of dawn filtering through airborne sand reflected off her crystalline gaze.

It was all Doc could see. She couldn't look away from those glowing eyes. So focused on that tiny round face she barely noticed what was happening around her.

Jahnsen's voice came across her headset, but she couldn't

hear him.

A hand settled on her shoulder, barely registering in her consciousness, but enough for her to breathe out the words, "Her eyes." Doc's voice was already a whisper, but her words fell away as the sand swirling around them cleared.

All the children were now visible, a small huddle of girls. The child closest to Jahnsen had midnight black hair that seemed to be curling up into ringlets as she watched. Doc could feel a slight vibration throughout her body along with a low-pitched hum in her ears that gradually grew louder with each passing second. As she took in the scene in front of her more closely, she realized all the children were focused on the little redhead at her feet with unnatural intensity.

A voice crackled over their headset, "Stingray, we see you. There's a... a clearing in the storm, and we see you, over." Even over the radio, they could hear the pilot's confusion on the other end.

Jahnsen looked into Doc's eyes. "Sheila, what is this?"

She looked down at the six little girls. "I have no idea."

Glass Prison

# ABOUT THE AUTHOR

M.J. Thompson is a retired Combat Weather Forecaster who occasionally jumped out of perfectly good airplanes, sells real estate, renovates houses, and writes fiction novels.

M.J., her husband, and four children live in Sanford, NC. Her debut novel, Glass Prison, was born after a jump accident found her with a traumatic brain injury that temporarily plunged her into a dark and silent world in which the only thing she found tolerable was writing with her eyes closed. During those lost days, she occasionally wrote snippets of her experiences. One of which gave life to the women in the debut of her Prisoner Series.